SANCTUARY

Ginny Fite

MILFORD
HOUSE
an imprint of Sunbury Press, Inc.
Mechanicsburg, PA USA

MILFORD HOUSE

an imprint of Sunbury Press, Inc.
Mechanicsburg, PA USA

For information about special discounts for bulk purchases, please contact Sunbury Press Orders Dept. at (855) 338-8359 or orders@sunburypress.com.

To request one of our authors for speaking engagements or book signings, please contact Sunbury Press Publicity Dept. at publicity@sunburypress.com.

FIRST MILFORD HOUSE PRESS EDITION: November 2024

Set in Adobe Garamond Pro | Interior design by Crystal Devine | Cover by Ginny Fite | Edited by Gabrielle Kirk.

Publisher's Cataloging-in-Publication Data
Names: Fite, Ginny, author.
Title: Sanctuary / Ginny Fite.
Description: First trade paperback edition. | Mechanicsburg, PA : Milford House Press, 2024.
Summary: The year is 2039. Jean Bennett's husband and sister are dead. Chased by government goons and a virus that might kill her at any time, Jean must be braver than she ever thought possible as she races a thousand miles to Canada to take her five children to safety. On a ride unlike any they've ever taken, Jean must overcome each new challenge as she begins to understand what she must do to save her children.
Identifiers: ISBN : 979-8-88819-177-4 (paperback).
Subjects: FICTION / Dystopian | FICTION / Science Fiction / Apocalyptic & Post-Apocalyptic | FICTION / Thrillers / Suspense.

Designed in the USA
0 1 1 2 3 5 8 13 21 34 55

For the Love of Books!

To
Kristyn, Andrew, Jamison, Hayden, and August.
I believe in you.

Also by Ginny Fite

Leave Everything You Know Behind

The Physics of Things

Possession

Blue Girl on a Night Dream Sea

No End of Bad

Lying, Cheating, and Occasionally Murder

No Good Deed Left Undone

Cromwell's Folly

Thoughts & Prayers (co-author)

)(

"By day, the banished sun circles the earth like a grieving mother with a lamp."

—CORMAC MCCARTHY, *THE ROAD*

)(

1

Jean

THE infection hit with such ferocity and speed that all public transport had shut down by the end of my husband's meeting in DC, sixty-five miles from home. No car, no commuter train, no way out.

In the five hours since he'd arrived in the city that morning, police had blockaded roads and barred highway entrances. Airlines delayed flights and then canceled them. Residents, under threat of arrest, huddled in their homes, and universities restricted students to dorms. Government officials shuttered public buildings, closing and locking the gates.

Television news showed black helmeted National Guardsmen herding panicked tourists back toward their hotels as they stampeded down unfamiliar streets. Coast Guard cutters patrolled the Potomac River; helicopters buzzed overhead. From Capitol Hill to the Ellipse, red lights on Constitution Avenue blinked on and off. Front pages of the morning newspaper skittered across empty streets.

I waited for Ted to call.

)(

Six months later, planting is the one activity that still makes sense. Elbow deep in dark, loamy soil, preparing this year's vegetable garden, Caro says, "Even demons believe in God." Her eyes are lowered, watching her own gloved hands transfer a tender tomato plant from its small pot to the ground.

Her sudden assertion doesn't surprise me; we've been playing this game all our lives. This will be another argument in my sister's perpetual attempt to crack open my agnostic armor. I'm accustomed to parrying her new thrusts.

She nailed a cross on her door when she was fifteen. I hung a bejeweled heart on mine. Ten years later, we argued about the sanctity of gurus

1

when she taped an image of Maharishi Mahesh Yogi on my refrigerator. I countered with a photograph of the owner of my local market. Three years ago, well before the infection, she began attending Friday evening Shabbat services; I took up Tarot card reading. These days, the figure of Death turns up frequently.

I sit back on my heels to watch her face. "I don't believe in demons."

"Maybe you should, Jean." Caro purses and twists her lips—her expression on the rare occasion when I take her rook with my queen. She always beats me at chess, although sometimes I surprise her with a move or two.

My neck clicks as I roll my head around to stretch out the knots. I'm the older sibling, not the smarter one. Pragmatism is my religion. When the world is falling apart, doing what works is a virtue. At least, that's what I tell myself to keep from going crazy.

Caro calls me a mechanic, but I understand her. It's comforting to believe in something, particularly now. I believe in what I can see, what I can do. Beyond the edges of my small map of the world, the little I know won't work. The real world is huge, and at thirty-nine, I'm still a journeywoman. It's unclear now that I'll have enough time to arrive at proficiency.

"Never mind," she says, giving me a reprieve from heavy arguments on an otherwise perfect March day that feels more like May. Next year it'll be warmer still; that much we can count on.

She plunges the baby tomato plant into the black dirt. We've already put in lettuce, broccoli, and onions. Tomorrow we'll plant eggplant and green beans. Relieved she's surrendered, I reach for another tender shoot, drop it into the soil, and pat the earth firmly around the roots. We've learned to cherish small wins when we can. I can almost smell the tomato to come, taste it sliced and salted, drizzled with balsamic vinegar, and sprinkled with fresh basil.

More than ever, life is what we make it. The last viral pandemic, the one dubbed COVID-19, I was young enough to feel impervious to disease. I used to think getting dirt under my nails was good for me, that the musky energy radiating from the center of the Earth would balance me. Now I'm watchful, careful about everything, xenophobic about interacting with even the tiniest forms of life because, this time, where the enemy comes from is a mystery.

The year before my son, Ren, was born, all we worried about was climate change. Ted and I put in forty-two trees on the three-acre meadow where we'd planted our house to balance our carbon footprint. We were such Boy Scouts, thinking the world would continue on the course we expected, believing we could be prepared for anything.

I am grateful for our industry, though. Those lovely oaks, maples, pears, birches, and fir trees block any neighbor's view into our yard. Redbud and cherry give us color; cedar gives us fragrance. My struggling magnolia throws out cream-colored satin buds the size of my fist every June, no matter what's happening in the world. From a drone's eye view, our house is an origami box floating in a sea of green.

Caro wipes sweat from her forehead with her wrist, keeping the dirt-covered fingers of her glove pointed away from her face. She doesn't want to streak her cheeks with mud. I love her for this unnecessary fastidiousness about her appearance. Aside from our small gang of five children, no one will see her gardening or doing anything else.

"What about angels?" she asks, pulling off her gloves and adjusting her broad-brimmed sun hat.

"Angels?" I laugh. She hasn't given up, only changed tacks. "What about them?"

"Do you believe in them?"

I look at her angular, still unlined face and wonder why she's struggling with this idea of deity today. "Why is this important now?"

"I saw something," she says. "Hovering over the kids yesterday when they were playing in the trees. Something I don't know how to explain."

"Heat haze," I guess. "Northern lights during the day. Electromagnetic activity caused by sun flares. Auras."

She lowers her eyes, a signal that she thinks I'm being flippant. In the world of all possible answers, I haven't stumbled upon the right one.

"It's a portent." She stares into my eyes as if to send me a telepathic message. "You know, like Mom said. Something we're supposed to notice."

I tense. Our mother was not an oracle I would believe, but whatever Caro saw has meaning to her. I should pay attention instead of making light of it, even though I can't resist teasing her. She's always so serious.

"Okay. What does it portend?"

"I did something you're going to be angry about."

I stretch my neck, close my eyes to shutter my annoyance, and wait.

)(

During the first hours of the lockdown, social media reports constricted my lungs. I checked my messages every two minutes: nothing from Ted—no text or email, no missed call.

I texted him. *What's happening?*

He didn't reply.

Two hours later, well after the world knew what happened, an emergency alert blared from my phone, the volume of the automated voice set on high. "Major viral outbreak in Washington, DC Lockdown enforced. No one allowed in or out. Those displaced will be transported to temporary quarantine camps. Anyone attempting to enter or leave the city will be stopped."

Words jumped out at me. *Displaced. Transported.* These words triggered ancestral memories; my body shook. *Camps.*

My husband had been quarantined inside the city with nearly half a million other displaced commuters, all looking for a place to hide. Where would they put them all? I fingered my locket, checked my phone again, and paced.

When I couldn't stand another second of not knowing what was happening, I texted my husband again: *Where are you? Tell me!*

No answer.

Television news taped furious members of Congress storming the planes at National Airport, demanding to be flown home. Befuddled university professors, ordered to leave their classrooms, mingled on the streets with zookeepers and museum curators, ambassadorial staff, and hotel workers. Herded by helmeted police toward white buses with impenetrable windows, commuters monitored their phones for instructions. Strangers shouted at each other, jostling in line, faces grim. Where was Ted in this mess?

On my phone, I watched a White House staffer whine, "Goddamn it." Her voice broke. "They've had seventeen years since COVID to figure out how to deal with this crap, and this is the result? This wasn't the plan. We can't all be infected. Test us and let us go home." Sweat streaked her perfect makeup.

I replayed her viral post on my phone, tapping the button over and over, hearing the strain in her voice, the shock, trying to extract from her words what she meant. What crap? What was she talking about? If she expected something different, then the government had a plan for this emergency. They'd known for a while that another deadly virus was coming, and they hadn't prepared us.

Networks picked up the staffer's post, and the twang of her anguish repeated on every screen in my house. The news camera panned, showing her huddled on the lawn with other White House staff not important enough to hitch a ride on Marine 1. The President's helicopter lifted off the ground; she put her face in her hands.

Choppers rose from rooftops simultaneously all over the city like butterflies migrating on cue to Mexico. On Twitter, I watched the rich and well-connected fly off, their escape documented in videos by those left behind.

Be back when it's over, tweeted the President. *My thoughts and prayers are with you.*

My gut twisted. I called my husband and left a message. "Ted, where are you? For God's sake, call me. Tell me what's going on."

)(

Caro sits down in the garden and speaks quickly as if she might not have enough time to get through her confession. "I talked to our neighbor. She was forlorn about her dog dying. I reached over the fence to touch her cheek. She's a widow, like us, but alone, and she needed human contact. How could I not help her? We weren't wearing our masks. Her cheek was hot. It was only a moment, but I knew what happened the minute my fingers touched her skin."

My own cheeks flush and chill; my heart plummets. I'm instantly too tired for what comes next. "Caro," I whisper. "The rules." All possible consequences lay themselves out like cards falling from a deck. I gather my patience and scrutinize her face. "When was this?"

"Ten days ago."

The shock of her answer runs through me, but she looks fine. Maybe she's immune to the virus, or she wasn't infected because she was out-doors and the wind carried the microbes away. She would have washed her hands and face afterward. I have to believe she hasn't already infected us. Everything in me wills it to be okay.

"We've had enough work for one day," I say. "Let's jump in the pool to cool off and then make a picnic supper for the kids."

My mind switches gears, already listing chicken salad, sliced avocado, grapes, and almond cookies—a fantasy meal from days gone by. My stomach growls. We live well, I remind myself, even if we never leave our gated community. We treat ourselves to asparagus, fried eggplant, and fresh cantaloupe as if we were rich people. It's a point of pride to make our own bread, pies, mayonnaise, and ice cream. I feel vaguely guilty about people starving in the cities, waiting for the government food airdrop. They didn't have my choices.

)(

The day the virus struck, Amina, fresh off the bus on what turned out to be her last day of school, backpack hanging by one strap from her shoulder, hair blown in every direction as if she'd walked through a tornado, entered the house through the garage.

"What's going on, Mom?" She eyed the jumble of clean sheets on top of the dryer in the laundry room. "Don't you normally, like, fold them?" My newly teenaged daughter, who shares my instinct for order, has always admired the systematic way I do laundry.

Eyes glued to the TV, I said, "I couldn't get the corners to square."

She stared at me like I'd lost my mind while I clutched a pillowcase to my chest as if it were going to save me. Unable to form full sentences, I tried to explain the lockdown, the outbreak, her father stranded in the city, unable to come home.

Her eyes grew wide; her lip trembled. "Mom, we have to get him. We have to go now."

Helpless, I nodded. "I don't know where he is. He has to call."

To calm us both, I brushed and braided her hair the way my sister and I used to do for each other when we were afraid—the long strokes, the slight tug at knots, fingers running through each strand—but my hands shook.

We watched a television news reporter trying to interview a man on the street, sticking a mic in his face. Behind him, people broke into a pharmacy; the sound of breaking glass muffled the reporter's question. Wild-eyed, the man stared at the microphone, his mouth open but silent as if his words had been stolen, and then he shook his head and bolted.

Ted had to come home; we *had* to find a way. Gritting my teeth to stop my hands from shaking, I texted him again.

Walk to Georgetown, use the canal path, and walk west. I'll pick you up in Glen Echo Park outside the city. You can make it; no one will notice you. I can be there in an hour.

Steal a boat from the marina, row across the Potomac. Hide out at Roosevelt Island until dark. I'll be in the pullout on George Washington Parkway.

They've got too many people to watch. You look so respectable. They won't notice you.

He didn't answer.

I texted my sister, thinking she might know something useful. *What's happening with Nate?*

She responded in seconds. *No word.*

Maybe their cell phones aren't working? Or they've already been transported?

Don't panic yet, she replied.

In my head, I heard Ted's perennial joke. "Don't panic yet; there'll be plenty of time to panic later."

I planned more escape routes. A map of DC on my phone displayed a cat's cradle of roads leading away from the city. There were forty ways to flee. Was Ted even looking at a map and, if not, what was he doing all this time? My patience ebbed away; I was never good with uncertainty.

Frazzled by his silence, I threw my phone on the sofa cushions, turned in a circle, and picked it up again, worried it would buzz and I wouldn't hear it. I sent him more solutions, one after the other.

Wait behind the gorilla compound at the zoo. If they're using dogs, animals will mask the smell of humans.

Walk out through the back alleys. I'll pick you up at the Bethesda Library. I can be there in an hour.

Please, try anything. Please.

The thought of dogs chasing him made my breath come in short spurts as if I were climbing a steep hill. Instead of pacing the house again, I made the bed, smoothing the sheet with my palm, seized by a memory of how we used to lie together on weekend mornings before the kids were born, luxuriating in the touch of skin and lips, of how I made my home in him.

I cleaned the kitchen floor, baked bread, and did more wash. Finally, my phone pinged.

Total chaos here, he texted. *You have no idea how bad it is. People are going crazy. Seeking shelter.*

I was out of ideas, blind to what was happening to him. His urgency rumbled through me. He was exposed, in danger, and afraid. What was the one thing I could say to support him?

Tell me the minute you're safe.

The chyron below the same video streaming on every television channel read, *CIA headquarters now being evacuated.* Headquarters was on the Virginia side of the river, the safe side. Over the course of that day, I began to understand the reality—there *was* no safe side. The virus was spreading, and the government couldn't do anything about it.

At that moment, a man crowed on Twitter that he'd stolen a skiff from the Georgetown marina and rowed across the Potomac River to freedom. He posted a photo of the city on the other side of the river, the tall spike of the Washington Monument in the distance behind him. I hated him because he did what my husband would not. Ted was too honorable, too rational, too fair to sneak away; he followed the rules. The very traits I loved about him now trapped him.

He texted, *Going to stay with a friend who owns a townhouse on Vermont Avenue.*

A few minutes later, he sent photos of a beautiful kitchen with enough light from tall windows to coax a lemon tree into fruiting, the lush yellow of the fruit beaming among the dark green leaves.

See. I'll be fine here. This is the sane choice. Don't come into the city. It's dangerous. Your job is to keep the kids safe.

I wanted to object, but instead, I typed, *Stay safe yourself. Love you.*

This was the coward's way out. If I were heroic, I would have jumped into the van, driven at breakneck speed down Rt. 270, careened into the city, and saved him despite what he said. Instead, I convinced myself that getting back to normal was just a matter of waiting. He'd be home for dinner in two days, or three. Four at the max. I pictured family pizza night with Ted standing at the kitchen counter, pressing the dough into a circle, laughing as it sprang back while the kids splashed red sauce and shredded mozzarella everywhere. I so wanted this to be true, I almost believed it.

Time rolled out in front of me, demanding to be filled, nights empty of our quiet conversations, his eyes lighting when I agreed with him on some point he made. My fingers tingled from clenching my phone.

"It'll just be another week until the panic dies down," he said the last time we spoke, the last time I saw his face on my phone. "Two weeks, the longest. They know what they're doing. I'll work from here until the all-clear sounds, and we can return to our lives as they were. Don't worry. Stay strong. Kiss the kids for me."

I knew that tone. He meant to reassure me. It's the tone he used when my mother died—measured and calm—the tone that said, "Something terrible has happened, but you can handle it."

)(

My sister tosses off her clogs and hat and leaps into the pool, shrieking as she did when she was a child. I step gingerly down the stairs into the shallow end.

Six months of lockdown have changed everything. It doesn't matter that we're wearing our gardening clothes; we'll hang our wet duds over the porch railing to dry. Lots of things don't matter anymore. We cut our own hair and wear the same jeans and T-shirts for days. Long gone are the days of nail polish and pedicures.

Somehow, the banking system still works, and our husbands' survivor pensions are automatically deposited in our bank accounts. I've stockpiled toilet paper, tampons, and pads for the girls when it's time. Masks, gloves, and five different kinds of bleach products are now stored in the basement closet, but I no longer browse the lipstick selections online. We purchase food we don't grow from a local farmer's market website. The guard texts when boxes of meat, dairy, eggs, locally grown and milled wheat flour, vegetables, and fruit are delivered to the gatehouse, and we ride over on our bikes to pick them up.

A stash of supplies in the van ensures we always have what we need if we ever go anywhere again. The house and its three acres are our safe zone, the place where we're free. Sometimes I feel like a sultan in Dubai, floating on my back in the pool's aqua waters, watching the peerless blue sky scroll around the earth. Then I remember that the rich in Dubai died in the first wave. We're in the second wave. It's not a good comparison for my karma.

The kids come running over, slide out of their flip-flops, and join us in the pool. Shock and grief have made them more compliant and quieter than they once were, but they still know how to play. In the water, they're more otter than children; it's their element. Ren performs his customary perfect dive with barely a splash. My beautiful Amina, who never calls attention to herself, slips over the side into the deep end and glides beneath the surface toward us.

Pam sits with Owen and Mira in water up to their armpits on the steps in the shallow end and shows them how to put their faces in the water and blow bubbles. Watching her, they shriek with delight. Even in the pool, my twelve-year-old niece wears her father's ancient Mets baseball cap. Pool water soaks the brim, and the babies' dripping faces resurface with wide grins.

"I did it!" Owen yells. At five, most of his conversation is at the top of his voice.

Mira grins, and light beams from her face. She reminds me of my sister at four years old and how I always envied her easy beauty. Sometimes, like her mother, Mira is eerily wise, as if she's reading my mind.

The kids make the loud, cheerful sounds children at play are supposed to make. Those sounds echo back to us from the surrounding mountains that hug our valley. They make me feel more fully alive, but I wonder momentarily if those same sounds cause heartache in other houses.

)(

It took twenty-four hours from the first symptoms—headache and vomiting, then diarrhea, palsy, unconsciousness—until Ted's friend died.

At least blood didn't leak from his eyes, he texted

My stomach turned over in sympathy, and a blaze lit in my belly. I pictured my husband attending the death throes of a man I didn't know—Ted's calm face and soothing words, the warm pressure of his hand. I closed my eyes, trying to unsee what he'd written. A vise squeezed my chest.

I wanted to scream, "Get out of there! Run for your life!" But I had to be calm, for his sake, for the kids. I had to stay strong even as every cell in my body revolted. My thumbs were barely able to land on the right letters. *It must feel like you're in hell.*

He replied. *Not doing so well myself, actually.*

My heart twisted.

Really tired. To the bone. Everything hurts, even my eye sockets.

I had to know if he was infected, but I couldn't ask in a text. I needed the sound of him in my ear, craved the breath between his words. He didn't accept a video call; my phone calls went right to voicemail. His recorded voice sounded so normal, a buoy in a storm sending a reassuring signal: this is the distance you are from home. I called him again just to hear his message and remembered his gift for understatement, for making light of the worst.

"Hang in there," I recorded through the knot in my throat. "You'll be home soon." I knew those words were a lie as soon as they left my mouth.

Apprehension followed me into my dreams. I woke up sweating, my throat raw as if I'd been screaming. To calm myself, I ran through my list of advantages: this was the 21st century, I lived in a first-world country, in a house of my own with every modern convenience, in luxury, truly. Two decades ago, there'd been a vaccine and treatments; surely, they had a cure for this virus too. Why wasn't anyone talking about defeating it? The government had just thrown up its hands and surrendered.

)(

A day after Ted's friend died—three weeks after the virus first struck—we ventured as far as the Post Office to mail my husband a care package of clean clothes and a tin of homemade chocolate chip cookies without knowing if it would be delivered.

Ren pointed to huge barriers being installed along Frontage and Millville Roads, where the US Customs and Border Patrol training campus sprawled across two hundred acres. "Look, they put barbed wire on top of the concrete barrier that was already there," my son said. "Like someone would want to get in."

I tried to grin, but my face wobbled. "The government must be predicting that we desperate rabble will storm the gates to steal their toilet paper."

Ren glared at me. "Not funny, Mom. More like their weapons and food."

Startled he thought this way, I noted that even with high walls, guards, and a trillion-dollar arsenal, government officials didn't feel secure. They knew something we didn't. Suddenly I understood: it was going to get worse. I pictured myself with a pitchfork, standing shoulder to shoulder with millions of starving, dirty people, forcing our way into their pristine bunkers, and in that instant, I understood the government's fear: there were more of us than there were of them. At what point would they use weapons to subdue us, to keep the infected at bay?

Ren, on the same wavelength, asked, "If they're not here to protect us, who are they protecting?"

No answer came to me. CBP trainees in desert camo with matching headgear pulled up next to our van in their unmarked black vehicle at the stoplight. The driver turned his head to scrutinize us, his face concealed behind an N95 mask and reflective sunglasses, reminding me of a praying mantis. Fear slid through me like a ghost.

"Whatever they're protecting, it's not us."

On the car radio, the newscaster rolled out the number of dead, a count that ticked up every minute, second by second, in every country. "The US," he intoned, "is up to a sixty-seven percent positivity rate."

Experts contradicted each other daily—how many would get sick, how many would die, what to do to avoid contact, the latest miracle cure. They were a smokescreen for a government that built walls to protect itself instead of solving the problem.

Sending Ted a care package was my way of claiming the world was still normal; I didn't know what else to do. I refused to imagine him sick, unable to move, lying alone and moaning on the floor of a stranger's house, but each day of his absence made it harder to breathe. I couldn't let the kids see my helplessness. I had to keep going. But periodically throughout the day, regardless of my perennial argument with Caro, I stopped wherever I was and silently begged an unhearing universe not to take my husband away from me. Tears gathered in my throat like early mourners.

Two more days passed, three, with no acknowledgment from him that he'd received the package. When I couldn't stand another second of not knowing what was happening, I phoned my sister. She was still waiting to hear from Nate. Caro understood the silence between words, how I couldn't say aloud what I feared because that might make it come true.

"Remember what Mom told us about portents?" she asked.

"No. What about them?"

"She told us how trees turn their leaves upside down before a storm to catch the raindrops. That's how you know when it's going to rain, even when it's sunny, because of the leaves."

"Caro, you can be so infuriating. What do leaves have to do with anything? I'm worried about Ted. I have no idea what you're talking about."

My sister sighed as if she were the long-suffering one in this relationship. "She was trying to tell us to watch for signs, so we'd know what was coming. So we'd be prepared."

"More new-age hooey from a woman who didn't want us around most of the time."

She waited silently while I huffed for a few seconds.

"Okay, what are the signs saying?"

"Protect the kids," she said.

I spent another week talking to myself, lying on our bed in the afternoon, my face in the pillow to stifle my moans, remembering Ted's warm palm on my knee, the way he said my name.

When Owen asked, "Where's Papa?" I pulled my five-year-old onto my lap and hid my face in his curls.

"He's staying at his friend's for a while." My voice broke.

My baby looked up into my face and put his hand on my cheek. "Really?"

Somehow, he knew I wasn't telling the whole truth. I nodded because I couldn't speak.

Three days later, the phone rang. My hands were wet from doing dishes. The screen said, "Unknown caller." Ted was calling from someone else's phone, or he was in the hospital. I swiped to accept the call and pressed speaker.

"Hello?"

"This call is to notify you that Theodore Bennett of four-three-two Redflower Lane, Harpers Ferry, West Virginia died September twenty-one from the Pandoravirus," the automated voice said. "For more information about his interment, go online to . . ."

I sank to the floor. Ted had died four days before, and I had no idea. We never said goodbye. I'd never hear his voice again, never touch him, never see him. I opened my mouth to wail, but no sound emerged.

I could only manage one thought at a time. They had a name for the infection. The government knew my husband's name and home address, the number to call. They had so many calls to make, they automated them. I sat on the kitchen floor, water dripping from my hands.

How did they know the body was him? Did a robot go through his pockets? Was he on some kind of list? How did they know where to find him? Then I remembered our federal IDs. DNA databases. Drone surveillance. Online tracking, even on our phones. Our lives were real-time data maps for anyone who knew where to look. None of that mattered anyway. My husband was dead.

Stay strong, I heard Ted say in my head. *Stay strong.*

I stumbled upstairs to our bedroom, closed the door, and lurched into the shower. My hands fumbled with knobs, and I stepped under streaming water to muffle the cawing sound that ripped out of my chest.

All the things I never said. The way he looked at me over his glasses. The feel of the soft hair on his legs spooning mine. His lips on my neck. His face when I smiled at him, like that was everything he'd ever need.

Stay strong, he said. *Keep the kids safe.*

)(

Caro got the call about her husband the next day and moved into my house with her children a month later, boarding up the windows and abandoning her home in Frederick, Maryland, before they closed state borders. It took her a month to talk about Nate's death.

Unable to tear ourselves away from the TV, we watched news coverage of removals. Protected in Mount Weather, their underground base in Virginia, the US government sent crews to mark buildings and collect bodies. Halfway across the world, drone footage showed the dead dumped into mass graves by remotely operated machines.

I stopped keeping track of the number of dead and carried dread high in my chest as a hedge against mortality. Every morning my muscles ached as if I'd been digging graves in my sleep. It was my job to ensure that no one else in my family got sick, that no one else died. Keeping them safe preoccupied me.

Caro tried to lighten our fear with logic. "We're a state away from the disaster's epicenter. People here don't crowd into elevators in high-rise buildings, take cabs, or ride in subways or buses. They don't line up to get into restaurants. We can walk for miles and never meet anyone."

"You're saying the infection can't travel through empty space indefinitely."

She nodded vigorously. "Right. It needs carriers. It's not like radiation from a nuclear blast, carried on the wind for miles. The virus needs people to transport and transmit it."

"So fewer people with greater distances between them out here means there's less chance of us getting sick."

We sighed, feeling momentarily like we'd received secret scientific data and solved the problem. Caro and I agreed to behave responsibly. If we isolated ourselves, we could evade the virus. My heart rate slowed, but hubris hovered in the back of my mind, daring me to notice.

And then an epidemiologist on the news used the words "exponential spread" and "airborne" to explain the three-hundred-million people already infected nationwide, blowing apart my temporary calm. I felt like a 1920s silent film damsel in distress, tied to the railroad tracks in front of an accelerating train—the whistle blew, the ground trembled, ten tons of steel came right at me, and I couldn't move.

"He's saying eighty percent of all the people on earth will be infected." I pointed to the expert's grave face on the screen. "That's more than five billion people!"

Caro shook her head. "Think about it the other way. Not everyone gets sick. If we stay away from people, we wear our masks, our chance of getting the virus decreases. That has to be true."

In the next breath, the same expert claimed children were immune; they weren't even carriers. Caro and I locked eyes. Our five kids sprawled across the family room, reading, playing games, building a Lego city, arguing over who controlled the remote.

I stopped listening to the experts. Nothing made sense anyway. New rules of what we could and couldn't do went up on the refrigerator: masks on the minute we went outside, no touching anyone except each other, no overnights, no contact sports with neighborhood children.

We took temperatures every morning before brushing our teeth and watched the kids for listlessness. The tell-tale signs of illness—pallor, swollen eyes, raspy voice—looked the same as grief. Hugging the children before bed at night, I pressed my lips against their foreheads, testing for heat. We recited a new catechism—*How does your stomach feel? Are you shaky? Do you feel weird?* —and waited for the right responses.

"I'm not weird," Pam said the first time I asked her, her lips twisting like her mother's. "My dad died. I'm sad."

My niece was right. When the people we love most die, when there is more death in the world than we can count, when each new death increases our sorrow exponentially, then sad is the only sane way to be.

Four months in, with West Virginia Public Radio reporting state infection numbers were low compared to neighboring states, the state layered eighteen-wheelers sideways across the bridges to stop traffic from other states. Only essential vehicles could get through. State troopers monitored roadblocks to guard against people abandoning their cars and walking across. A desperate Maryland woman leaped off the bridge onto the rocks below, leaving her children clutching the rail and screaming. How easily that could have been me.

Stay strong, Ted said in my head.

Online the rumor spread that government officials had been infected in their safe bunkers. The news reported that thousands of sailors were dead in warships prowling the seas on autopilot. TV pundits calmly discussed using drones to firebomb cities with over eighty percent positivity. Police officers were dying in droves. A new militia dubbed the USVPD clad head-to-toe in orange hazmat suits appeared on the streets without explanation.

We followed on maps as the infection zigzagged across the country in what looked like a planned attack, first decimating large cities, exhausting resources, and devastating medical personnel, and months later, swerving into less populated areas with limited defenses like ours.

Motorcycles grumbled along our streets at 3 A.M. for two weeks running. Sleepless anyway, we watched panic-struck from our windows. After an online debate, our exurban community used the homeowner association funds to install a high fence with steel gates at every entry point from the main road and issued electronic devices to open them. Armed guards now staffed gatehouses fitted with bullet-proof windows to protect us from the infected.

"I can't fathom anymore how we shook hands with strangers." Caro's face displayed her disgust. "All those germs."

I agreed. Grasping a stranger's hand in greeting, a high-five slap of bare palm against bare palm, or kissing a friend's naked cheeks now seemed the most wanton incivility.

Frustration built in my teenagers. Just when they needed to be set free, they'd been grounded by the lockdown—no playdates, no school, no track or soccer for Ren, no real-life meetings with friends. He immersed himself in his online games with a vengeance. Through his closed bedroom door, I heard heated exchanges in the middle of the night between him and players in California, Hawaii, and Taiwan. My friends, he called them when I asked who he was talking to, friends he'd never meet in real life.

"What are you talking about?"

"How to win." His eyes blazed. Framed photographs on the hallway walls shuddered as he slammed his door.

The girls huddled together over apps I'd never heard of and talked to friends online for hours about nothing. Sometimes Pam stared into space for too long, or Amina fell quiet in the middle of a sentence, or both were abruptly shrill, fighting over who owned a shiny red barrette. They sobbed unexpectedly when memories of their fathers caught them unprepared, but they had each other the way Caro and I did, someone who spoke their language and understood what they were going through. They no longer confided in us.

Owen's and Mira's orange, blue, yellow, and green drawings of our new family configuration went up on the refrigerator: two mommies and five children wearing masks and holding hands surrounded by mountains and trees while a brilliant sun burned overhead. They stopped asking where their fathers were.

)(

"The thing I saw, the apparition. It had wings, a huge wingspread, and was dark green," Caro says, floating on her back, talking to the sky.

I give in. "Okay, Caro. Was it menacing or protecting?"

"Neither. It was just there, hovering."

"What makes you think it has something to do with God?"

"It wasn't man-made. Maybe it was an omen."

My skin prickles. "What do you think the omen means?" I've seen the cards, but I couldn't say the answer out loud.

We're now in the space of the unspeakable, the things we never say for fear of making them come true. We don't even whisper our fear that despite our precautions, Caro and I will die from this infection before we've taught the kids how to survive, that they'll be alone, helpless without us to protect them, that they'll die. This is the specter we defy simply to keep going.

We live in the moment for a reason. We don't speak about a future, any future. We don't suggest the children will go to school or college or ever have jobs, much less professions. Life consists of doing chores that keep the house in one piece—dusting on Monday, vacuuming on Tuesday; Wednesday is for washing clothes. Thursday, we clean the bathrooms and the pool. On Friday, double-masked and gloved, wearing hats and long sleeves, we take garbage to the dump. In the spring and summer, we add gardening and mowing. That's our structure, the order that keeps us sane.

I no longer expect quarantine to end. Every day, ambulance sirens whine through the streets, even out here where houses are a quarter mile apart. We stop what we're doing and listen for the direction the sound heads, holding our breaths. When they pass us, we sigh.

Not our street, not us, not today.

Caro puts her feet down on the bottom of the pool and tugs at my hand to pull me upright. We walk through the water and sit on the steps in the shallow end with the little ones. They smack their feet against the water, and droplets fly around us in perfect, round rainbows. Mild waves lap against us when the older children cannonball into the pool. Endless sunlight creates mosaic tiles on the water.

Caro leans her head on my shoulder, and we watch the children play. This is my whole family now. I can't afford to lose any of them; every one of them matters. We are a tiny galaxy in a vast universe, spiraling faster and faster across space.

"I vomited blood this morning," she whispers.

2

Ren

WE don't bury my aunt. We burn her.

Mom hands me gloves and a mask. We dig a trench and lower Aunt Caro into the ground, wrapped in the sheets she died on, her clothes, and anything she touched in the last two weeks. I don't ask why. I just do what Mom says. We go from playing in the pool one day to cremating my aunt the next.

Mom yanks out the plants Caro put in the ground the day she gave in to Pandora, tosses them into a paper bag, and throws the whole thing on the fire. Her face twists, and she shudders as she throws the rake and hoe, the spade, Caro's gardening gloves and hers, her towels and toothbrush into the blaze. She doesn't stop to wipe the tears off her face.

The smell of burning hair makes me gag, but I have to be brave the way Dad was. His lips would turn down at the corners, and his eyes would half-close, but he never cried. I knew he was feeling stuff, but he didn't talk about any of it. I'm the one who has to be strong now.

We huddle on the back porch steps and watch Mom stand next to the fire—a wavy black shape outlined in red. She lifts her chin, her hands in fists at her sides, and screams at the sky. Every shriek makes my stomach clench. The girls stopped crying this morning. Now, Amina, Pam, and Mira sit silently with their arms around each other. They're so sad it makes them tired.

Owen wraps his arms around my neck and puts his cheek against mine. "What's Mommy doing, Ren?" he whispers.

"She's remembering Aunt Caro," I say, because, truthfully, I don't know either. It looks like she's obliterating her sister, totally deleting any sign she was ever here on Earth.

"Does Mom have the 'Dora too?" His body shakes.

"I don't know, Owen." I worry she's losing her mind.

"Don't come near me," Mom says, her hand up in the STOP position when she comes back to the porch. Owen abandons his leap from the steps mid-air and drops to the ground. He looks up at her, his mouth open, eyes blinking, confused that his mother won't catch him mid-jump, won't comfort him.

Her voice sounds strangled when she tries to explain. "I dripped water into her open mouth. I washed her face; she breathed on me. There's virus in my hair, on my skin. I've breathed it in. You can't come near me for fourteen days—if I live that long."

Like I need that extra idea. I'm already wrecked. Mom can barely drag herself upstairs, but she makes sure not to touch the banister.

"What about us, Mom? Are we contaminated too?" Amina calls up the stairs. Her face looks like she's been up late watching slasher flicks.

Mom's face, already gray, gets paler. "I don't think so." She holds her cheek with her hand. "God, I don't know. It's just an extra precaution. Keep doing what we always do—temperatures in the morning, symptom checks every day."

Amina looks at me, and I shrug because what can I say?

Mom stops at the top of the stairs. "Ren, spray the steps, anything I touched, my bedroom door. Use the bleach I keep under the kitchen sink. You're in charge. No one can come near me until I come out of my room. Can you take care of each other?"

Amina and I nod. What else can we do? Mom is counting on us. First, I think we have to be in this together, and in the next second, I almost say, "Why me? Why do I have to do everything?"

"Stay out of the pool," she warns us as she closes the door. "Maybe there's virus in the water now. We don't know how it spreads. Watch each other like hawks. You know the drill—vomiting, cough, fever, chills, sweats, headache, diarrhea."

Owen giggles. Amina shoots him a look, and he stops.

From the other side of the door, Mom says, "Look under the pelican magnet on the fridge. I put instructions there for what to do if I die."

We race into the kitchen. Amina pulls the handwritten list off the door and reads aloud: *If I die, don't touch me. Leave my body in the room and abandon the house.*

Shaking starts in my legs. I fall into a chair. Mom can't die. That can't be what happens next. Amina takes three shuddering breaths and closes her eyes. In a few seconds, she clears her throat. "I can do this," she says and raises her chin.

I like my sister. Even though she's only thirteen, she knows things, and she's not a drama queen. Dad would be proud of her. She throws her braid over her shoulder, stands straighter, and reads. *Go to Aunt Dee's house at 112 Leo Street in Sault Sainte Marie on the Canadian side across the Saint Mary's River from Michigan. She'll take you in.*

Amina sips some water and clears her throat. *Take the van. Get the gas cans from the shed. Follow the GPS directions. Select no tolls, no highways on the app. Drive as far as you can on back roads.*

She looks up from Mom's instructions. "Can you drive, Ren? I've got no idea how."

I nod because I think I can. Dad let me drive on the beach in the Outer Banks, steering his Jeep over hardpacked sand, the ocean roaring in on one side, high dune grass on the other. I felt like a test pilot breaking the sound barrier.

He grinned from ear to ear the whole time. "Never tell Mom I let you do this." Then he winked. Mom must have known; she knows everything.

My sister inhales the way singers do. *Take the paper map for when the GPS stops working. Dress in layers; don't take suitcases. Pack food, water, and toothbrushes. Put my phone and wallet in your backpacks. Leave everything else.*

Amina winds her braid around her hand one way and then the other like she's thinking of the things she has to leave behind. *Don't go through cities. Don't ask anyone for help. Keep the little ones safe.*

My sister looks at me, her eyes wide. I feel like someone is crushing my ribs together. We're too young to be responsible for everything. We're supposed to have time to grow into adults, not *boom*, and there we are. This is so not fair. Why do we have to leave home when everything we need is right here? I want to yell, "It's too much. I can't do it," but I don't. Mom's counting on me.

Amina reads Mom's final instruction. *You must make it to Canada. You'll be safe there. I love you forever.* Her voice breaks. She raises her face and stares at the ceiling. Tears drip off her chin, and she wipes them away with her shirt. She's quiet for a while and then, her voice rough, says, "Savage."

"Totally."

"We can't tell Owen and Mira."

"Tell them what?" Pam asks as she walks into the kitchen and plops down on a chair. She looks destroyed, like all the lives she had blew up at the same time, and it's game over, no coming back.

Amina and I look at each other. Pam's mother just died; it's amazing she can walk and talk. We have no idea what to say to her. Amina reads the instructions to Pam. It's easier the second time around.

Pam picks up the salt and pepper shakers and clinks them together. "I thought it was over." She puts down the shakers and stares into space like there are instructions on the wall she's supposed to be paying attention to.

"I don't want to go anywhere," she says. "Why can't we stay here? My mom is here."

She's saying what I wish I had the balls to say. Then it hits me. My cousin's an orphan at twelve years old; she's got nothing left to lose except her sister. We're her whole family now that her mom's dead.

In the last few months, she's become my best bud. We play the same games, and she thinks like me. If she doesn't live with us, she's alone. And then, like the second half of the house falling on me, I get that if Mom dies, we'll be orphans too. Inside, I'm like Mira, crying for my mommy to come back, but I can't let anyone know.

Even if Mom survives, my life is messed up. She thinks I'm ready to be in charge of the family, but I'm like a baby bird that just broke out of its shell. I can't fit back into the cramped space of being told what to do every minute, but I don't know how to get along on my own. My shell is broken, and I have to be ready to fly. That scares the crap out of me.

I take the instructions from Amina, fold the paper eight times, and put the small square in my jeans pocket. I can't lose them; they're my link to Mom. Amina has her eyes closed, but her face is calm. She's processing, like my avatar, when it's downloading a new skill.

We take turns sitting by Mom's door, checking in with her, and that night, the three of us older kids memorize the instructions, reciting them in the dark before we fall asleep on the couches in the family room. In the morning, we study the map, testing each other throughout the day. We don't know what will be important, what will save our lives. It could be the smallest thing.

Amina grips the edges of the map so hard, the paper rattles. Like Dad used to say when my sister drove me crazy, we deal with stuff in different ways. I catch myself constantly holding my breath and have to let it out in spurts so I don't blow apart. We have no idea if Mom will live or if we'll survive. We watch each other for symptoms the way Mom said. Amina takes our temperatures; I watch how the little ones eat to check if their stomachs are upset. So far, so good, as Dad used to say.

Once a day, Owen has a meltdown. He runs up to Mom's door and pounds on it. "Why is everybody staring at me?" he whines. Tears fly out of his eyes, and he buries his face in his arm. I get where he's coming from.

Mira sits beside him, puts her head on his shoulder, and pats his back. "You don't have to be scared," she says. "It'll be okay." Her hand is so tiny, but somehow, it comforts him.

When Mom paces her room, her footsteps creak above us. Some days, there's no noise, as if she's not moving. I lie on the sofa staring at the ceiling and make a rule for myself that if she goes three days without moving, I'm going into the room to check on her. Every day, when I take the tray of food upstairs, I call out, "Food's here, Mom." It's another way to make sure she's alive.

"Leave it by the door, Babe," she says. "I'll get it after you walk away."

I feel better just hearing her voice. Sitting on the floor in the hall across from the door, I talk to her just to be sure she's okay mentally. The second day, she starts telling me stories about her childhood, like she's handing them down to me so they won't be lost if she dies.

She tells me about riding her bike down a hill so fast she knew she couldn't manage the turn at the bottom, so she ditched the bike on purpose before she crashed into a tree. "I could feel the angle between me and the earth steepening," she says, "like gravity was pulling on me." I know there's a lesson in that story she wants me to learn, but I can't figure out what it is. Is it about knowing something will be a problem and solving it or doing stupid things?

"I'm not as smart as you think I am, Mom. I don't always understand you." But maybe, I think, it's a warning to save myself before we crash.

She coughs when she laughs. "Yes, you are. You're way smarter than I am."

We're quiet for a while, and then she says, "I feel like I failed you. I wasn't strong enough, and Dad said . . ."

The rest is muffled, and I don't know how to answer her anyway, so I tell her about something I saw on CNN that I don't get. She finds it on her tablet, and I replay the story on my laptop so we're both watching police in riot gear with plastic masks drag people out of their homes into white vehicles painted with infinity symbols on the sides. The people thrash, hang onto door jambs, sob, and scream as the police use their batons to get them to move.

She says, "Oh, my God."

"How can they do this?" I ask. "Those people were in their homes. They weren't bothering anyone." It's hard not to cry.

"They must be sick," she says, using her calm voice. "This must be from another country, like China, where they have a different kind of government. The police are removing the sick to protect the healthy."

"This is CNN, Mom. It's from here. In Brooklyn, it says right on the screen. That's in New York, right? How do the police know who's sick?"

"I don't know," she says, her voice low. "Maybe the police monitor social media. Or the people who do the virus tests report them."

"Why would people report each other?"

"To keep themselves safe? Or maybe their phones identify contact with someone who's been infected and automatically send the information to a database the police monitor." Then she whispers like someone else is listening. "Ren, you need to be careful what you say online, to anyone, about anything, but especially about us. Don't tell anyone Caro was sick."

I try to remember whether I told my gamer friends about how we cremated my aunt, but I don't want to believe they would tell the authorities. What's in it for them to do that? Does the government pay for each sick person someone reports? The thought is too weird and complicated and doesn't help me deal with what's happening right now.

"How did this pandemic happen?" I ask for the millionth time because no answer ever makes sense to me.

"I don't know," she says. Before Aunt Caro died, Mom's answer was different every time. Dad said he liked the way she thought. Every idea was a Rubik's cube with multiple moving parts, and if she just kept turning the pieces over and over, the answer would fall into place. I never understood what he meant.

I think I'll know the truth when I hear it, but so far, nothing makes sense. "I heard we were attacked," I tell her. "My gamer friends said that cleaners for public spaces—you know, train stations, subways, airports, offices—"

"Oh yeah, the maintenance people who clean post offices and librar- ies, malls."

"Right. Those guys entered the buildings at night while no one was watching, the way they always do, and used contaminated cleaning sup- plies to wash the floors and bathrooms. Wherever they went, they left invisible viruses on everything. The workers got sick too. It took only one night to infect enough people to cause a pandemic."

"On purpose?"

"My friends said so."

"Was it just here in the US?"

"It started in the US and spread because of people flying everywhere."

Mom is quiet for a while and then whispers, "That might make sense. People I follow in L.A. and Chicago, Miami and Houston, Atlanta and New York City say the virus struck there the same day. Then Mumbai, Rome, Paris, Madrid, Moscow, Beijing, and London fell in the next few days."

"Mom, do you think it's true?"

"Yes. Maybe. I don't know."

"Mom."

"Well, I saw another theory that claimed it was eco-terrorists trying to rid the world of excess human population—cull the herd, they called it."

"Mom, that's like a crazy idea."

"Yeah. It is crazy. Wild speculation, but otherwise, we're talking about a million-year-old deadly virus embedded in Arctic permafrost that thawed because of global warming, or a microbe that escaped from a lab during an accident no one reported because they didn't want to be fired, or some poor fool infected by a feral pig, spreading it to millions of people."

I hate this. Knowing there's no explanation or that the government deliberately keeps the answer a secret doesn't help. Guesses don't do any good; I just feel more helpless. "What happened to Dad?" I can't stop myself. This is the question I need the true answer to. It's like popping poison ivy blisters with a pin—I have to ask, even though I don't want to hear her say it.

"What I told you before. He got sick and died."

I have to wait a few seconds until my voice comes back. "How do you know?"

"They called me."

"Who called?"

She takes a breath this time like she's wondering about this too. "The government."

"What did they do with his body?"

She's already told me so many times. This answer never changes, even when she tries to make it easier to hear. Knowing the truth won't change the fact that I'll never see that oh-my-god-my-kid-is-so-smart look on my dad's face again. The way he smiled at me.

I have to deal with what the government did to him, but I can't get over it. The only way to move on is to hear it again and again until I get numb. "Did they have a ceremony? Did anyone say his name or play music?"

Mom gasps and coughs. Even though I can't see her, I know her eyes are half-closed, and her head tilts as she thinks how to say this part. Her face will look like she's taking five Gs of force, the way it did the first time she told us. She never gets used to saying the words, no matter how many times she tells it.

"No, baby. Nobody said anything or played music or prayed. The police collected the first batch of bodies, cremated them, and buried boxes containing their ashes in trenches they dug in the old football stadium a few blocks from the Capitol."

This is the brutal truth. Saying it kills her every time. I can't breathe for a second. My head's going to explode. It's totally unfair. We never hurt anyone. We don't even call people names. Why does anyone want to hurt us?

Then I get it. The answers to my questions don't matter; even my questions don't matter. It's just the way it is. Life is like my games; it comes with a built-in setup. Each game will always be the same, no matter how many times I play it, but if I keep playing, my skills will improve.

I'll learn the rules, anticipate the bad guys better, win this round, and go on to the next level. That's what I have to concentrate on—improving my skills and getting to the next level in this new game.

"Mom, will we ever have a normal life?"

"Experts say it will take a generation for humans to adapt to the virus. Maybe more."

"Are the experts right?"

"I don't know."

"Will the bad guys attack us again?"

"I don't know. I've been doing some reading. They don't need to. People will spread the virus now without any help from anyone." She sucks in her breath like thinking about it will end her.

"How long will it last?"

"Till it runs out of people to kill."

My chest feels like it's going downhill on a roller coaster. "Then how do we win, Mom?"

"You never give up." Her voice sounds like her throat is clogged. She clears it. "You do whatever you have to do to survive. If you don't know what that is, close your eyes, ask yourself the question, and wait for the answer. Then do that. Or ask your sister. Amina will know."

When she starts crying, I go downstairs to give her privacy. Dad is gone, and Aunt Caro. Mom could be next. I touch my pocket to make sure her instructions are still there.

)(

Ten days later, we're in the kitchen, and we hear her door open. We pound up the stairs and wrap ourselves around her. She's shaky, but she's showered and smells like soap. I picture how we look from the ceiling—like an animated illustration from my biology unit of one squirming organism about to replicate itself.

"Are you okay?" she asks each of us, her palms on our cheeks, staring into our eyes. When she gets to me, she reaches up for my face and says, "Oh my God, Ren, you're a giant. And your hair is long and curly. How did that happen in two weeks?"

"I've been like this, Mom. You were just used to it. We celebrated my fourteenth birthday a month ago. Are you okay?"

She hugs me. "I survived. So happy to see you, Sweetheart, so glad I'm alive to see you."

It's all I can do not to put my head down on her shoulder the way I did when I was five, close my eyes, and hold on. I was safe in her arms. Whatever she said was the truth. That was back when we had a perfect life, when Dad was alive, and when I went to school and had real in-person friends. That's over. I could tell myself everything will be okay like Mira does, but I'd be lying. More bad stuff is coming. I can feel it. That's how games go; they always get harder.

The next time we pick up our meat and vegetables order from the farmers' co-op at the gatehouse, the guard tells us through the glass that our neighbors are dead. Mom doesn't ask how he knows. That afternoon, a windowless white bus with "USVPD" and the infinity symbol painted on the side rolls up the street. We watch from our second-floor windows, taking turns with the binoculars Dad used to watch birds.

People in neon orange hazmat suits go into the house. They bring out two large, black plastic zipper bags that look heavy. Then they drag the kids, dressed in head-to-toe white space suits, out the door. An officer with "Sgt. D. Cooper" stamped on the sleeve shoves the kids into the vehicle.

Amina points. "Are those . . . ?"

"Some kind of government personnel," Mom says. "The virus police, must be."

"The kids are alive." Pam presses her nose against the glass, her cap pushed to the back of her head. "The kids didn't get sick." She waves and places her palm on the glass. The neighbor kids can't see us. "They must be scared. I would be."

"We didn't get sick from our neighbor even though Aunt Caro did," Amina says. "Does that mean kids are immune?"

"I heard that kids don't get sick," Mom says, but she doesn't sound sure.

Through the bathroom window on their second floor, we see smoke. Mom says it's the chlorine gas they use to fumigate buildings. The police board up the doors and windows on the first floor. One of them sprays an orange ∞ symbol on the door.

"What does that mean?" Amina asks.

"The house is contaminated." Mom's voice is flat like the feeling's been pressed out of it. "Forever. It's a warning so no one will go in there." She stands at the window looking out for a while after the government vehicle leaves.

"We have to go," she says. "Whoever told on Paul and his wife must have told on Caro. They'll come for us tomorrow or the next day because she died. I don't know why it didn't happen sooner." She puts her palm on my chest. "Ren, get our camping gear and the plastic gas cans from the shed and bring it all into the garage. Amina, fill our water bottles. Owen, find our sleeping bags and pile them by the back door. Pam, Mira, come with me. We're going to pack food. We leave tonight."

"Why tonight?" I'm not defying her. I just want to know.

Mom looks me right in the eyes. "It's time. The virus is here, in our neighborhood. When they come for us, they'll take me away from you because they'll know Caro made me sick. You and Owen will be separated from Amina and Pam. They'll put Mira somewhere else because of her age. You'll never find each other again. I can't let that happen. We have to stay together."

I'm dizzy, like I just inhaled glue fumes.

"We're going tonight so we don't panic our neighbors into a mass migration. The less movement a satellite or drone detects, the more likely we'll get away from here without being noticed."

Mom's right. Even though cops don't patrol our neighborhood, drones fly overhead every day. The government must keep track of everyone.

Pam's mouth opens in an O, her eyebrows raised. She glances at Amina and then blurts, "But my mom is here. You're leaving my mom—and everything—here."

She's braver than my sister, or it's just that she'll say what's on her mind, and Amina won't. My sister looks down at the floor like she warned Pam not to say anything, and now she's blown it.

"I know, Sweetie," Mom says.

"I want to stay here," Pam says. Tears leak out of the corner of her eyes.

Mom squeezes Pam's hand and tugs the brim of her baseball cap down. "You and Mira are going with us. We're not leaving you behind. You're part of our family. You'll always be part of us."

Pam's face turns red. "You don't get it!" she shouts. Her fists fling out in front of her like she's going to fight. "I don't want to be a part of *you*. I want the family I had with my own mom and my dad and Mira."

Mom looks like someone dropped a bucket of ice on her head. "Honey, you can't stay here alone. It's not safe. How will you take care of yourself?"

"We'll be fine. Me and Mira. Why can't you just leave us here?"

She's fighting against her tears, but they keep coming. I can't decide if she's brave or crazy. If I were her, my insides would be mush. Pam watched her mom go up in flames. I don't know how I'd handle it, but probably not as well as she is.

Mom puts her palm on Pam's cheek without saying anything, and slowly, Pam leans against Mom like it's okay again, but her lips are pressed together, which tells me it's not. Mom rubs her shoulder, takes Mira's hand, and walks into the kitchen like the showdown's over and everything's okay.

Pam adjusts her cap and follows her. She's decided something; I can tell by how she won't look at me.

I'm hollow. I look around the house I grew up in. We've been safe here, and now, we aren't. I look up Aunt Dee's address on Google Maps. It's a thousand miles away, far from here. Anything could go wrong. What if we don't make it?

Amina throws her arm around my waist and squeezes. "Hey, wake up. Don't forget the water purification stuff in the shed."

Dad always said my sister was the sensible one. If you ask Amina what she wants to be when she grows up, she smiles and says, "I just want to be grown up." That is the last thing I want to be.

I tug her braid. "How come you're so calm?"

She shrugs. "What else are we going to do? No one's coming to save us. We have to do it ourselves."

)(

"Coronavirus research has contributed to the understanding
of many aspects of molecular biology in general, such as
the mechanism of RNA synthesis, translational control,
and protein transport and processing. It remains a treasure
capable of generating unexpected insights."

—HOWARD HUGHES MEDICAL INSTITUTE,
UNITED STATES, 2008

)(

3

Sgt. D. Cooper, USVPD

IN the pep talk before our first assignment out in the boonies near Harpers Ferry, West Virginia, LT reminds us that we might encounter lethal resistance from anyone in the residence or from neighbors. "All those second amendment proponents out there got guns," she says. "If they panic, they might not hesitate to use them."

We're ready. There's no knowing what we'll find when we enter a home, but we're armed, too, with guns, tasers, batons, and tear gas, just in case. The job of the United States Virus Protection Directorate is to remove the infected and dead from society so the healthy will survive. It's the same as deadheading plants so they grow the right way. People should think of us as gardeners.

The whole country's in lockdown, and the damn virus is still spreading, so we have to step in. It's not like we want to be cruel, but we're prepared for a backlash and physical resistance even though the President called us frontline heroes in his latest speech from the bunker. I'm not surprised folks don't see us that way; I don't find talking heads convincing, either.

LT points to a vintage image on the screen behind her of a woman holding a baby. "Don't make a Ruby Ridge out of it," she reminds us. "Just get the targets on the bus. It's not an arrest, but it's okay to use appropriate force to detain them."

Of course, LT knows what happens when regular folks like me get permission to use force. Things escalate. Maybe the powers-that-be are counting on that outcome.

Our assignments come from headquarters. Intake clerks assemble daily lists of tips from neighbors, landlords, healthcare workers, local police, and health departments—even disgruntled exes. The names aren't vetted beyond the initial report, but there's an eighty percent chance a target will be infected when we reach their doorstep. It's pretty obvious who's sick—their eyes look empty. We'll know what's what when we get there.

LT stares at the ceiling tiles of our HQ assembly room for a second and adds, "Don't shoot 'em." She needs to underline that for the younger team members who weren't born in 1992 or didn't listen in history class. "They're not criminals. Think of them as rabid animals," she advises. "We're just going to quarantine them."

Putting them down on the spot and burning the building would be simpler, but I don't say that out loud. I've got an outlier view of things, but my way would certainly be quicker. Why waste all those resources on someone who's gonna die anyway?

We're supposed to be in and out of a dwelling in twenty minutes to minimize contact with viral particles in confined, contaminated environments. The less time we spend with infected bodies in enclosed spaces, the better. After six weeks of training, my squad can clear a single-family home in fifteen minutes, but we're novices at this, and hours of practice with dummies or compliant colleagues haven't prepared us for the real thing. We know that going in, though.

In training, they told us at least half of everybody infected dies from this virus, which is not as bad as Marburg, Ebola, or AIDS. This killer spreads from person to person, but they haven't figured out how yet. They do know it's more contagious, so they expect eighty percent of the US population will be infected before it's over. The Centers for Disease Control, the government agency that's supposed to know this stuff cold, says more than half the US population is already compromised. Boggles the mind. And half of those infected folks don't know it, the agency claims, because they're asymptomatic. Despite the lockdown, they're roaming around the country spreading germs. They have to be stopped.

It's not all bad news, though; the virus isn't a sixth extinction event, and it *will* eliminate the weak. That's got to be the upside. LT said the top estimate is a hundred million deaths in the US by the time the contagion has spent itself, but that's got to be wrong. It'll be more like two hundred million dead, and all those sick people mean job security for me. When it's over—a date nobody seems willing to guess—there'll still be enough people, which is good because my own company bores me silly. I've seen up close what happens to people who drink alone. It's not pretty.

We suit up before we leave headquarters, thinking it's only an hour and a half drive to Harpers Ferry. Once I'm inside that suit, only my eyes and eyebrows show through the clear plastic visor, but wearing this gear is the safest I've felt since the pandemic started, even if the sweat trickling down my cheeks under the headpiece makes me cranky.

I can't wipe my face without removing the headpiece, visor, and gloves, and that's too much trouble since it takes two people to dress one. Got to remember to wear a headband next time. I wonder if this is how astronauts feel walking around the moon. Wearing a five-and-dime spacesuit is the closest I'll ever get to that kind of glory.

"You okay in there, Diana?" LT yells like I'm hard of hearing.

I give her a thumbs up. "Yeah," I yell, but I sound like a robot. Everyone in these get-ups sounds like they're eating rocks.

When Manny pulls the vehicle up to the gatehouse at our target's location, we're knocked off our seats. It's completely different from the wooded hills with falling down shacks or the open farmland with scattered homesteads we expected. Not a pig in sight, no cars jacked up on cinder blocks. It could be any suburban neighborhood in Maryland with large, manicured lawns and fancy landscaping. I never knew rich bitches lived out in West Virginia.

Riley says out loud what we're all thinking. "Entitled rich bitches with guns. The worst kind."

Manny shows our credentials to the guard, and we wind along a narrow, paved road to a two-story house with a couple of acres around it. I should be so lucky. Grass and trees as far as the eye can see. It's like living in a park. I'm guessing my 400-square-foot studio in the dorm has less space than their master bathrooms.

No one opens the door to our polite knock or our repeated yelling, "USVPD, open up!" So, we resort to standard procedure and storm it. The place is a mess—dirty plates, open cereal boxes, bags of chips, garbage everywhere—and the decomp stink is nauseating, powerful enough to permeate my headgear.

Three kids sit on the floor in the living room, playing a game of Monopoly. I don't know how they tolerate the smell. They must be used to it. They look up at us without moving or speaking, a blank expression on their faces.

They must have been alone in the house for more than a week and are traumatized by their parents dying or shocked at the sight of us, or both, but it's still disappointing that they don't greet us as saviors. Even though they aren't listed on the assignment sheet, protocol says we can't leave them in a house contaminated by two dead adults.

LT says, "Cooper, you evacuate the kids."

At first, I think she gave me the easy job, but the second I say, "Okay, let's go," in my robot voice, the kids freak out, run around the house in different directions, hide in the bathrooms, and lock the doors.

I let them scream for a while to exhaust them, and then I break down the doors one at a time and drag them out. That lets them know who's boss. They settle down after that. The littlest one isn't sobbing too loud.

Day one of the pandemic, we learned if you let people get away with a little, they're gonna try to get away with a lot. Like that New York mayor said, someone who can spit on a sidewalk can rob a convenience store or something like that. Add weapons and looting in the cities, and by the fourth month of the pandemic, it was constant street skirmishes with resisters. The government finally figured out we gotta stop 'em in their tracks before things get out of control.

Easy for them to say; they were all holed up in air-conditioned bunkers, but cops dropped like flies in the early months, and nobody could figure out why. If they had thought about it, they could've seen from the beginning that this virus is sneaky. It slides inside you when you least expect it. Obviously, detentions were contamination central. You're out there detaining a guy who's resisting, and after you pop him once or twice, blood gushes, he's squalling, there's spit and sweat, and the virus gets on you. You wipe sweat off your face, and bingo, you're infected.

Transferring from state highway patrol to USVPD was the best career move I could make. A nice bump in salary, a better apartment than the place I had, and nutritious meals in cute takeaway boxes stacked on a table outside the decontamination suite after we've showered off from that day's job are definite pluses.

As a bonus, my drunk ex-husband can't sneak past the guards in the dorm lobby to bang on my door in the middle of the night. I'm so over him I wonder why I ever started. The way he lied about everything. It must have been that misleading puppy dog look, that black curl hanging over one eye. I hate myself now for buying his baloney.

After Riley and Popova remove the parents, they help me. "Jesus, stop squirming," Riley yells at the kids. That just makes them wriggle more.

"See what I'm talking about," I say, my hands gripping the middle boy's ankles so Popova can get the suit over his feet while he thrashes.

It takes another twenty minutes to zip them into the suits. We're way past our time limit in the house, which makes us tense because longer exposure means greater danger, and we might apply a little disproportionate force. Our detainees incur a few minor injuries in the process, which I duly report to LT, who doesn't think it's necessary to note that on the official removal report.

"We're doing this for your own good," I tell the kids. My dad used to say that to me before he smacked me, so I figure they've heard it before. "We're taking you to a nice school where you'll be fed, have a bed, and someone will take care of you. It'll be clean there. You'll be safe."

"We don't want to go anywhere," the tallest one yells like I'm deaf. "Leave us alone. You can't put us in cages. We're Americans." He flails his arms like a windmill and gets the younger kids riled up again. Tears spurt out of their eyes like juice from a cut lemon.

"Settle down." I use my firmest voice, but I have to whack the back of his knees anyway to calm him. He's an annoying kid.

Like putting them in cages is even a thing we do. Although we only drop kids off where we're told to, so I don't know about the conditions of their confinement. After a tense phone conversation with HQ, LT gets these children ordered to the closest destination for orphans in this area—a private boarding school the government commandeered in Hagerstown, Maryland, half an hour north of here.

The littlest one clings to the front door jamb when I try to herd her toward the bus. I feel a little bad about knocking her fingers with my baton to wrench her free, but she's resisting. She made me hit her, although, unlike *my* father, I would never hold a grudge against a kid who didn't know any better.

"Can you make sure I stay with my sister?" the middle-sized boy asks as I help him climb into the bus.

I shrug. "Not my call, Bud." I try not to be annoyed with their whimpering.

They should be glad we aren't taking them to one of the contamination camps the Corps of Engineers set up in stadiums. Rumor is the virus is more lethal in those camps because of crowding and bad airflow. I've seen the videos on social media of women clinging to the fences, mouths open, shrieking, "Where are my children?" It's not a good look for America. Officials need to get control of the stuff going out on the Internet.

"Is anyone in government thinking about what to do with the orphans after this is over, how to reconnect them with surviving family?" Popova asks as she holds the girl down in a seat while I secure the seatbelt.

My suit rustles when I shrug. Popova's naïve. This Pandoravirus—open the box you're not supposed to open, and every terrible thing flies out—has blown up our way of life, and the only thing we can do is mop up afterward. Time for Popova to grow up. "No one knows if there'll be a future."

Her eyes blink like "message received."

Now that I'm thinking about it, though, I can see myself managing an orphanage and protecting children from ruthless predators. I mean, what were their parents thinking, leaving these kids in the house with no preparation? It's reckless, not having a plan for your kids' survival. Every family should be required to have a plan. I might draw one up and pass it up the chain of command for publication and get noticed so they already know my name when I apply for lieutenant next year.

We drop off the kids, and fifty miles later, right when we arrive back at our Montgomery County base, we get an order to extract a female adult from the house next door to the one we just did—another seventy-five miles back the other way. We look at each other through our visors.

"Bosses," LT says and rolls her eyes.

"Computers," Riley says.

Everyone breaks out laughing. We'll get to her tomorrow. It's not like she's going anywhere. As far as I'm concerned, anyone infected who thinks they can wander around the country deliberately putting other people's lives at risk is a criminal. Catch 'em, lock them in the camps, and let nature take its course—that's my plan.

4

Jean

I HAVE to believe we'll be safe at Aunt Dee's house in Canada. Caro and I visited once as teenagers when Mom needed us out of the way for the summer. My aunt's welcoming smile when she saw us standing on her doorstep, her hugs and chatter, eased the sting of being inconvenient and discarded.

Dee's sedate Tudor-style house glowed like a Matisse painting inside with unexpected colors, patterns, and textures; it was our sanctuary. Amid that visual liveliness, my adolescent otherness diffused. I could laugh even when I was confused and sad—exactly the medicine my children need now.

A thousand miles, a three-day drive. I can manage this. Once we're over the Saint Mary's River and across the border, we're free from any federal officers chasing us. Except, when I stop giving myself the pep talk and realize I'm about to embark on a thousand-mile mad dash, running from the authorities and a deadly infection with five children in tow, my sense of dread grows.

The memory of that goon dragging Katie from her house next door— the baton hitting her hands—flares. I picture armed officers snatching Mira, yanking her from Pam's arms. My skin shrivels. I can't let that happen; the children can't be taken from me. No matter what.

The calculus of contagion that Caro taught me—more open space with fewer humans to catch and spread the infection—should make transmission more difficult. I imagine the virus's protein shell drying and cracking in the open air, splitting apart, and dying before it inserts its DNA into another human cell. Its death gives me deep satisfaction.

Between instructions for packing, the kids stand in the garage, limp-armed, staring around at the neighborhood as if they were already orphans who had lost their way. What if something happens to me, and they're left alone? They're completely unprepared.

"Mom." Ren startles me out of my anxiety attack. "How are we going to get past the checkpoints at bridges?"

My smart boy, already thinking about the obstacles ahead and formulating a plan, snaps me back to reality.

"We'll take backroads the police aren't watching. I know a way that takes us far enough upstream that we only have to cross a one-lane bridge way out in the middle of nowhere. Dad and I went that way once. No one will be monitoring that spot. We'll head north first and then west."

"What if someone else stops us?"

I don't have an answer. Other bad guys never even occurred to me. My son has jumped far ahead, leapfrogging over the end of government as we know it. His question assumes someone, for good or ill, gives a damn about what we do. I don't think anyone does, except for virus police organized enough to swarm our little outback when someone dies. He imagines a much creepier future with more bad guys than I've considered. Is he right, and the virus police will come after us no matter where we go?

"Mom? How are we going to avoid the feds?"

"I'll trick the GPS."

The device has always been a mystery to me. I picture a ring of satellites circling the Earth, signaling to banks of redundant servers powered by alternate energy. The servers are housed in large warehouses hidden in remote Arctic locations and maintained by robots. Images of a world empty of humans but with automated gizmos still working buzz my mind. I envision a monkey tapping on my cell phone. I'm losing it.

"How, Mom?"

"Type in a city as if that's our destination, even though what we want is only the general direction."

"Can you do that?"

"Dad used to do it all the time with the old system." How my husband had tortured that device, trying to make it see the world the way he did. "He didn't like the roads it told him to use."

His mind was always too complicated for me.

I hug Ren's shoulders. "I don't think anyone is watching us, honey. They've got more important things to do." He gives me a guarded look like I don't want to know what he's thinking. "We'll use your phone. Maybe they won't check that. And I'll turn mine off."

We pile into the minivan, do a last-minute check of supplies, chargers, and water, and pull out of the driveway. From the street, I look back at the house I love. Howling starts in my head, but I turn it off. No time for melodrama or goodbyes.

The girls make hearts with their hands against the windows as we drive through the neighborhood, framing photographs in their minds. They wave to the night guard at the gatehouse. I don't stop to tell him what we're doing or where we're going in the middle of the night, and he doesn't stop me to ask. The less contact, the better. That's the new social contract.

I drive south on Route 340 to Withers Larue Road and turn right. I remember this lane from the ancient past when I drove to a yoga retreat up in the mountains. The dark, winding road, up and down hills past old farms puts the kids to sleep.

Ren, riding shotgun, holds the phone in his hands, following the map view as I steer, and points as the automated voice of the GPS lady calls out turn-by-turn instructions.

According to the map in my mind, her directions feel counterintuitive, but I obey. I've learned she's always right because she knows where the roadblocks are. If only she could tell me what happens after this, what the map of our future looks like, and if I'm driving in the right direction.

Night reduces the visible world to the slice of the road illuminated by my headlights. Our route's circuitous; no one would be able to guess where we're going by the turns we take until we hit Route 11 and head west. Even then, the whole country opens up from there. We could be going anywhere, not that anyone cares.

We have the road to ourselves at three in the morning. Even trucks aren't lumbering over the asphalt. Every once in a while, Ren spots a light in a house in the distance and points to it as if it's a beacon of safety, a lighthouse in a sea of monstrous waves and sharp rocks. We have no idea what's happening in those houses, but if lights are on in the middle of the night, it's nothing good.

Even if those homes were safe havens and the area was virus-free, with the vehicle's hybrid fuel system, a full tank, and twenty gallons of gas stored in plastic jugs in the trunk, I don't plan to stop at a station for a fill-up for five-hundred miles, about halfway to our destination. That should cut down on our contact with other people.

The steady rhythm of the kids' breathing calms me. Owen's curly head leans back against his car seat, his cheeks rosy, his perfect lips slightly parted. Mira's eyelids flutter as she dreams, one finger patting her lips. Pam rests her head against Amina's shoulder, Amina's cheek on her hair, like angels resting in a Renaissance painting. Their beauty makes me breathless.

Outside the safe confinement of the SUV, the countryside divides into the precise geometric shapes of planted fields and cleared circles around houses briefly lit by our headlights as we pass.

It's as if the pandemic had never struck, and then I spot a truck flipped sideways onto the shoulder, where the driver didn't slow for the S curve. Glass is strewn across the road. No one has come to collect it yet. Adrenaline shoots sharply through my legs. I swerve, avert my eyes, and don't stop to call it in, either.

Three times the mountains rise steadily as I take turns, my ears popping as we descend. Ren drowses in his seat, his head lolling against the window. I slow down to avoid waking him on the curves when his head tilts to the other side. Hours pass, my eyes close, and something brushes against my arm.

Go slower, Caro whispers in my ear. *There's a problem ahead.*

I whip my head around to see her as if she were in the backseat, but only the children are sleeping there, their faces glowing in the early morning light. "You fell asleep, idiot," I mutter to myself.

Ren jerks awake. "What's that, Mom?" He looks around, rubbing his eyes with his fists. "Where are we?"

"We're outside Breezewood, Pennsylvania. I need a pit stop."

He grins. "Yeah. Me too."

In town, we crawl through a pretzel-shaped intersection to stay on the main street and pass a small brick post office building. A gray pickup sits in front. Oddly, there's no other sign of activity, no mail trucks or postal employees arriving for the morning mail-sorting shift.

Brick cottages and ranchers with lots of grass around them spread out from the cross streets at the lone traffic light. It's quiet, but maybe nobody's sick here. Or they're all dead. I tell myself we're far from a major city, and it's six in the morning—logical that everyone would be in bed—but I don't believe that's why it's so quiet.

Two motels, four gas stations, a truck stop, and a gaudy rest stop for highway drivers fan out from the highway intersection with Main Street. In a town this size, it would only take one church picnic to infect everyone. And then I realize what's strange about this scene—no cars moving anywhere. That's unusual, even under lockdown rules.

Not here, Caro says in my head. *Keep driving.*

Not that I ever listened to my sister when she was alive, but I trust whatever is talking to me. Too many viral carriers, I think. I must be a carrier also, but none of the kids got sick. They were in the pool; they played with Caro. Mira slept in her lap. An idea breaks over me like a wave: not everyone gets sick.

"Too many people here," I say.

Ren looks around and back at me. "I don't see anyone."

"Who knows who's inside the buildings."

He nods like he knows what I'm talking about. Maybe he does. What we used to call paranoia has become good common sense now.

The kids stir in the backseat. "I'm hungry," Mira says.

Amina rummages in her backpack and pulls out one of the last of Caro's homemade granola bars. Mira peels back the wax paper wrapping, sniffs the bar, and whines, "I want one with chocolate." Amina plunges her hand back into the bag and extracts the correct offering. Mira smiles and takes it from her.

"Thank you," the child remembers to say. We are still civilized.

Amina smooths Mira's hair back from her face. She bites into the bar rejected by her four-year-old cousin and chews. "Peanut butter," she says to Mira.

Mira makes her "that's disgusting" face. "Yuk."

Owen yawns and stretches his arms. I remember the silk of his cheek under my thumb. "I have to pee," he calls out.

Pam hands him an empty bottle. I glance at his face in the rearview mirror. "Ew," says my son, looking at his cousin with a mixture of disgust and curiosity. "I'm not peeing in that. You drank out of it."

Pam raises her eyebrows so high that they disappear under her cap's brim. "You're worried about my spit?" The kids giggle.

"Okay, guys. Settle down." I need to focus. Their bickering will distract me. "After I deal with whatever's right ahead of us, we'll stop somewhere, and you can run around while I rest for two hours. I'm bushed."

My word has always been good; I keep my promises. They settle and watch out the windows. In ten minutes, according to the GPS, the old two-lane Lincoln Highway narrows to a one-lane bridge that crosses the river's headwaters into the next state.

From a quarter mile away, we spot something in the road at the entrance to the bridge.

Careful, Caro says.

I slow down to twenty-five miles an hour, then fifteen.

Ren tenses and blinks. "What. Is. That?"

At seven-hundred feet away, the gargoyle at the bridge takes shape. An old geezer in shorts, a sleeveless undershirt, and a faded red baseball cap sits on an aluminum folding chair, a rifle lying across his legs. His knobby knees glisten in the early morning light. He shades his eyes with his hand and watches my vehicle approach with the rising sun behind me.

He waves us closer with his claw-like hand. At five-hundred feet from him, I have no idea what to do. Panic rises in my throat. I reduce speed to ten miles an hour; we roll forward.

"I think that's the toll taker."

"Not an official one," Ren says.

When we're two-hundred feet from him, the old man raises the butt of the rifle to his shoulder and points the barrel at my windshield. He grins. I note that he has no teeth and that the rifle isn't for his protection. He's not kidding around.

"Ren, is there a sign that says how much we have to pay?"

Ren's head swivels from side to side. He leans forward. "Nope."

One hundred feet from the bridge, I grab the coins in the change cup and toss them out of the window, hoping to distract him. The old guy doesn't even blink. That's not what he wants.

I should return the way I came, but the road is too narrow to turn around. The old man could easily shoot us before we get away. Besides, the only other way west is the highway, which I want to avoid because it'll be monitored by authorities. He knows people crossing this bridge are running from something and that we have to pass.

"Mom!" Amina's voice is shrill. "Mom, there are people in the road behind us."

They emerge from shrubs on the verge of the road, like shadows—shadows carrying baseball bats. They beat them against their palms as they stomp toward our truck. Their faces are obscured by masks, but I don't need to see their features to understand their intent.

I scan the area again. No houses in sight, no place to run to, no help available. No one would care if we screamed. My heart pounds. If I go forward, the old man's bullets will shatter the windshield, piercing my head or chest, hitting Ren.

My brain is stuffed with steel wool; I can't think, can't move. These strangers want everything—my cash, the car, the gas, my children. A pang, like the gong of a bell, strikes against my bones. My hands shake. I don't want to give them anything.

"Why should I pay this scumbag? He doesn't own this bridge."

"Wait, Mom," Ren says. "Something else is wrong."

I jam my foot on the brake. "Wrong like some guy thinks he can shoot random people on a bridge if they don't pay him or wrong some other way?"

"Mom, there's guys in the trees too. He's got more backup."

Ren points, and I turn to see armed men perched on the low branches of the huge oaks near the foot of the bridge. That's their trick. The old man's a decoy; the batboys are herders. If I stop the car to pay him, they'll rob us. If I drive through without paying, they'll shoot us and then take whatever they want. Either way, they win, and we lose.

I have no weapons, nothing to negotiate with. I've never had to make a calculation like this. My mind stutters, unable to decide. Seconds tick by. One by one, men drop out of the trees and slowly saunter toward us, rifles at the ready, sure of their tribute. They don't even bother to cover their faces. They're whistling like this is a walk in the park. I hate their confidence.

"Floor it, Mom," my son says, his voice as taut as steel suspension cables. "Everybody, get down!"

The kids unbuckle their seat belts with simultaneous clicks and slide onto the floor. I grip the steering wheel, slam my foot on the gas pedal, and blow by the old guy as fast as the vehicle will go, skimming his chair. I hear the screech of metal on metal.

His face twists with obvious surprise as his chair topples over sideways. A sound like a firecracker lands too close to the rear bumper, another to my left. My heart lurches with each blast, my shoulders hunch, but I don't let up on the gas.

Eventually, Ren puts his hand on my arm. "It's okay, Mom. You did it."

I lift my foot off the pedal, check the rearview mirror, and coast. The odometer tells me we're ten miles from the bridge. "God, I'm wiped. I have to rest."

"The map says a country club with a golf course is coming up in another ten miles. You can rest there."

"Is another ten miles enough?"

He turns around in the seat and looks out the back window. "Nobody's following us."

I lean against the headrest and realize my mouth has been stretched open in a silent scream. My fingers ache from gripping the steering wheel. Sweat streams down my back and between my breasts. I'm so weak I can barely keep my foot down on the accelerator.

"We can't leave the car where it can be seen."

In twenty minutes, Ren points to a sign indicating the country club entrance. "There, Mom. The entrance. Pull in there behind those trees. No one will be able to see the van from the road, even if they are following us."

I inhale and swing the minivan toward the club parking lot as if I've been following my son's orders my entire life. I glance at Ren. Something's different between us. He seems more mature, but I must be imagining that. He's still only fourteen, the same boy he was yesterday.

The golf club unfolds as we drive up the lane. It's beautiful, sunny, a cool seventy-nine degrees at 7 in the morning, according to my car's dash, and no one is here. Locals are following the first rule: stay away from people.

I turn off the engine, and the kids spill out of the car, racing toward the clubhouse and the shimmering pool behind the building. The quiet order of the open space beckons. Twenty-four hours with no sleep plus crashing after an adrenaline rush makes me dizzy with exhaustion, but this is almost too good to be true. On the other hand, my bladder is bursting. If it's a choice between a toilet or trees, I'll take the more civilized option.

"Masks on! Stay together," I yell as the kids gallop over the grass. "Bathroom first. Then we'll eat something."

If there's food here, I can save what we brought along for the remaining eight hundred miles of our drive to Sault Ste. Marie. For a second, I question the sanity of this stop, but the tranquility of the place makes me want to weep with relief. I've been awake for more than twenty-four hours, and I'm desperate for sleep. Just an hour or two in this quiet place will revive me.

"Don't touch anything," I shout as I trot toward the building. Too late.

Ren grabs the front doors of the clubhouse and pulls them open. The kids dash inside and can't hear me. I chase them, barely holding in the pee. If the doors are open, people must use the place, and somebody might routinely sanitize the building. We *are* in the middle of nowhere; infection numbers could be low. I hear myself mitigating the risk and almost laugh. Ted always said I could talk myself into anything.

The kids are washing their hands by the time I relieve my bladder. "Sing happy birthday," I yell at the girls.

The virus is not the problem here, Caro says. She must see something I can't.

The sounds the kids make as they run through the empty building—voices liberated from the close confines of the vehicle—make me happy. The building looks immaculate. I give up on quarantine protocols.

In the clubhouse kitchen, I find potato chips, pickles, tuna, deviled ham, and canned peaches in the pantry. Management must operate the golf club remotely, with members staggering tee times to keep their distance. It seems odd that people would play golf during a pandemic, but I understand the need to get out of the house, to relax in the serenity of a manicured space with a blue sky above. All that air could lull someone into a false sense of safety.

I open cans, bags, and jars, hoping the food or containers aren't contaminated. We eat with our fingers until we're full, then throw the debris in the trash and wipe the counter down with the bleach spray under the sink. I leave ten dollars on the counter to pay for the food we consumed.

We can be considerate, even if we're breaking and entering, even if we're stealing someone else's supplies. I almost laugh at the lies I'm able to tell myself.

The kids stare out of the windows at the pool. I know they need a break from being trapped in their seats in the car. Like Jacks I've let out of the box, they vibrate slightly.

"Refill water bottles while I put gas in the car. Don't wander away where I can't find you."

Listening to the drone of a lawnmower in the distance, I pour five gallons of gas into the van's tank. With the hybrid assist, that should get us another three hundred miles. The continual buzz of the mower and the glug of the liquid are the only other noises besides my children. We're alone here.

When I'm done, I find the kids standing on the pool's edge. It's a light jade green with some leaves floating on the surface. Whoever maintains the grounds hasn't quite got the chemistry right. I remember Caro saying it wasn't our pool that made her sick. This is no worse than a pond. I collapse onto a chaise and, lulled by the quiet hum in the distance, fall into a trance, imagining I'm back in my former life when we were safe.

"You're the lifeguard, Ren. Keep an eye on everyone."

My eyes close, and in the next minute, I'm dreaming my sister is talking to me about watching afternoon shadows flow downhill and something else I don't quite catch, something about how I should be planning an escape, and I shouldn't wait too long.

5

Ren

MIRA and Owen sit on the top step in the pool, screeching loudly and splashing each other. Mom zones out, except for her hands and feet, which twitch. I think of swimmers readying themselves for a race.

Pam removes her baseball cap, and the girls slip off their hoodies and clogs and dive in. The pool water smells like a creek and turns Amina's hair slightly green. They lie down on chaises in the sun to dry off. I pop off my tennis shoes and sit on the edge of the pool near the little kids, struggling to stay awake.

Someone touches my arm. I turn to see a girl standing next to me. Sunlight shines through the blond curls around her head, making a halo. She points to Mira, standing on the bottom step, water up to her mouth.

I jolt up, heart racing, and jump into the pool, catching my baby cousin under her arms as she lowers herself down the last step. I lift her almost weightless body out of the water. "Hey, you decided to learn to swim today, huh?"

She giggles. "I can swim. Pammy taught me. I can put my head in."

"Well, let's not take any chances." I take Owen by the hand, walk out of the pool, and sit the little ones on the concrete deck. "How about we dry off in the sun, so we can get back in the car."

The sun's hot enough that my jeans dry in five minutes. I remember Mom's written instructions, pull them out of my pocket, and lay them flat to dry out next to me. Some of the words have washed away. I'm not sure why I'm keeping the note; Mom didn't die. But they're like the security blanket I dragged around till I was five.

I look for the girl who warned me about Mira, but no one's here except us. "Amina, did you see a girl here talking to me?"

She gives me her boys-can-be-so-peculiar look. "You were dreaming."

Pam pulls on her cap and looks around. "I didn't see anyone."

I shake my arms, shoulders, and head to get rid of the feeling of being watched.

Owen yanks on my hand. "I didn't bring any toys to play with." His eyes fill with tears.

I totally get him. "Maybe we can find something on the golf course." I hold out his shoes for him to put on. "How about a treasure hunt for a lost ball?" He grins at my idea and nods like a bobblehead doll.

Outside the pool area, a lawn of green grass leads to a group of trees in front of the golf course. A wide asphalt path winds toward a tee.

"Let's go run around on the grass." I point, and the kids are up and running before I have my shoes on. Grabbing the instructions, I stuff them back into my pocket. "Amina, Pam," I call out, "we're going to scout our environment." I wave my hand in the general direction of the golf course.

The minute I say it, I realize we should have done a security check first thing. Why didn't Mom think of that? She must be too wiped out to think. I have to kick myself into a higher gear to handle things better.

"I'll stay with Mom." Amina pulls her braid over her shoulder, leans back on the chaise, and closes her eyes. Sometimes my sister doesn't pull her weight.

Pam stretches and stands. "I'll go with you. It's boring just lying here." She ties her hoodie around her waist and puts on her shoes.

We walk through the gate, and I make sure it's latched so the little ones can't wander back to the pool alone when I'm not looking. Pam and I chase them up a slight hill. Ahead, a small group of trees flank a sand trap and putting green. A flag stands in the hole like an advertisement for the perfect golf resort. Owen and Mira race for the hole, and I follow them, wondering where the golfers are and who takes care of this place.

Owen pulls a small white ball from the hole. "I found one!" He jumps up and down and runs in a circle around the green, holding up the ball like a trophy.

Mira races after him, yelling, "Yay! We win."

Pam calls, "Good job."

We trot through a clump of trees on the other side of the green, and I spot the girl I saw in my dream sitting at the edge of another sand trap. I stop in my tracks. She stares at us like she's deciding whether we're real.

I'm not sure if she's real, either. She could be a decoy like the old man on the bridge. I turn in a circle to scan the area around her for danger. She's alone. I walk up to her slowly, in case she's not really there. Even if it's the end of the world, I don't want to look like an idiot in front of my cousin.

"Your mom needs you," the girl says, her voice calm. She seems way too mature for her age, which spooks me.

Pam gives her that "what do *you* know?" look she always uses on me and runs after Owen and Mira. I'm glad Pam sees her too.

I squat next to the girl. Her face is streaked with dirt, and her green striped shirt and red shorts are dirty like she's been sleeping outside, and no one is taking care of her. "What's your name?"

"Ruby."

"Are you here alone?"

She nods.

"Where are your parents?"

"They went to find another place for us to live five days ago. I don't think they're coming back."

"Why didn't they take you with them?"

"Dad said it would be faster without me."

My breath comes out in a huff like somebody punched me in the stomach. Her parents abandoned her. She tells me this like it's no big deal, like it's just a fact of life. Would my mom ever do that to us? I blink the thought away.

"How old are you?

"Eleven."

"How'd you get here?"

"Dad left me in the parking lot. We used to come here, before the sickness. Mom liked to golf; my dad and I used the pool. He said I could use the bathroom here and get water and eat the food. He was in a hurry."

"Why didn't he leave you at home?"

"The government was coming to get us. Dad didn't want them to take me to a camp. He said this would be better. I'd be free."

I have to wait a second to get my voice back. "So, you're living here?"

"Not inside the building. Dad thought I could sleep on the sofas in the club room, but it's dangerous there. I stay out here in the woods, where there are lots of ways I can get away fast. I sneak inside the clubhouse to get food and use the bathroom when he mows."

"When who mows? Why is it dangerous?"

"There's a man who sleeps in an outbuilding. My parents called him the groundskeeper. He keeps the golf course pretty, but he's a bad man. My mother said he used to watch women in the locker room. He was always bad, but now no one can stop him. Really, you should get your mom."

I wonder why it's so quiet and realize I no longer hear the lawnmower. "Get the kids," I yell to Pam, sprinting toward the clubhouse with Ruby following me. From a distance, everything looks the way it did before. Mom and Amina are asleep, the sun shining on them. The water in the pool ripples in the breeze. A large shadow inches across the concrete deck toward Mom.

"Mom!" I yell as loud as I can. "Mom, get up, wake up! Amina!"

"They can't hear you from here," Ruby shouts.

I race toward the pool, my legs moving faster than I knew they could, as if they're longer and propel me through the air. I pull on the gate, but it's locked from the inside. Pam and the kids are running toward me. I reach over the fence, fumble with the latch, and open the gate just as the man grabs Mom.

6

Jean

HIS hot, rank breath hits me before I open my eyes. The sound of alarm in Ren's distant voice rings in my ears. Feet pound over the ground. Amina squeals. Heat envelopes me; my arms are clamped in a vise against my body. I can't get free no matter how much I writhe and push. That smell overwhelms me.

Opening my eyes, I see a bulbous, purple-veined nose, one eye covered with a grimy black patch, greasy gray hair, and yellowed teeth. I blink. This can't be real; I must be asleep, lost in a nightmare. My body shakes uncontrollably. I squeeze my eyes shut and then open them. All my instinct focuses on one internal command: *get free*.

Amina screams in short bursts, like a school alarm system, and every screech redoubles my heartbeat. In the next second, she slams an aluminum chair against the man's back. He laughs, ignoring the blow from the chair. His breath is foul.

He lifts me off the chaise like I'm weightless. When I open my mouth to scream, no sound emerges. He throws me over his shoulder and jogs toward the clubhouse. Black hairs sprout from the pale skin of his sweating back. I hear my children shrieking. The rank odor of his body fills my nose. My heartbeat thrashes in my ears as I wrench myself back and forth and beat him on his head and back. I kick, trying to find his softest spots.

He lumbers, undeterred, toward the building.

What happens to the kids if he kills me? A sob rises in my throat. I can't let that happen. My mind races, looking for a way to escape.

Ren, Amina, and Pam yell in unison, "Hey! Stop! Mom!" as they chase after him.

"Stay back," I yell. They don't listen. I see Owen take Mira's hand.

Pam darts in front of the man with her arms spread wide like she's trying to halt a panicked horse. She yanks the cap off her dark cloud of curls and waves it, her brown eyes wide and clear. "Take me!" she yells at the man. "Take me instead." She has no idea what she's offering.

He stops. His body hums against me, his grip loosening. I thrust myself away from him and lunge for Pam before he does. Ren runs up behind him and slams a metal umbrella stand against his head. The man groans, his face going blank as he falls to his knees and collapses on the ground. The kids surround me; they're sobbing.

I hug them, tears filling my eyes, then find my voice. "Let's get out of here."

I pick up Mira, grab Owen's arm, and we run toward the car. A girl stands next to it, holding a long, shiny rod. I stop moving and clutch the kids against me. "Who is that?"

"That's Ruby," Ren says. "We have to take her. Her parents ditched her here."

"She could be sick. She has a weapon. Maybe she's with that man."

"If she were sick, Mom, she would have died already. She's been alone here, hiding from that monster for over a week."

"How do you know?"

"I talked to her."

I stare at his guileless face. "We don't have room for her."

He looks at me with disbelief. "Of course we do."

"But Dee is expecting only five of us."

His expression changes. Is that disdain? "Mom, we can't leave her here with . . . that man."

The girl looks at me, and I notice streaks of dried tears crisscrossing her dirty cheeks. "I dreamed my parents died," she says so quietly I hate myself for thinking of leaving her.

Guilt at my selfishness and pride at my son's compassion sweep through me. There's no time for a contest of wills. "Of course, you're right. We'll take her."

I hold my hand out for the rod she carries, and she gives me a broken golf club shaft with a sharp, jagged end. I turn it over, wondering how she uses it.

"It was my mom's," she says as if that's the only explanation needed.

This is what she has left of them. The thought leaves me hollow. Hard to imagine this lightweight wand could ward off the thug who lifted me into the air. I unlock the van to toss it in the back, but I pause, feeling the coldness of the metal in my hands.

Ren yanks open the doors, and the kids scoot in the back. "Come on, Mom. Let's go before he wakes up."

Ruby snuggles in between Owen and Mira. They hold her hands as if they're old friends, or maybe they mean to comfort her.

I think about that man's breath on my face, his hands on my body. Did Ruby break that club on him? His smell is in my nose. My stomach roils at the thought that he got her, and my bones ache. Hands shaking, I turn over the shaft Ruby handed me and picture its sharp end piercing his flesh.

Kill him.

The thought is so irrational it startles me; we're not people who kill people. I have never fought anyone physically, and rarely do I call names or even toss insulting gestures.

"Mom!" Ren shouts. "Come on, he's coming!"

I look up and see the groundskeeper lurching out of the building. He's not my problem. Get in the car, jam my foot on the gas pedal, and we're out of here. We'll never see him again. A flash memory of his hands on my skin, the harsh violence of his lust, and a shudder rocks me. After he was finished with me, he would have attacked my girls without mercy. My chest burns, and the muscles in my legs throb from adrenaline.

I can't let this alone. He could terrorize other children who hide in the shadows, hoping to sneak food from the golf club's pantry. I lick my dry lips and ignore my dizziness. Ruby's golf club is in my fist. Another shudder passes through me, drowning me in all my losses, all my fury, my fear. I slam the rear door shut.

"Ren, get in the driver's seat. Lock the doors. Drive away if something happens to me. Run him over if you have to."

Ren's jaw clenches. He nods, climbs over the middle tray between the seats, slides behind the wheel, but doesn't look at me. The door locks click.

Amina and Owen call to me. "Mom, Mommy, get in the car. Mom!"

Pam bangs on the window. "Aunt Jean, what are you doing?"

"Mom!" Amina screams. "No!"

The groundskeeper is ten feet from me, roaring as he races toward us. He'll be on us in a second. Blood from his head wound soaks his shoulders. This man is my enemy; he intends to kill me. I have one shot at this. If I miss, I'm done. He could snap my neck with his hands.

I grip the shaft of Ruby's broken golf club in my hand like a javelin and, bellowing like a madwoman, run at him. With every ounce of my strength, I scream and thrust the sharp jagged end of the rod at his face. It pierces his one good eye. He drops to the ground, clutching his head, howling.

Glee rises like bubbles in my chest. My triumphant giddiness terrifies me more than he did. I race back to the car and throw myself into the passenger seat. "Drive," I say.

"God, Mom," Ren says and starts the van. He throws a sideways glance at me. His face is ashen. Tears streak down his cheeks. His hands tremble on the steering wheel as we lurch out of the parking lot.

My heartbeat pounds in my ears. When my breathing slows, I hear Mira sobbing. My body vibrates against the leather upholstery, making a shushing sound. Looking around, I see Amina and Pam holding each other, eyes wide and full of tears. My mouth is dry.

"Did you get him, Mom?" Owen asks, his lower lip quivering. "Did you get the bad guy?"

I nod and whisper, "I did."

"Are you a bad guy now?"

I can't answer. I would have to say yes.

After twenty miles, Ruby says, "There's a place up ahead where we'll be safe, I think."

For no reason, I believe her. After all, she knew when to hand me a weapon. Maybe she knows other things. She's probably been there with her parents; there's nothing strange about her saying this. My children often know where they are around our home by landmarks they've memorized.

Ren taps on the GPS and follows a new route with his finger. "Here, Mom." He turns the device so I can see the route he's plotting. Route 30 to Route 8 takes us right into a town about 150 miles from here. That makes me nervous—too many people, too much infection.

"It's called Wilbursburg," Ruby says from the back seat, though she can't see the screen. "It has big old houses. Mostly children are left."

"Did you live there with your parents?" I ask.

"No," she says. "I just know about it. Like someone sent me a text message."

"Well, are your grandparents or any aunts or uncles there? We could take you to them."

"They're dead," the child says quietly.

The girl is so calm. Is this what will happen to my kids if I die, that quiet numbness? My babies just watched me mutilate a human being. I shudder again, picturing it from their perspective, and hope they'll be able to forget it ever happened, forget this entire year.

I understand in a rush why Ruby's parents abandoned her. They felt death creeping over them, that weakness Ted mentioned, when every breath is an effort and thinking requires too much energy, the languor that comes just before the end.

But why did they wait until the last minute to make a plan to save her? They must have hoped they would survive. Leaving Ruby would have been their last option; that choice alone would have killed them. I shouldn't make the same mistake.

I twist in my seat to look at the children. They are the reason I'm doing this. But Owen's right. I've become a bad guy, and its only day two of our journey. What other horrifying acts will I commit in the name of protecting them? As my fury ebbs, I want to weep. "I'm sorry about that, guys, that I, that you had to see . . ."

"Thank you," Ruby whispers. "Thank you for saving me."

7

Ren

TWO hours after Mom destroyed the groundskeeper, we're on the wide, empty streets of a city that GPS and Ruby say is Wilbursburg. I point to a huge house with dark windows, its front door wide open.

The blank windows and open door make me think of someone shocked by what they see, kind of how I feel about Mom attacking the monster. If I close my eyes, the whole video of it will run. I'm awed by what she did and terrified at the same time. Who is she? In a game, that would be the winning move, but I didn't know she had that much courage. I don't know if I do.

Mom gazes at the house I point to and nods. She's been mostly silent since the golf club, and her face is blank. She's still shaking and hasn't said anything about my driving. I was nervous at first, the way the van goes on its own even without my foot on the gas, how it swerves if I look in the wrong direction. But she's acting as if I've always driven, like I was born being able to do it, and she already knew that.

"Victorians," she says finally. "Some of them used to be rich." She drags her finger along the GPS map. "We're near Pittsburgh. This must have been a suburb where robber barons lived." She looks out the window as I drive slowly past house after house. "Look for a place we can rest."

"Lots of the houses are empty," Ruby announces like she just got a notification from some app. "The virus police were here, and they took folks away. But the house I see in my head is sort of a museum. So, maybe there's food and water and bathrooms. And rooms with beds. I might have come here once with my parents when I was little."

"Do they have treats?" Owen asks.

"I don't know," Ruby says. "But I don't see any monsters like the groundskeeper."

I only half believe her.

Amina and Pam sigh loudly. "Maybe you don't see anything," Pam mutters.

In the rearview mirror, I watch Amina lower her chin, raise her eyebrows, and give Pam a sideways, *you read my mind* look. They smile, and I feel sorry for Ruby.

"I have to pee in a TOILET," Owen says, looking directly at Pam. Everyone laughs. Owen, clearly unsure what's funny, grins. "Well, I do."

"Okay." Mom's voice sounds like she's decided. She points to a brick mansion set far back from the road. "Let's check out the one with the blue and white striped awnings and the park around it. There's a sign. Maybe it's open to the public. Go there."

The house is so big, I can't imagine anyone ever living here. Robber barons must have had it pretty sweet, living in places as big as a hotel. But if you were their kids, you'd always have to be on your best behavior.

"Pull up as close as you can," Mom says. "Find a spot where no one can see the vehicle from the road. We don't know how far behind us the virus police are."

I drive up a service road on the side of the mansion and, with only a little jerking, park behind high bushes. Historical markers are set along an asphalt walking path leading to a greenhouse and stable. I catch a blur of movement in a rear window of the house, but when I look hard at it, nothing's there.

What if there's someone in there, someone who doesn't want any visitors? I want to double-check with Ruby if bad guys are inside, but I don't ask because I don't want to look scared. And the girls would laugh at me. Somehow, even with my dad dying, the virus police, and bad guys everywhere, the girls laughing at me is still the worst.

"Stay together," Mom says. She takes Mira's and Owen's hands and walks slowly toward the back porch, stopping at a small sign stuck in the grass near the steps that says, DELIVERIES ONLY. The rest of us bunch up behind her. She goes up one step and pauses to listen.

"Mom, are you sure this is a good idea?" I ask. Not checking out a place first didn't work out at the golf club. "Shouldn't we scout the area before we go in? There might be bad guys hiding anywhere, and . . ."

"I *am* going to check it out. No one's going in until I know it's safe."

"But . . ."

She hands the little ones to me. "Stay here with Ren," she tells Owen and Mira. She puts her hand on my shoulder. "Ren, you know the drill."

The drill is to run for the van, lock the doors, and drive away. She's not taking this seriously enough. It's not like we're in one of my games and can break to get a snack or pee. There's no chat, no site to look up the cheat codes. Didn't she learn anything from the last level, or will she now kill everyone on sight? My regular mom has disappeared, and I don't know what this one will do.

"Mom," Amina says, her voice squeaky like she's about to cry, "you could get attacked in there, and we'd be out here and not even know it. We won't be able to help you." She looks over her shoulder both ways and shivers. "I don't want to be left alone."

Mom looks at us for what feels like forever, takes my face in two hands, kisses my forehead and then Amina's, and says, "I'll be back. I promise." She turns the knob on the door, pauses, then pulls it open. "Don't wander off," she says, giving me a look that means, "You're in charge," before she disappears inside.

I don't want to be in charge. Why can't Amina be in charge for a change?

"Aunt Jean," Pam calls. "I'm coming with you. In case . . ." She leaps up the porch steps and runs inside after Mom before we can stop her. Why didn't I do that?

Mildew, mold, and something disgusting like potpourri float toward us from inside the house when the door opens. I shake my head and take the babies' hands. It's quiet here, too quiet. No sign of life. It's more like a cemetery than a museum. I expect a ghost to come lunging out of the door at us any second. Amina sits on the back step, and Mira lets go of my hand to lean against her.

I'm still spooked about the groundskeeper and what Mom did to him. Bad things will happen now, I get that, and Mom might do something awful. The thing is, I don't know what will scare me more. It's the not knowing that makes me queasy. Amina's biting her bottom lip—a sure sign she doesn't think stopping here is a good idea.

"Amina," I say, the rest of what I meant to say after that disappearing into thin air.

She stares at me and shakes her head.

I don't know whether this means it's okay or if it's a bad idea to go inside, or she has no idea what happens next. She's not helping.

"It's okay, I think," Ruby says.

Why should I trust Miss Know-it-all? I wish we hadn't taken her, then I feel bad I thought that, and then I hate that my mind is a revolving door that keeps turning around and around, and I never know where I'll come out.

"How do you know it's okay?" What if she's just screwing with us and doesn't know any more than we do?

"I get pictures in my head, like in dreams."

"What do you mean?"

"Like when you dream, you don't know if you're awake or dreaming. Everything in the dream feels real. It's like that, only I'm awake when it happens. And most times, I don't know what the dreams are telling me."

I'm more confused than before. "I don't think that what I dream is real. Why do you?"

Ruby looks down at the ground, and I can't figure out if she thinks I'm dumb or if she's sad that I don't believe her.

Owen jiggles and shakes my arm to get my attention. "I have to pee. And I'm thirsty." Amina tries to distract him with a game of I Spy. We've been waiting for Mom forever. My watch ticks off another minute, then two. Three. My chest starts to tighten. Bad things are going to happen. Four.

Pam throws the door open wide. "The coast is clear." Her grin is as wide as the door. "This place is cool." She stares at her shoes for a second. "You were right, Ruby. It's okay here."

We walk into a huge kitchen with two dishwashers and two large refrigerators. Amina opens one like she owns the place and hands out water bottles. "I think they must have catered parties. When people had parties, that is."

It's like my sister and I grew up on different planets with different facts. She reads; that's how she knows stuff. My games don't explain anything about real life unless there's a magic sword hidden in the garden that will give me an edge in the next battle. There will be another battle. I *have* learned that, and if I beat these bad guys, there'll be more of them on the next level, and it'll be harder to win. But I'm prepared. Amina thinks we're at a party.

"I have to pee," Owen says yet again. Mom takes his hand and leads him out of the kitchen. We hear him as they walk through the house. "How come they have so many rooms? Do those windows open? Can I ride on that rocking horse? Do they have toys? Can I have a toy? Who lives here . . . ?"

Sucking on the water bottles, we wander from room to room until we find one with comfortable chairs and sofas. We collapse into them, falling asleep in a second. I wake to an old lady's voice asking if we want food.

She leans over me and taps my shoulder. Pink circles are painted on her wrinkled cheeks. Above her marble-blue eyes are drawn-on black eyebrows. Her hair is white, and she smells like she's been soaking in super sweet potpourri. "Does your family want tea, sonny?"

All of a sudden, I realize she's not wearing a mask. I pull my shirt over my mouth and nose and leap off the sofa. Everyone but Ruby is asleep. She's watching me. She got us into this mess on purpose. My brain goes into overdrive, trying to figure out what to do. I stall.

"Who are you?" I poke Amina awake. She shakes Mom.

"I'm the docent, dearie," the woman says. When she smiles, bright red lipstick smudges her gray teeth. She must be as old as the house. "I didn't know if you people were dangerous, so I hid for a while."

"What's a docent?"

The old lady laughs. "It is a funny word, isn't it? I'm a guide. I know things about this house. All the secrets. Where the bodies are buried . . ." She giggles like that's funny.

I don't think it's funny.

Mom stands, adjusts her mask, and walks over to the docent. She towers over the woman. "What's your name?" she asks like this is the old times and people can be friendly with each other.

Watching my mom, something clicks in my head. If I were the docent, Mom would be the dangerous one. For a second, I think the old lady's going to curtsey.

"I'm Mrs. Pittman. You must've traveled from far away to get here. I haven't had any visitors in the longest time, and I'm happy to serve you our traditional afternoon tea in the café. Gratis." She smiles, and I think her eyes switch to snake eyes for a flash. "Just to have the company."

Mom takes in Mrs. Pittman's outfit, which looks like a costume from a movie about the old west, where she's the doctor's wife. "That would be lovely, Mrs. Pittman," Mom says. She turns around and signals us to stand up.

"Wait, Mom," Amina says. "What about the 'don't ask strangers for help' rule?"

Mom raises her eyebrows and half-smiles like she's pleased Amina remembered the rule. Amina turns her palms out and glares at Mom—her "what are you doing?" look.

Mrs. Pittman doesn't notice. She heads into the hall, and we start to waddle behind her like ducklings. "The café used to be the stables a long time ago when horses were the main means of transportation," she says in a travelogue voice. "It's a short walk from the house through the legacy perennial flower garden and quite charming. I'll lead the way."

Mom holds up her hand, and we huddle. "The minute we're outside, run for the car," Mom whispers. She picks up Mira and takes Owen's hand.

Everyone nods but Ruby. Her head is tilted like she's listening to far-away music. "She won't hurt you."

"How do you know that?" Mom asks her.

"She told me."

"When was that?"

"Just now."

Mom gets this weird look on her face. "Right now, while we're talking?"

Ruby nods slowly.

"Why do you believe her?"

The girl looks up at Mom. "I don't know."

Mom considers this for a second, her eyes closed, and then she surprises me again. "Okay, let's see what happens. I would like to rest for a while, and that sofa was comfortable . . ." She stares off into space for a few seconds. "And we could use a snack."

My shoulders get tight. Mom's not making good decisions. We can't afford to trust people anymore; strangers are trying to hurt us, and we should be on our guard. We have to get to Canada before the virus police find us, before Mom runs out of steam, before anything happens to one of us. If I know that, she knows it too. I don't understand what's gotten into her. Maybe being brave is hard work, and that's why she's so tired.

In the tearoom, tablecloths cover the tables, and light from chandeliers blinks off fancy water glasses. Mrs. Pittman must dust them every day. We sit on chairs Mom would normally call dainty and watch Mrs. Pittman wobble around. Having an old lady wait on us makes me feel guilty.

She serves us iced tea in pitchers and plates of small cucumber sandwiches and some with brown paste I think is supposed to be chicken salad on crustless white bread. The bread's a little stale, but we don't say anything about that. In summers before the pandemic, Mom spread peanut butter and honey on homemade bread for us to eat at the pool with green grapes. We'd lick our fingers and play Bananagrams and Twenty Questions while we waited until she'd let us get back in the pool. My mouth waters, and I gobble five sandwiches without thinking.

Owen crams two sandwiches and three oatmeal raisin cookies into his mouth before he says, "I'm gonna puke." Everybody stops eating with the next bite halfway to their mouths.

"Crap," Mom says. "The food must be spoiled." She scoops up Owen, Mrs. Pittman points, and Mom runs toward a sign that says restrooms. We hear Owen gagging before the bathroom door closes.

Mira glares at Mrs. Pittman. "You made Owen sick on purpose. You're a mean old lady."

Mrs. Pittman tsks. "I never." She pours everyone more iced tea. "Cookies, anyone?"

"It won't work," Pam says. She puts both hands on either side of her baseball cap as if someone had threatened to remove it.

"Why, whatever do you mean, child?"

"Giving us bad food on purpose, or by accident, won't keep us here. We're going someplace far away where no one will hurt us."

"Mrs. Pittman," Ruby interrupts as if to stop Pam from saying anything more, "what was it like here before, when you were young?"

Pam gives Ruby a look that would kill me, but she doesn't say any more about where we're going.

"Do I know you from somewhere, dear?" Mrs. Pittman asks Ruby. "You're so familiar. Did your family come here often?"

"No. I don't know you. Why did *you* come here? Like originally."

"Well." Mrs. Pittman sits at the table with us and puts her hands in her lap. "I first came to the house as a young woman, over sixty years ago." She smiles as if she's watching a movie of her younger self.

"So, you're like ninety," Pam says. The look on her face says she's amazed by that age.

Mrs. Pittman smiles. "Well, dear, I'm actually one-hundred-and-four."

"Wow," Amina says. "Why didn't you retire?"

"I did," Mrs. Pittman said, "but then my husband died, and I had nothing to do with my time, so I came back to work here. The foundation doesn't pay me. I volunteer."

"Oh." Pam looks sad she said anything. "Sorry about that, your husband dying, I mean."

"Our daddy and mommy died too," Mira says. Pam leans over, kisses the top of her sister's head, and smooths back her hair.

Mrs. Pittman clucks. "Fact of life. People die. When the other grownups on my block died, I started coming here every day. Lately, I sleep over; the house protects me. It's a little lonely with no one visiting now, and food deliveries are spotty, although I did get a big shipment this week that could last me for months. I guess everyone on the board isn't dead. Someone must be paying for food delivery."

She gets this faraway look on her face. I think she's gone to sleep with her eyes open for a second. When she goes back to telling her story, the creaky sound of her voice calms Mira and Pam, although Amina still looks doubtful. While she's talking, Ruby removes the plates and takes them into the kitchen. I follow her.

"What are you doing?"

"She's a harmless old woman. There are beds here, and your mom needs to rest, or she won't be able to drive. It's going to get worse out there."

"She doesn't have to drive; I'll drive. Anyhow, how do you know about it getting worse? How do you know anything?"

Ruby shrugs. "I just do. I don't know how the pictures get in my head, but they mostly turn out to be true, some of the time anyway."

Does she mean the way she showed up in my head at the golf club? Wasn't that just a dream? Unless being psychic is her superpower. It might be a new power that she doesn't know how to use yet, which means it could get us in trouble instead of helping us.

I wander around the kitchen, opening cupboards and drawers. When I open a door with a big metal handle, cold air blasts me from a room-sized refrigerator. Inside are shelves of food. We could stay in this house for a long time. No one would know we're here. I'll bet there are even toys for Owen to play with. It feels like a window opens in my mind, and fresh air comes in, and I can be unafraid for a minute. And then, just as fast, the window slams closed. I can't trust it. It's too good to be true, like Dad always said.

I walk back out to the table where the kids are listening to Mrs. Pittman tell them a story about the old days. "We're going north," I tell Ruby like she's a grownup I have to negotiate with. "We're going as soon as Mom's ready."

She shrugs. "Up to you."

Mom comes back with Owen and stares at our faces as if she could read on them what we said to each other. I tell her about the huge refrigerator. She opens the door and scans the shelves. "Ren, get our backpacks out of the car. We're going to take some provisions."

I'm glad she's thinking what I'm thinking. Time to leave.

Mrs. Pittman grabs Mom's arm. "What are you doing? That food doesn't belong to you." She tugs on the bag of apples in Mom's hand.

Mom wrenches the bag away from her. The old woman staggers and clutches a shelf to get her balance. Mom looks shattered like she attacked her best friend and didn't mean to. "I'm so sorry, Mrs. Pittman," she says. She bows her head and shakes it. "But we need the food. We won't take everything, just what will keep for a day or two—some apples, cheese, peanut butter, bread."

"But it's stealing," the old woman says, her chin quivering. "What am I supposed to eat?"

"I'm leaving plenty for you," Mom says. "But I have six children to feed. They're used to eating constantly."

I can't figure out why taking this food is so important, but it is. We're like squirrels who know winter is coming. We gather whatever we can carry in the two backpacks and herd the kids out to the car. What can Mrs. Pittman do about it?

She rushes after us, her hands gripping her apron. As we climb into the van, she grabs Ruby's arm. Her fingers dig into the girl's skin. "She stays here with me. That's the trade for the food."

Mom turns and steps back toward her. "What?"

"I need the company. She's like me. She knows things. She should stay here."

Ruby tries to wriggle herself out of Mrs. Pittman's grasp like she suddenly gets it—this woman isn't safe. "What are you talking about?"

"You know what's coming," Mrs. Pittman says to her. "I know what that's like. It's difficult at first to know what's real and what's not."

Ruby tries to yank herself away, but Mrs. Pittman's hands tighten.

"I remember how it is," Mrs. Pittman says. "It can be confusing and dangerous. Interpretation is tricky, and the fact that no one believes you until it's too late can drive you crazy. For people like us, the fewer other people we see, the better. You'll be safer here, where their memories and feelings, their futures, can't rub off on you. They'll use you and blame you for how everything turns out."

Ruby looks from Mom to me to Mrs. Pittman. Clouds cross her eyes. Her lips turn down. "I'm not like you," she says to Mrs. Pittman in a quiet voice. "I'm doing what I want to do."

"Do you want to stay?" Mom asks.

Ruby shakes her head. "I'm supposed to be with you."

Mom's eyebrows go up, but she says, "Ruby comes with us." Her voice is firm; she's made up her mind. "She belongs with us now. She chose. That's where she's supposed to be."

Tears fill Ruby's eyes. She doesn't say anything, but her face changes when Mom claims her. She's on our team now, not just a spectator, not tagging along. She's one of us. Our future is her future.

Mrs. Pittman's face changes from a mild-mannered old lady to a demon in a second. Her eyes bulge. Her cheeks get red under the pink circles. Her eyes turn green, and her fingers dig into Ruby's arm.

"This one belongs with me," she says in a deep voice. "Going with you will be the end of her."

Mom wraps her arm around Ruby's shoulders. "That's ridiculous."

Pam peels Mrs. Pittman's fingers off Ruby's arm.

"It will be bad for you out there," Mrs. Pittman says to Ruby, low in her throat like someone else is speaking through her. "You won't survive. There are too many for one small boat. One of you will die."

Mom looks at her as if she smells like spoiled milk. "Get in the car," Mom says to us. "Get in." Everyone loads into the van and shuts the doors. She turns to face Mrs. Pittman through the window. "I know you're lonely. I'm sorry about that. But you can't have her."

Mom starts the engine and zooms down the driveway before Mrs. Pittman turns into the dragon she sounds like and scorches us with one breath.

When we're halfway down the lane, I look over my shoulder and see an old woman covering her face with her apron. She's not a demon; I only imagined she was. I set the GPS for north, where I told the docent we were headed, figure out the nearest back road, and give Mom the directions.

8

Dee

PICASSO barks and dances around the front door. I peer out the window, hoping Jean and her family are in my driveway. No one but some boys skulking past the house, slowing down to scan my yard, making a note of things they can steal.

Where could my niece have gone? She couldn't have died; that isn't acceptable. It's been three days since Jean promised to touch base with me on each step of her journey. Her last text came when she left home, and by yesterday, I caught myself wringing my hands—such an old lady gesture that I momentarily despised myself. And this morning, to top it off, I discovered my phone's gone out. She could have been trying to contact me for days and got no response. My heart turned over.

Just to be sure, I squint to read the words *No Service* in one-point font on the top left side of my screen. Patting my chest, I take deep breaths and practice logic. The cell phone is charged because I plugged it in last night. My town prides itself on its transition to all-green technology; my house has electricity. To prove this to myself, I flip the house lights on, in case the tiny 100 percent charged notation on the right side of the small screen is only mobile technology propaganda. There's nothing wrong with the power in my house. This user interface is the problem—it was designed for a ten-year-old.

A vehicle rolls by on the street, and I jump up and run to the front door to greet my family, but when I fling it open, no one's there. My nails are already bitten down to the quick, but there's nothing left to do except curse faceless technocrats who will never know how distressed they've made me. Then I remember Georgia's constant reminder: "The world doesn't revolve around you."

Standing in the middle of the kitchen, complaining to the dog about my phone and tugging on what little is left of my white hair, I grasp that

I'm losing the last shreds of my sanity. Picasso sits at attention, turning his head left and right to follow my movements. His ears twitch. I lean over and pat his head; he's such a good dog.

"At least *you* understand."

I'm not going to dawdle around the house, not knowing what's going on. Mask on, I readjust my glasses, so they won't cloud up and scoot my walker across the yard to my neighbor's house. On the porch, I talk to Geraldine through the glass storm door. No point in making small talk; we aren't supposed to socialize anyway. "You guys got service on your mobile phones?" I wave mine, so she can see what I'm talking about.

"Nope. Not for a week." Geraldine gives my jeans, long-sleeved t-shirt, knit scarf, and puffy vest the once over like I'm yesterday's cat puke. "Says no service on it, just like yours."

"Thanks." I wave at her and hobble down the steps. She still hasn't forgiven me for the stale cake I brought to her place the day she moved in thirty years ago.

Must be a cell tower outage that interrupted service. I try to connect with Jean using FaceTime and Duo, but they don't work either. Her phone rings and rings, but no lovely face appears on the screen to reassure me.

Stricken by the thought that I haven't heard from her because she's changed her mind and isn't coming, I review our phone conversation. I was so happy to hear from the girl, maybe I gushed too much; I don't like gushers either. Sweetness is suspect, and some people are too wordy. After five minutes, they exhaust my capacity for politeness. Of course, Jean didn't gush; she didn't sugarcoat anything.

"She died, Aunt Dee," she said so quietly that I almost didn't understand the import of what she was telling me. "Caro got the virus, and she died."

I heard the tremble in her voice, the intake of breath, the tamped-down tears.

"Ted and Nate died too. I'm alone with the kids, and it's not safe here."

"Oh, no." What could I say? I recognized that strained tone; she was holding herself together. Displaying one little bit of emotion would cripple her. Her mother was like that too. Truth be told, our whole family smothers their emotions like it's too dangerous to feel things, leaving you too vulnerable to attack. Better to harden your hide, lift your head, and get on with life.

"I'm worried government virus goons will catch us. They'll separate us, and we'll never find each other again." A small sob escaped before she continued. "I can't let that happen. Do you have the virus there? Can we come to you?"

I fell into a chair. "Oh, my goodness, oh, my poor girl. Yes, of course, come right away. It's okay here. The town has very few cases and no deaths."

But since I told her that, people have started dying. From one minute to the next, people keeled over all at once like they'd been shot. Now I'm not sure it's safe here either. It might not be safe anywhere, but I don't know if I should tell her that. What would I say?

When I was young, everything that came into my mind came out of my mouth. Georgia would cock her head, raise her eyebrows, and tilt her hand, and I would know I was going over the top. "People genuinely don't want to know what other people think," she said. "They're more interested in hearing themselves talk, and they'll like you better if you let them."

After emptying a few rooms at parties and losing a few best friends, I learned to repress most of what I thought. So, I didn't tell Jean what I'd figured out: that this virus preys on weakness and picks its victims. It kills people who think they can brazen it out and won't be felled as well as those who do everything to hide from it. It's deliberately cruel as if it were human.

We're just hosts to a villain whose only intention is survival. Scientists may claim a virus can't have intention because it isn't alive, but how else can they explain the virus' behavior?

I didn't tell Jean that either. She's better off thinking she can protect her family and keep them together. Being together is everything. Georgia would have reminded me that having someone next to you while you're watching hockey on TV is so much more fun than watching it alone. I remember the feel of her shoulder against mine, my hand bumping hers in the popcorn bowl. How she chewed with her mouth open. Remembering it makes me smile.

I have a soft spot for my nieces. Jean and Caro were the only family members who sent flowers and condolence cards when Georgia died of cancer five years ago. I called to thank each of them, charmed the girls had reached out when I needed someone to care.

They were in their thirties then, knee-deep in little children and their careers. I never forgot their thoughtfulness. How unfair is it that my beautiful niece lost her life to this insane virus, and I'm alive, an old curmudgeon with no one to love me? That is plain evil, nothing random about it.

The world is upside down. There's a heatwave at both poles, for God's sake. It's hotter in the Arctic than where Jean lived, yet the winters in Sault Ste. Marie are as frosty as they've ever been. No wonder ancient viruses are waking from their icy graves. They're as confused as we are.

Before I talked to Jean on the phone, the world's big-city problems hadn't mattered. "A tempest in a teapot," I told Picasso. "Who cares about them? Damn Americans, always screwing things up." Even though my town was on the main route from Ottawa, where the prime minister was sick, that was a long way away.

In the Soo, the river flows deep blue, cumulus clouds hang overhead on sunny days, my sturdy house is the same as it has always been, and I can pretend every day is like the one before it. Unless two inches of ice coat the sidewalks, I toddle every morning along the river walk, wave to people, chat with acquaintances and strangers alike, exchange a book at the library, and shop for my dinner at the local market in the afternoon.

Our first nine cases changed all that. I read everything about the pandemic I could get my hands on. Shocked, townsfolk blamed tourists and military personnel returning from overseas tours. Humans always think the bad stuff comes from somewhere else. They can't imagine their own bodies might harbor the worst killers. Regardless, local people kept on as usual with the addition of face masks and gloves. Unlike our southern cousins, we Canadians are a fairly compliant bunch. A week later, when the number of local cases rose to sixteen, everyone blamed the Americans, so wrapped up in their own entitlement, that they didn't care if they spread a deadly disease during a three-day gambling spree. Still, we had no deaths.

In the space of a week, our town had 200 confirmed cases, and then the province was up to 2,200 cases, and everyone was staying home voluntarily, suspicious of every human contact. We watched the virus course through our streets like a flood, swamping everything in its path, but the effect was nothing compared to what was happening below the 49th parallel. When the mayor died, we immediately shunned all people. Everyone was a possible carrier, and outsiders were no longer welcome.

I'm glad Georgia didn't live to see this. She was so gregarious that the absence of friends and acquaintances would have wounded her. I can hear her saying, "Fuck it, I'm going out there and talking to people. I'm going to shake a stranger's hand. Watch me."

In the last three days, this infection has brought everything to a standstill in our small town, and no one knows how to get rid of it. We're up to four strains in our province, each with its own effects, and people with no symptoms walk around shedding cells riddled with virulent disease. Whenever I see someone on television sweating profusely, I know that poor sap has it.

I've stopped reading about it. If I can't absorb another bit of data and can't assemble the bits into a coherent picture, it's better to focus on myself and my own little life. To get my mind off death, I've taken up painting what I see outside my front windows. The sky is a clear blue, colors pop in that pure light, and shadows are well-defined. Strange how nature isn't foreshadowing the doom we all feel coming.

Meanwhile, I can't forget that Jean is out there on her own, unprotected, without an adult companion to help her with those children, and I can't do anything but wait. "Enough of this whining, Picasso. I have to do something. Let's bake a cake and prepare for the kids' arrival."

Just then, a rock pings against my front door. I peek out the side window and see a boy, arms akimbo, standing in my driveway, taunting me.

Before the cake, then, I'll clean the guns and check my ammo.

9

Jean

I DRIVE away from Wilbursburg, blindly following GPS instructions over back roads, that old woman's curse ringing in my ears. "You won't survive. There are too many for one small boat. One of you will die."

"Ruby, do you know what she was talking about? Mrs. Pittman. The boat thing she said?"

The child shakes her head and stares out the window as any other kid would. It looks like the scenery is the only thing she sees. But after an hour, she says, "There's a place called Elyria in Ohio, sort of near Lake Erie," as if a Google map image just popped into her head.

I put together the "lake" she mentions and Pittman's warning about a "boat," and the muscles in my shoulders knot. We don't have a boat. When is this boat accident supposed to happen?

If Ruby's gift comes in dreamlike snatches, she needs a good interpreter, and that's not me. Is it fair to use her gift to save ourselves? Could her visions save her also, even though Pittman said the opposite is true? Doubt, like smoke, obscures the answers.

Ren, also doubtful, finds the city on the GPS. "There *is* an Elyria," he says with a dash of surprise. I nod, and he adjusts our destination.

We should be choosing our own way instead of following the hazy hallucinations of a traumatized eleven-year-old. Unless all she's doing is seeing where we will go, no matter what. I try to push my concern aside, but apprehension pushes back. Taking Ruby changed our fate. Maybe we weren't supposed to take her and leaving her with Pittman was the way to fix that error, so now we're doubly cursed.

No, that can't be true; taking her was the humane thing to do. This constant dread that I'll do the wrong thing and we'll perish makes me question everything. I need to calm down, as Ted would say.

A billboard announces the city's name as we approach the Cleveland suburb. It's real enough, even though the name makes me think

73

of many-headed serpents rising out of a roiling sea to snatch wailing princesses off volcanic cliffs, bearded men in loincloths holding spears, and blood rites. I shake myself. These are modern times. The city won't be an ancient village on the Adriatic once conquered by the Greeks.

I'm so tired, my mind spews up nonsense as if I'm dreaming. Flashes of the jagged edges of a titanium golf club piercing the groundskeeper's face race through my mind over and over. His shock. Blood spurting. Each time the memory surfaces, I shudder. I can't do that again; I'm not a good murderer.

The double yellow lines in the middle of the road blur, and for a second, the vehicle strays onto the shoulder, spraying up gravel, the sudden racket shaking me awake. Caro whispers fiercely, *Be careful!* I jolt awake.

"You need to sleep, Mom." Ren searches the map for a place to rest. "There's a park and a community college nearby. Maybe we can find a safe place there."

At a stoplight, I rub the back of my neck and stretch. Pushed to the edge, I'm a killer, not an eco-mom. That's my real self, as Owen would say, a fact that takes my breath away. In one act of fury, I'm revealed—Judith, capable of beheading Holofernes to save my city. If every human turns murderer in the face of danger and each of us is the other's enemy . . . I can't let my thoughts reach the obvious conclusion. There must be another solution, another way.

I follow Ren's directions toward the community college campus, longing for an empty infirmary with rows of beds, white sheets, tucked gray wool covers, and polished floors. I hope the epidemic hasn't reached here and there are adults I can talk to, people who will help us.

What a luxury it would be to ask for help. The farther from home we travel, the more trapped and uncertain I feel, as if we're in one of Ren's games, living in a simulation on a spaceship in the middle of a galaxy billions of parsecs from home, no communication with anyone and resources running low.

Our route takes us into the city through a neighborhood that could be anywhere in the country, the same supercenter stores, identical chain restaurants, and cookie-cutter public school buildings, except something is wrong, and I can't put my finger on it.

We pass a gas station where cars idle, drivers waiting for their turn to fill up. Is this the effect of the nearby college and the hospital—people are still employed, going about their normal lives? Ranchers, cottages, brick, and clapboard split foyer residences fronted by well-tended yards abound, their porch steps decorated with pots of bulbs about to burst into spring bloom. No guards, no tanks, no barbed wire, no sign of gloom or dread.

Closer to campus, a block of narrow brick or clapboard two-story shops with colorful facades, each one different from the other, is open for business. Lights are on inside stores with fruits and vegetables, flowers, or items arrayed for sale outside. I tap the brakes to slow the car to the posted twenty-five miles an hour, and we stare out the windows.

"Look, Mom, look!" Ren rolls down his window and points. "People! People are walking around the way they used to."

I turn where Ren directs, and we find ourselves in the heart of this commercial area with shops and cafes on both sides of the street for a few blocks. We stare out the windows as if we're on a Disney ride peering at an animatronic display. I listen for a theme song. Astonishingly, people look normal. They're every age, their faces aren't drawn, their eyes aren't darting around scanning for danger, and they're not wearing masks.

A mother holds her child's hand to walk across the street. An old woman leans on her cane and hobbles into a bank. People going into stores smile and laugh and talk to each other. A man in a gray suit carrying a black leather briefcase moves briskly along the sidewalk but stops to greet a woman pushing a stroller. My heart bangs away in my chest, like warning drums.

"Is this real?" Amina echoes my thought.

When I stop at a red light, before I can object, Pam puts on her mask, leans out of her window, and asks a woman standing on the sidewalk, "What town is this?"

The woman's smile lights up her face. "You're in Elyria. Best kept secret in the heartland."

Owen asks, "Do they have—"

"TREATS!" the kids shout in unison.

Owen grins. "Yeah."

The woman peers into our car. Her eyes sparkle. I'm instantly suspicious; I have never believed happy people.

"There's an ice cream store right around the corner," the woman says. "Charlie's. You can't miss it. There's a giant ice cream cone outside the store."

"Does he have rainbow sprinkles?" Owen asks.

"Of course," the woman says. She waves at us and crosses the street.

The kids cheer, "Ice cream, ice cream, ice cream!"

As I drive, my distrust of pleasant people and their ulterior motives nags at me. But it's clear we have to stop for ice cream, or I'll have a mutiny on my hands. I set aside my anxiety, park at a meter, and feed it quarters.

"Everybody put on your masks." All my senses are on high alert. The place is so pre-calamity normal that part of me wants to fall into the deep feather bed of it and never get up. That's the reason I'm suspicious—it's seductive. I want to stay here, stop traveling, and sleep for weeks.

Inside the ice cream store, the man behind the glass case wears a white paper hat and a long white apron. His sleeves are rolled up. On the inside of his wrist is a tattoo of the infinity symbol. I flash on the hazmat guy spray-painting the symbol on my neighbor's door—contaminated, toxic, forever altered. Feeling squeamish, I push my mask firmly into place.

"I want chocolate!" Owen yells.

"Strawberry," Mira says.

Ruby looks at me, and I nod. "Chocolate chip, please. My dad always got me chocolate chip."

Amina, Pam, and Ren study the list of flavors and order mango, watermelon, and blueberry.

The man smiles, and the corners of his eyes crinkle. Usually, I take that as a sign of sincerity, but something holds me back. He pulls on translucent plastic gloves to scoop ice cream into cones. "What about you, Ma'am?"

Ruby's eyelids fly open in warning as if she now realizes there's something odd about this town. "Nothing for me, thanks," I say. Best not to be lulled into the manic optimism of a sugar high before I know what danger we face. The kids lower their masks to lick their cones while I put cash on the counter. "Keep the change as a tip," I say and scoot the children out of the small, enclosed space in the store.

We need somewhere to sleep for the night, preferably a place with bathrooms. I long to wash my hands and face with hot water and soap. We've been cooped up in the van for two days, except for our brief forays into Mrs. Pittman's fantasyland and the golf club, which were decidedly not restful. I need to fill up the gas tank. It would be good if I could buy gas and save my stockpile. Something else troubles me, but I can't put my finger on what it is. I should call Aunt Dee to tell her where we are, but that's not it.

While the kids walk ahead of me, looking in store windows, I consult the map on my phone. We're blocks from the community college, but if the town is truly normal, college security folks won't let us use the facilities. We're refugees, the people no one wants in their cities and towns; we're the people others shun. I need a Plan B.

Ren falls into step beside me. "It feels weird here, Mom."

"Yep. What do you think we should do?"

At that moment, we're surrounded by five adults in front, behind, and on either side of us. None of them wear masks. They lean toward us, so close I can smell them through my mask.

"We can help you," the woman who told us about the ice cream store says. She's returned with reinforcements; I was right to be uneasy about her. She sizes up Ren, who's tall for his age. "This one only has a year before he's susceptible."

"What are you talking about?" I scowl at her and peer around her shoulder to see Amina and Pam have rounded up the little ones. They hold hands and stare at us. Mira's chin trembles. Ruby says something to them. That I don't know what she says worries me.

The woman touches my arm to get my attention. "We have a treatment for the virus," she says. She also has a tattoo on her wrist. "That's why everything is normal here."

The skin cells on my arm where she touched me curl up. "What kind of treatment? And what do you mean he only has a year?"

I put my hand on Ren's shoulder, pulling us out of the circle the Elyrian citizens made around us. We walk toward the kids. The Elyrians follow us like ghosts crowding Pacman.

A bald man with rimless glasses shoves his face too close to mine as if he wants to examine the pores of my skin. "The virus infects eighty percent of adults and kills fifty percent of its victims."

He sounds like he's accustomed to lecturing in a classroom. These facts mean nothing to him personally; he's detached, unconcerned about humanity. This data is intended to immobilize me with fear, like a spider's venom paralyzes a fly.

"The frail and elderly who don't die from the virus often die from the after-effects of the infection—pneumonia, organ failure. Those who recover carry the virus in their bodies for the rest of their lives, like the chickenpox pathogen. Symptoms return when the immune system weakens from age or some other insult."

My mind races to Caro. "Is the virus in swimming pools? Can it spread that way?" I hate myself for asking him, but I have to know.

The expert scowls. "Pools? No. It's airborne. Infection is transmitted from person to person. Someone infected talks to you, breathes near you, even fifty feet away, and the virus jumps to your body. It's quite a simple mechanism." His volume increases as he gets to his punchline. All I can think of is that he's breathing near me, and he's not wearing a mask.

I twitch and push mine up on my nose, praying it works.

"If you've been in contact with someone who was sick, even if you didn't get sick, you're probably a silent carrier. The virus resides in you until it finds a more hospitable host to whom it can leap, which means you could give it to your son when he becomes an adult."

I step back away from him and collide with the Elyrian behind me. "What are you saying?"

Ren steps in front of me. "You're not making any sense. I'm fine."

"*Now* you're fine," the man says. "Children and a few adults have natural immunity. The gene that makes you susceptible to this virus doesn't get turned on until you're around fifteen. That'll also be true for your brother and sisters when they turn fifteen if the virus remains in the environment." He waves his hand toward the kids. "Of course, you must be around infected people to catch it. The virus doesn't survive very long on non-animal surfaces, and if no one around you has it, you won't get it. But it's highly unlikely you wouldn't come into contact with the virus given the prevalence of infection in this country."

The hair on the back of my neck lifts. He's saying that half of my children will die from this thing, and there's nothing I can do about it. That can't be true; I won't let it be true. The shrill voice coming out of my mouth doesn't sound like mine. "So, you what? You made a vaccine, and you inoculate strangers for free, for the good of humankind?"

Heat flushes my neck and face. Images of the monsters we've already met flash in my mind. This man is one of them, even if he's wearing a starched white shirt, bowtie, and tweed jacket. We have to get away. The van is one hundred feet from us. My kids are ten feet from me. How fast can we run away from these people? This feels like one of those verbal math problems I can never solve.

I raise my head and lock eyes with Pam. Amina nods. Ren steps closer to me so that our shoulders touch. I reach into my pocket and press the key fob to unlock the doors. *On my signal*, I send the kids telepathically and hope that kind of communication actually works.

Another woman slides up beside me and twines her arm around mine, holding me in place. The Elyrians surround me. My teeth clench when I try to pull away. I glance at Ren; he lopes to the kids and gathers them around him.

"We were doctors and scientists working at the cancer institute before the virus hit," the woman confining me says. "We'd already been looking at ways to hijack RNA signaling as a method to cure certain cancers. We simply applied what we knew to the new problem."

She waves her other arm to indicate the townsfolk on the street who have stopped what they're doing and are staring at us.

"We nearly have it perfected." She holds out her wrist with the tattoo emblazoned on her skin and smiles at me. The pedestrians around us raise their arms to display their tattoos.

The air in my nose turns ice cold. I shake my head and try to extricate myself again. She grips me with two hands. The bald man approaches me, and another closes in behind me.

"The procedure is quite simple. We draw blood to type you. If you have natural protection, that is, if your T-cells are strong enough to fight off the invader, you won't get sick from the virus, although you could be a carrier. If you're not naturally immune, our infusion awakens your T-cells and knocks the virus out of your system. There are side effects for some."

"No, thank you. I'm not interested." I yank my arms away from the woman and step around the man.

He wraps his arm around my shoulders and holds me in place. "It's quite easy. We only need your informed consent to transfuse you. You're bedridden for a week or so. Only a few fatal complications have occurred:

heart failure, for example, and a few people have gone blind or been paralyzed, a few strokes, but not many, not more than fifteen percent. Statistically, very few. Certainly not medically significant." He looks my kids over as if they are different delicious ice cream flavors. "During this time, we would, of course, take care of the children. We'll do the older boy, also, as prevention."

"You're not doing anything to my aunt," Pam yells, her cheeks red and her eyes blazing.

Pam is my personal superhero; I'm so proud of her. The kids grip each other's hands. I push away from the strangers and rush to the children. Ren stands behind them.

"You do not have my consent," I say, trying to keep my voice calm, trying to sound reasonable and be perfectly clear, even though I want to scream.

In my head, Caro is yelling, *Run!*

I nod to the kids and jerk my head toward the van. Ren picks up Mira, I take Owen's hand, and we streak as a pack to the vehicle. Pam yanks open the doors as the surprised strangers surge toward us from across the street. The kids dive for their seats.

Cars stop as the drivers stare and point at us. More people come out of the shops and raise their fists. The man with glasses thrusts his arm through my open door to drag me away as I enter the vehicle. He grabs my arm and tugs. I try to pry his fingers loose. He moves closer. I can feel his breath on my neck. The kids are screaming.

I kick him away with both feet, shoving hard into his soft stomach. He loses his grip. I slam the door shut, push the lock button, start the vehicle, and swerve into the street.

"Turn right," Ren calls out.

In my rearview mirror, I see the townsfolk standing, their mouths agape, watching us speed off. Another car pulls out behind me, speeding toward us. I make the turn Ren points to and zoom down the street, ignoring the red stoplight. Holding my breath, I listen for sirens and pray they don't have the police on their side. In two more turns, the car following us disappears.

We zip through the commercial area into a residential section beyond the college. None of us speaks. In this part of town, no one is outside. Doors and windows are shut. Not everyone in Elyria is part of the experiment. Or they're dead, victims of hope, the original snake oil. The man never said how many people died, went blind, or were paralyzed by their concoction.

"He's a bad man," Mira says. "He wanted to hurt you, Aunt Jean."

"They're experimenting," Ruby says as if she recently learned the word. "They need more guinea pigs."

"I want a guinea pig," Owen says. "They're furry and soft."

We smile at Owen and feel better because we're smiling.

"Ruby, did you know Elyria was dangerous?" I have to ask her, at least to allay my suspicions that she set a trap for us. This would be the second time, unless Mrs. Pittman was a test, one we passed by keeping Ruby with us instead of abandoning her at the first convenient opportunity.

"I'm sorry," Ruby says. "I saw the town. It looked safe."

I watch her face in the mirror. She looks distraught.

"I can't tell if what I see is a warning or directions or just what will happen." She puts her hands over her eyes. "I didn't see those people before they found us, and then I saw everything like a movie in fast forward. You were on a gurney with something in your arm, and blood was coming out. A word flashed, but I didn't know what it meant. P-L-A-S-M-A. They were going to take it out of you until it was all gone. It was too late by then to tell you. They were already surrounding you. I'm so sorry." Her voice trembles.

"Oh, honey," I say, not knowing whether it was a mistake to bring her with us or not. The minute I think that, though, I understand that taking her was the test of our humanity, the hurdle we had to leap to prove we were up to whatever is ahead. Ren knew that instinctively; I was the one who had to learn it.

Amina pats Ruby's shoulder. Pam clears her throat. "It's okay now; we're out of there."

Ren leans over and says, "No harm done. Everyone's present and accounted for," something Ted would have said.

There are limits to her powers. Or she's just a kid with no special powers, and we want to believe her because we need every bit of help we can get. "Did your mother get pictures in her head also?"

"She said no, but I think she did. She used to space out a lot. My grandmother definitely did. My mother told me to ignore them cuz they're confusing."

"*Can* you ignore them?"

"Not really. It's like when you're hungry, and your stomach growls, and you can't stop thinking about food."

A glimmer of how difficult this experience must be for a young girl breaks through my frustration. It would be hard for me to figure out. I rerun our encounter with the Elyrians. The idea that Ren will get sick when he turns fifteen hits me so hard, I gasp.

"Mom?"

I wave it off. "Just remembering." I could be remembering any one of a hundred horrible things.

"Turn left," Ren says, his voice tight. Knowledge has infected him also. "Do you think they're right, that I'll get sick next year when I turn fifteen?"

"I don't know." I glance at him. His face is pale, his eyebrows drawn together. I have never loved him more than I do this second. "We'll find a way to keep that from happening."

He puts his hand on my arm. "The truth, Mom."

"If they're right and not getting sick has something to do with genetics, and I didn't get sick, maybe you won't get it."

Ren looks out of his window. "Dad got it. He died from it."

"Not everybody gets it. Nobody knows why that is. Not even the Elyrians."

I concentrate on making a right at the next intersection. After ten blocks, we see a sign indicating we're outside the city. The space between houses increases, and a river meanders to our right. "Where are we going?"

He consults the GPS. "We're headed toward a campground on Lake Erie. Maybe we can rest there."

"Good plan, honey." I glance at the fuel gauge on the dash. "We only have a few miles before we have to stop to fill up the tank."

Ren consults the map. "We'll make it." He looks at me as if waiting for my answer to his unasked question.

I taught him basic probabilities last year. He knows what a fifty percent chance that he'll die means.

"We'll fix it, honey. I promise. We'll find a way out."

I focus on the road ahead because I can't look at him. Every day I find new ways to lie. I'm astounded by the metamorphosis happening inside me; the virus is changing my very DNA.

10

Sgt. D. Cooper, USVPD

LT and me, we clash a bit. I tell her we've got to go back and pick up the other infected in Harpers Ferry first thing. We got that order on day one, and I've got this urgency thing about it like we're missing our main chance to do the right thing. But LT says there's no particular order we have to go in as long as we fill the minimum weekly target set by headquarters: seventy percent of assignments completed. The department has standards.

If a pickup's delayed by a day or two, she says, it's only a difference of destination—quarantine camp for the living, crematorium for the dead. How can she be so blasé? The longer the infected walk around, the more other people get sick.

She ignores me because I threaten her authority, so, it's two days before we head back out there. And then, of course, we discover the target has given us the slip. "See. I knew it. I told you," I say as we walk through the first floor. They left so fast that they even left the door unlocked.

LT turns her back on me and starts opening cupboards and drawers in the kitchen as if something in there will give her a clue.

I yell from the upstairs bathrooms, "There's no toothbrushes." They left clothes, food, pictures on the walls, toys, books, and dishes. The beds are made. I run down the backstairs to confront LT in the kitchen. "They fled, they fled!" I flap my arms, but she's not listening.

In her omniscience, she says they've gone shopping. I see her note the disbelief on my face. Nobody goes shopping nowadays.

We scour the grounds and find a charred female skeleton in the backyard. That would be the one we got the report on. First time I've seen this—homemade cremation. Makes me shake my head, the things people get up to. The flames probably alerted the neighbors something

83

was wrong. One of them must have anonymously reported a possible infection on the USVPD website.

People like telling on each other. Even in the old days—drugs, theft, vandalism, leaving trash cans out on the street for a week—folks getting away with breaking even the silliest laws riles up people, makes them antsy. They complain to the authorities to balance things out. Life is a seesaw, and if your neighbor is up, you're on the ground, and you gotta do something about that. Telling on people makes you even, or it gets you in good with the powers-that-be, so you won't get arrested for your own misdemeanor. Could be true there's a little tit-for-tat with some officers, but not me. I pride myself on being a straight arrow. The law's the law.

LT tells us to hang loose; we'll wait half an hour for the Bennetts to return. There's nothing to do except go through the laptop left on the bed in the master bedroom. I scan emails, check search history, and click on maps. The most recent map search was someplace in Pennsylvania. I'd bet that's where they're headed.

Looking for more evidence of where they might have gone, I stumble on a wedding video. Jean and Ted Bennett didn't have one of those posh weddings with the whole Disney princess theme, but light beamed out of their faces when they looked at each other, even from across the room, just like in the movies. I've never seen two real people that happy. Jealousy grabs my gut and makes me want to shake those memories out of her. For sure, she took them with her, even if she left everything else.

I flip through a book on Bennett's nightstand called *The Road* and stuff it in my pocket; it might be a roadmap to where she's headed. I also pinch a pair of turquoise earrings she left lying on her bureau. I can't help myself, and who's going to stop me? When I hold them up to my mask and look in the mirror, I see how that color blue makes my eyes glow. Maybe they were a gift from her husband, and she thought about wearing them on the journey and forgot them in her rush to leave. Her loss. My gain.

A small bronze statuette of some goddess with six arms on a bookshelf in the family room calls to me, but it turns out to be surprisingly heavy and would be hard to conceal. Not that the rest of the squad isn't taking things. Popova slips a sparkly green bracelet onto her wrist over her gloves. I watch in the mirror as LT pockets an opal ring she finds in a wooden box on Bennett's dresser. I mean, these people have everything, and they're never coming back; they won't miss a few things.

Neighbors watch us from their windows when we leave the house. LT thinks they might get defiant and reminds us that they're armed. "Best to leave before it's dark." She sounds nervous.

When we return the next day, Bennett is still gone, like I said she would be. This makes me so antsy, like my blood is flowing backward in my veins, that I can't stand still. "I told you," I say to LT, but she ignores me, just like my mother did.

Popova pulls the driver's license, vehicle tags, and credit card data on the adult subject from our onboard computer, but for some reason, we can't track her mobile phone, and her vehicle's too old to have an onboard tracking system.

"I told you she fled days ago," I say. "You should've listened to me."

"I've got this, Cooper. Don't get your panties in a twist," LT says. She puts out a BOLO on Bennett. Every police department in the contiguous forty-eight now has the details. We'll find her. I don't have any worries about that. LT adds to the alert, "Approach with care. Likely infected," so everyone'll know.

The adrenalin rush hits three hours later when we get the go-ahead to track Bennett out of our immediate area. Finally, we're doing the right thing, going after someone spreading the deadly virus. Far as I'm concerned, she's a serial killer on the loose, armed and dangerous.

Not only has she done a runner, but she's taken a passel of kids with her. I saw the photos of them on the walls of her house. All those smiles made me a little sick to my stomach. How come she gets to have a happy family, and I get nothing?

I know about women fleeing, like my mother. I know how out of control and selfish they are, running around the apartment throwing things in a suitcase, sweat beading their faces. Unlike Bennett, my mother didn't take any of us along. We'd slow her down, she said, but we knew it was because she couldn't stand being with us. We reminded her of our father. Of course, her leaving made Dad even angrier, and he already liked being cruel. His open hand was the size of my whole face.

LT calls a planning meeting where she lays out how we'll proceed. "We've never been out of our region before, so this is big," she says. "We're going to work in concentric circles outward from the Bennett house until we get a firsthand observation of her intended direction and then track her from point to point. The whole nationwide network of cameras has her headshot for facial recognition and her license tags. The data's been shared with the drone system also. We'll get her the first time she stops to pee." LT gives herself a little nod of approval.

I suggest we head straight to Pennsylvania because of Bennett's map search, but LT says we're sticking to her plan. She's het up about the fact that a target slipping by us is bad for her rating. I'm feeling pretty intent myself. My career's riding on the success of this mission too.

After we apprehend Bennett—with or without those kids—it's a straight line to detention for her. She thumbed her nose at us, and there's a cost for that. Nobody's above the rules or the whole country falls apart. The USVPD is like the mortar in the walls of our civilization. This mission could turn out to be the most important one of my life.

)(

"The 1970s and early 1980s was the period in which
coronavirus virion proteins and nested-set arrangements of
mRNAs were identified and the discontinuous nature of
coronavirus transcription was initially demonstrated.

"The first published sequence of a coronavirus gene
appeared in 1983, starting an era in which the whole of the
genomes of four coronaviruses were cloned—in pieces—
and sequenced.

"This decade has seen the manipulation of these
clones . . . to study coronavirus RNA replication, transcription, recombination, processing and transport of proteins,
virion assembly, identification of cell receptors for coronaviruses, and processing of the polymerase."

—MICHAEL M. C. LAI AND DAVID CAVANAGH,
ADVANCES IN VIRUS RESEARCH, VOL. 48 2008

)(

11

Ren

CLOUDS of dirt blow up alongside the van as Mom drives slowly over the dry road into the campground. We stop to read the big green sign with white lettering that says, THIRTY DOLLARS A NIGHT . . . PAY IN ADVANCE for a campsite, but no one's in the gatehouse, and the metal arm is up. The owners have abandoned the place, or they're dead. We're starting at level three of a new game.

We pass campers with doors ajar, folding chairs set up around a fire pit, and supplies scattered on the ground. It's like in school when the alarm went off, and everyone ran—that tightness in my chest, the feeling I couldn't get enough air in my lungs. I don't need superpowers to know that something bad will happen.

In the recreation area, wooden shutters are pulled across the door and windows of a cantina. Picnic tables near the food stand are crawling with ants scavenging from paper plates. I check Mom's face. Her lips are pressed together.

"Mom, maybe this isn't the best idea."

She glances at me and rocks her head. "Maybe there *are* no clever ideas anymore."

Sometimes I wish she wouldn't tell me the truth.

Deeper into the woods, the kids roll down their windows. "The air smells like spring here," Amina says. "Like green ferns poking through the soil."

Pam pushes the brim of her baseball cap up. "How do you know what green smells like?"

Amina gets that superior look on her face that drives Pam crazy. She tosses her braid over her shoulder. "I just know."

How could two girls who were once so much the same I could barely tell them apart if my eyes were closed be so different now? Then I remember again that Pam's mom died a week ago, and Amina's mom—my mom—is alive. That enrages Pam, and she's not afraid to show it to everyone. Even her walk is more defined like her body has a double-bold outline around it. If I were Pam, I'd question everything too, and I might not be so nice about it.

"It's cooler here," Mom says. A breeze shakes tree branches just starting to bud. "Maybe that's an effect of the lake, or we're far enough north that we're in a different climate region. Did everyone bring hoodies?"

"Oh, no," Amina says, "I lost mine at the golf club."

"Can we go in the water?" Owen asks.

"We'll see. It's pretty late in the day. Keep your eyes peeled for the perfect campsite."

Mom has a way of distracting the kids without them realizing she's doing it. She gives them a job that makes them feel important, and they focus on doing it right. I need to learn this trick.

We pass a playground next to a miniature golf course. I imagine the place filled with families laughing and children running around. But it's empty, putters left lying on the greens as if folks dropped them and fled in the middle of their games.

"Golf!" Owen yells. "I want to play golf! I have a ball."

"Maybe later, Owen," Mom says. "Let's keep our eyes open for the best place to camp."

Up ahead, I spot a grove of trees with a ready-made fire pit. No sign of recent use. No adjacent campsites. I look around at Owen and point my head toward the spot. His eyes get wide, and he grins.

"There! There!" He points. "Look, Mom."

"That is perfect, Owen. Good job."

The little guy's face lights up. He holds up his tiny fist, and I bump mine against his.

Mom parks the van in a way that will shield our tents from the road. It hits me that we're alone in the middle of nowhere with no friends or allies, no one we can call to help us. I picture the bad guy at the golf club storming toward us and turn in a circle, listening for footfalls or a rustling in the woods. Nothing.

"Ren," Mom says, interrupting whatever's brewing in my mind. She has dark circles under her eyes and a pinched look around her mouth.

I've never seen her look so tired. "Should we set up three tents—one for me and Mira, one for Pam, Ruby, and Amina, and one for you and Owen—or should everybody sleep in a circle?"

The question she's not asking is, "Are we safe here?" If I have to guess, we're not safe anywhere. "I think we should sleep in the vehicle, Mom, with the doors locked, and we should set a watch outside. I've gotten some naps in. I'll go first while you sleep. Then we'll switch. Four hours each."

She looks at me with so much pride that I have to look away. It's embarrassing. Pam's watching us, and she smiles with half her mouth like she knows everything I'm thinking or feeling, or that look is because she's sad and missing her mom. I shrug at her because that's easier than finding the words to say. But I get what she's feeling. I take how I miss my dad and double it.

Amina puts her hand on my shoulder. "I can take a turn watching. I'm a good screamer."

Mom's eyes get wet, and her voice is froggy. "Okay, let's get everything out, lower the seats, and open our sleeping bags inside." She looks up at the sky, over both shoulders, and at each of us. "Then we'll scout the area, check out the lake, eat something, use the facilities, and get some sleep."

When I went camping with Dad, someone at a nearby campsite was always playing guitar or blasting their playlist. I could smell smoke from their fire and hear parents yelling at kids. Here, there's nothing, not even the call of birds as if a predator were prowling around.

I picture the virus police in their spacesuits raiding the campground and yanking people out of here. They might come back, this time for us. In my games, the bad guys hide behind fallen trees, silently signaling each other, waiting to spring out when we let down our guard. My shoulders tighten, and my stomach churns. I need to be ready, no matter who's taking the watch.

While the kids unload, I look for a weapon in the toolbox that Dad always kept in the back of the van. My hands wrap around a hammer and a screwdriver. In a flash, I see Mom driving the golf club into the groundskeeper's eye again, and my stomach lurches. I stuff the tools inside my sleeping bag.

Half an hour later, standing on the white sand beach, I almost forget we're running for our lives. The lake is slate blue and rolls out to the horizon. Low waves slowly flip over with a small shushing sound at the shore. Mira pulls off her shoes and puts her toes in.

Mom grabs her hand. "Watch out for the riptide. I read the great lakes have strong undertows."

To the west, the sun starts to go down. Owen stares at the water, his arms out from his sides, hands open as if he has to take the sight in with every pore in his whole body, not just his eyes.

Amina sighs. "It's beautiful," she says. "It makes me feel like everything will be okay."

Mom wraps her arm around Amina's waist. "It makes me think the Earth will survive us. It will recover when humans are gone."

My hands get cold. I shove them into my pockets and scan the shoreline. I'm proud Mom thinks she can talk to us like adults, like we would understand what she means, but her words scare me. She thinks humans won't make it, that we'll die off, and that makes me angry and sad at the same time. If she doesn't believe we'll make it, we won't. She's giving up too soon.

"We're going to survive, Mom. We're not going extinct. Not until the sun goes supernova, anyway, and that's a billion years from now."

She looks at me, and I see her course-correct on the spot. "Of course, you're right. We'll survive. We're as resilient as the planet is. We're made of the same stuff."

She hugs my shoulders. I know she's trying to make me feel better, but the look on her face tells me something else. Under her fear, I see the admiration that makes me proud and uncomfortable at the same time, like she expects something big from me that I won't be able to deliver, but this time, I don't look away. If what saves us is believing that we'll make it, I'll take it.

Waves lap up onto the shore over and over until I'm hypnotized. "We could stay here for a while, Mom. There are fish in the lake. We could just live here. Couldn't we? Wouldn't that be easier than driving up to Canada?"

"Maybe." Mom looks over her shoulders, and then she turns in a circle. "But if that's true, if this is a safe place to ride out the pandemic, why aren't other people here? Why did they run away and leave their stuff?"

I don't answer, but now I'm sure the virus patrol must have raided the place. If that's true, they'll be back, and there's no place to hide.

Pam does cartwheels across the beach, and Ruby imitates her. Mira and Owen try to follow them, falling in small heaps and then leaping up, yelling, "Ta-dah!" Mom applauds, but she constantly eyes the path and the woods for whatever comes next.

We watch the little ones build a sandcastle with Amina. I worry about how tired Mom is, whether she's making the right decisions. I'm tired, too. When there are no good options, how do you know the best choice? If this were a game, I could turn it off and think about it. I could search for winning strategies and ask other people who have mastered this level for cool tricks, but it's not a game. There's no hack for this. We have to decide now whether to stay or go.

How to decide stuff is the kind of talk Dad would have had with me. I wouldn't actually have listened because, in the end, I knew he would decide about anything important, but I liked the sound of his voice going on and on, even if I didn't realize he was teaching me something. It was just my time with Dad, and I thought I could have as much as I wanted, but I wish now I had paid attention to his words because they're gone, and I'll never hear them again. I need a do-over; the world needs a do-over.

"Hey, everybody," Pam yells, running toward us. "We found a boat! It has a motor. Can we go for a ride?"

Mom looks up. "A boat? Where?"

Ruby points. "Just around the bend."

"It probably belongs to someone," Mom says. "We can't just take it. Besides, six of us wouldn't fit in it, and we don't have life jackets."

Pam keeps pushing, as always, because sometimes that works. Watching her manage Mom, I get that I give up too easily.

"We could just try it out," she says. "We'll stay near the shore. We can swim back if it tips or has a leak."

"I don't think so, Honey." Mom reaches out and strokes Pam's cheek. "But you're quite the adventurer." She smiles at her.

Pam stomps away for fifty feet, puts her hands on her hips, and stares at the water. Mom doesn't do anything. Eventually, Pam comes back, sits beside Mom, and puts her chin on her knees. Her lips are pressed together. I can't tell what she's thinking.

"I'm a venturer, too," Owen says. He puts his fists on his hips and glares at Mom and Pam.

"Of course you are, Owen," Pam says. She tickles him under the chin, and he giggles.

We walk to our camp, make a fire, eat stuff, and do a bathroom run. I hear Mom insisting, "Everyone brush your teeth," through the thin wall between the men's and women's sections.

Owen raises his eyebrows at me. "Do I have to?"

I nod. "Just because we can't see Mom doesn't mean you don't have to do what she says."

He scrunches up his face the way he does just before tears. "You're not the boss of me. I don't have to do what *you* say."

It must be frustrating to be five years old. I was five once. What did I want from Mom more than anything? Then I get it. "Mom will be proud of you if you brush your teeth like a big boy without her having to watch you do it."

His face brightens, and he almost gives in. "I can't cuz my brush doesn't work right."

I push the button on his toothbrush and hand it to Owen. He grins and sticks the brush in his mouth. White toothpaste smears across his chin and cheeks. We're okay again.

Mom and I set our watch alarms for four hours when we'll switch who's on guard. Everyone but me crawls into the nest of sleeping bags. They look like the sardines in a can Mom bought for Dad, but nobody else ever ate. I fold up my sleeping bag on the ground, so I have something soft to sit on for four hours and put the hammer and screwdriver where I can reach them. Mom cracks the van windows for air, and they're asleep in seconds.

It's dark fifteen minutes later. I feed the fire and position myself with my back against the vehicle's rear bumper. Every rustle of the trees scares me. I remember there might be bears and jump up to put our food in the backpacks. I tie the packs with bungee cords, sling them onto high branches, and wrap the cord around the tree trunk.

Something thrashes around in the woods. My arms and legs go rigid. I hope it's not coyotes or something worse: humans. My breath balls up in my throat. I convince myself it's just my imagination and put in my earbuds. The last thing I remember is gripping the hammer.

12

Dee

AUTHORITIES have closed the US-Canadian border, stopping traffic over bridges and ferries in both directions. Only essential vehicles can cross. Border control officials are turning back everyone who isn't essential and detaining anyone who's sick.

Jean was supposed to have been here by now. This is my fault. I didn't listen to what she was saying closely enough. She must have told me how long it would take.

Georgia always said that was one of my many flaws: I don't listen. Even when I keep my mouth shut and stare at the lips of the person talking, the voice in the back of my head is always nattering away, blocking out the sound of whatever someone is trying to tell me.

The first time Georgia touched me was to put her fingers on my lips and say, "Shush. Let me say something." I was so astounded by the jolt of electricity that my whole body went quiet.

The minute Jean said she wanted to come, I began a list of supplies to put in before she arrived, but I forgot to make sure we could communicate no matter what happened. The whole world is going to pot, but it didn't occur to me that something might go wrong with the very technological advances that make a difference. If our phones go down permanently, everything changes. Which makes me think I should buy a horse and buggy before the rush pushes the price up.

I'm trying not to panic, but I have to find a way to connect with Jean and tell her they can't cross into Canada or get to my house without using the bridge or ferry unless they have their own boat. And how would they get one of those? Even if they had a boat, the river is patrolled. They'd be spotted and detained for breaking the law. That would be worse than taking shelter somewhere in Michigan.

Anxiety makes my head hurt. I ask myself, "What would Georgia do?" She was always good in an emergency. This morning on my walk

94

along the river, I searched for a solution—a fishing boat, a truck that makes daily crossings in which my family can hide, someone reliable I could befriend or pay to carry them across. But even if I made a deal for their crossing, how would I tell Jean? How would I connect them? A trip like that would cost something, and whoever I found might take my money and disappear. The questions nearly drove me crazy.

For two days, I've been weepy and hazy, dazed half the time. I hate being weak. Every morning, I take my temperature, hold my breath for ten seconds, and check my vital signs. I tell myself to calm down. I'm fine, those palpitations are anxiety. When I check the town website for self-care instructions, the only advice is to stay home and wash my hands. Drink hot water with honey. Take vitamin C. All code for nobody knows what the hell to do.

Twice today, I shooed a gang of boys out of the yard. Suddenly, people think they can just come on my property and poke around in the garage, open my car doors, or peek in the windows of my house. I never had to lock the car before. I often forget to lock up the house when I go for walks. That'll have to change.

"Get away from here," I yelled at the kids. I walked out on the front porch, the rifle cradled in my arms. "I've got a gun," I shouted in my most menacing voice.

They danced around and hooted, "Whatcha gonna do old lady?" and then laughed hysterically like something was funny, but they ran. So, mission accomplished, but the encounter left me shaken.

These kids are acting like I'm already dead, and they can pick over the remains. And in broad daylight. I shouldn't have shown them I have a gun. They might come back for that. The fact that none of my neighbors came outside to defend me stopped me cold. They're more afraid of the virus than of looters.

I load the rifle and put it under my bed where I can reach it. I just hope I don't shoot Jean accidentally if she arrives in the middle of the night when I'm asleep. I picture the scenario: a rustle downstairs, footfalls on the steps, whispering, a silhouette in my bedroom doorway. I see myself reaching for the gun, half-asleep, pointing, squeezing the trigger, the blast. There's a groan, a body slumps onto the floor, and I scurry to the body to discover I've just shot my only living relative.

The idea makes me want to vomit. The only worse notion is that I'll be dead when Jean gets here. I make a cup of tea and plump down into the big old stuffed chair I keep in the kitchen by the table. Would it matter if I got sick? I'm old, not contributing to the world, not essential. Are former teachers ever essential after they retire? But when Jean comes to live with me, I'll have something to live for, a new purpose. There'll be a big family to take care of. Picasso will have children to play with.

"What do you think of that, Picasso? Playmates for you. Eh?"

The mutt trots over to me and nuzzles my hand with his nose. We've been together for seven years. He sits at my feet, tilts his head, and looks at me as if I'm the queen of the world. I run my fingers through his thick, white ruff. I brought him home to comfort Georgia in her final years, and now he's there for me.

My recent recurring nightmare makes me shudder awake from my nap. I'm standing in the doorway, helpless, while some great brute drags Georgia out of the house. My heart squeezes together, and I can't even scream.

I jolt awake feeling dread and emptiness, the way I felt when my family tried everything they could to separate us after I told them about her. They insisted I choose, so I did. Afterward, my parents behaved as if I didn't exist, my sister too—the coldness of that, how sad I was. But I wasn't helpless. How brave I felt making my home with Georgia in a new country. That's what I have to do now. Be brave.

If Jean doesn't come, I'll be fine if I survive the sickness. Either things will slowly return to how they were, or everything will collapse. The virus kills our best people first—first responders, nurses, and doctors—as if it wants to prove that being altruistic is dangerous. After that, it's everyone for himself.

I'm ready for the worst. In case I'm surprised by an attack, I load the rest of my guns and conceal them in strategic spots around the house. Home invaders better think twice about busting through my door.

So far, except for those hoodlums, it's quiet. I heard someone broke into the community center looking for food, but other than that, there's no crime, no rioting. Meanwhile, my niece is wandering the country with her small band of children and has nowhere to rest. I can't just sit here waiting.

13

Jean

CARO'S lips brush my ear. *Jean*, she yells. *Jean!* Her voice sounds like God's.

I startle awake, my heart thudding, mouth dry. My mind ticks through the checklist of what my eyes see around me. Round forms of sleeping children, the woods beyond the windows, early morning light seeping through the trees, and I remember. We're at a campground in Ohio near Lake Erie. We're homeless. This is the third day of our trek across the country to a safe place.

I swallow and count heads, just to be sure. Amina's long braid, Pam's unruly hair, Ruby's blond head, Mira's silky curls. Where's Owen? I count again, touching their warm bodies. He must be outside with Ren. I crawl over them and gently nudge open the back door. Ren is asleep on the ground, his sleeping bag wrapped around him. Poor kid. He's as exhausted as I am. I check my watch. We slept through the alarm for the changing of the guard.

I walk around the van. "Owen?" I whisper and crawl back into the vehicle, touching each head again, smoothing hair away from faces. No Owen; my five-year-old is missing.

I'm instantly dizzy. Pressure builds in my skull as if my pupils are trying to increase the circle's diameter I can see in one glance. My breath comes fast. *Be calm*, I tell myself. *He could have walked away into the woods to pee.*

"Owen!" I call out, no longer worrying if I wake the kids. "Owen!" I expect to see his little face pop up from behind a bush in a hide-and-seek game.

"Mom?" Amina climbs out; she yawns and stretches. "What's going on?"

Ren jumps up from the ground, his face lined where it was pressed against his sleeve. He looks around wildly. "What?"

97

"Owen's missing. Did he tell you where he was going?"

Ren shakes his head.

My chest tightens, and my mouth dries. I try to think, but I can't focus. The woods around the campsite seem to close in and whirl around me. Where would he go? My breath comes in short spurts, and the ground drops out from under me. I can't lose my baby; it's not possible. Ted would never forgive me. I moan, wondering how long he's been gone.

Ren's mouth opens, and his eyes close. I see his remorse instantly, no need to ask any other questions. "We have to look for him."

"Owen, Owen," a chorus of my son's name comes from the other children. They sound like birds calling out to each other.

Pam jumps down from the van. "I'll go. I'll look for him."

The thought of the children wandering separately through these unknown woods, getting lost, unable to find their way back to me, comes at me full speed. I throw my hands out in the STOP position. "No, wait. We need a plan. Nobody goes anywhere alone."

I have no idea what I'm doing. Owen could be anywhere. He could have tried to go swimming in the lake. He could have wandered back to the road. Someone could have taken him away from me. Each option and its consequences make me gasp. The girls wrap their arms around me. Ren stands like a condemned soldier, shaking, waiting to be shot. I have to pull myself together.

"Amina, stay with Mira and Ruby inside the van in case Owen comes back. Lock the doors and windows. The key is in the cupholder. If you have to, drive away."

Amina's eyes shine with tears. "Mom, I'm not going to leave everyone here."

I take her little pointed chin in my hand and kiss her forehead. "You are going to do whatever you must to save your lives. Do you understand?"

Her eyes widen. She nods.

"Pam and Ren, you search the campground facilities together. Don't separate. Take the flashlights. Call me if you find him. Amina, you honk the horn if Owen comes back here. I'm going to search the shoreline and the woods to the west. We meet back here in half an hour. Got it?"

They nod. Amina, Ren, and I check our watches. "At six, right?" Amina asks.

"Yes. Six. A.M." The minute I say it, I know what went wrong with our wake-up call alarms. We were so tired that we forgot to select AM.

We run in separate directions. For a few minutes, I can hear Pam and Ren yelling to each other as they go through the woods, and then the sounds fade to forest noises. The sky lightens. At least the sun is coming up. That will help.

I trot to the beach we explored yesterday, looking in both directions as I run. I stop to search inside the rowboat Pam found, hoping my son curled up inside it and went to sleep. It's empty. The lake's surface is serene, the color of the water echoing the sky. I spot something dark floating about ten feet out from the shore.

My face freezes. No. No, no, no. It can't be Owen. It won't be him.

I splash into the water toward the object, my mouth stretched wide in a scream with no sound. The water pushes against me, restraining me. I move in slow motion, pressing against its power, my heart in my throat, unable to say his name, remembering his tiny hand wrapped around my finger. I can't lose him. Oh, God, please, I can't lose him. All my mistakes flash through my mind, and a hole opens in my heart. He's just out of reach, one step, two. I stretch out my arm to grab what looks like my baby's leg, and my fingers lock around fabric. I pull it toward me and find it's a half-deflated rubber raft.

I moan with relief. It's not Owen. I laugh out loud. Standing up to my armpits in the lake, waves surge against me as tears roll down my face. Then I scan the beach for his limp body.

Dripping, I run west along the shore, uncertain of which direction to go next. I picture him walking on tiptoes away from our camp, moonlight rimming his curly brown hair, his face intent. He would have picked up a stick for his sword and gone on an adventure in pursuit of bad guys to vanquish. I see him tiptoeing through the trees, his eyes wide, a smile on his face.

His story can't end here. I won't let it. "Owen," I call out as I crash through abandoned campsites. "Where are you?"

14

Ren

PAM explains our search strategy as we run through the woods. "Like in our video game. We search in grids. We keep ten feet apart and go twenty feet in one direction, then turn and go twenty feet in the other direction. We don't zigzag. We overlap. We don't miss anything."

I get what she means. "Right. We go east and then west, starting in the north and heading south. Quadrant by quadrant." I grip the hammer in my hand, just in case.

We can see each other the whole time. The thought of losing Pam in the woods feels like that moment when I used to take the next step out in the ocean and realize the bottom had just dropped off ten feet. The water closes over my head, the emptiness beneath me sucks me downward, and I'm desperate for air, sure I'll drown and miss my whole life—all these thoughts flash through me in a few seconds before I remember to kick. I look up to make sure Pam's right there.

We enter each vacated camper we pass, thinking Owen wanted to lie down on a bed. People left everything. Nothing's broken or turned over, no cobwebs; nature hasn't invaded. Nobody looted here. They left recently—a day ago, not weeks or months. Folks were having a normal vacation, and something scared them away—totally terrified them. Maybe they saw wolves. That would scare me, but I would take my camper. Unless they didn't have time to hook it up to their cars. They had to grab their kids and run away on foot. But if it was wolves, why not scramble inside the camper? Now, I'm freaking myself out.

Pam waves at me from the other side of the campsite. "Wake up," she yells. "You're in a trance. Nothing's here. Let's go on."

When we get to the amusement end of the campgrounds with the store, cantina, and miniature golf, we find Amina, arms rigid at her sides, hands in fists, glaring at Ruby. Mira sits on the ground, huge tears running down her cheeks. Ruby puts her hands on her hips and turns her face away.

"What are you doing here? What happened to Mira?" Pam asks as she runs to them. "You were supposed to stay in the van." She picks up her sister and hugs her. "It's okay, Mira. I've got you."

Amina's face turns red. "It's her fault." She points at Ruby. "This whole mess wouldn't have happened if I hadn't listened to her." Her voice catches.

Pam squeezes Amina's shoulder. "What mess? What are you talking about? We're supposed to be finding Owen."

"Owen is here," Ruby says. "I know it. I saw him."

All of us look sideways at her. I don't believe her anymore because what she sees is lopsided or half-true and always gets us in trouble.

Amina gestures to Ruby with her thumb. "That's why we're here instead of in the van. Ruby said she saw Owen playing miniature golf, but he's not." She closes her eyes and rolls her head around on her shoulders the way Mom does. "I thought finding him was more important than staying in the van."

"He was playing golf when I saw him." Ruby's heated. "There was a man." It matters to her that we believe her. For a second, I get how awful it must be to know something is true, to see it right in front of your eyes, and nobody believes you.

"See." The corners of Amina's mouth turn down. "What if I waited for you to come back and something happened to Owen? I had to check out what she saw, didn't I? I didn't have any way of telling you or Mom where we were going."

I feel Amina's chest splitting in two like it's mine. When we separated to look for Owen, she thought we'd never find our way back together again. It's like a cold wave smacks me from behind. This is the kapow moment when I get that I can't let us be separated. Ever. We have to stay together, and it's my job to make sure we do.

"What about it, Ruby?" Pam asks. "Do you see Owen?"

"He's here, but not . . ." She turns in a circle, her hand out, trying to explain. Her lips turn down, her eyes blaze, and her chin trembles like she's sad, angry, and confused at the same time.

Pam kisses Mira's cheek and smooths the hair away from her wet face. "What's going on with you, Mira?"

"There's a bad person, and no one will listen to me."

"Oh, Sweetie, there are lots of bad people. First, we have to find Owen. Then we can deal with the bad person."

Mira wraps her legs around Pam's waist. She sniffles and wipes her face with the back of her hand. "Promise?"

"Yes, I promise," Pam says and looks at me like I should know something that would help.

If I knew what to do, I would do it. I want to be the hero and save us, but I'm clueless, and I hate feeling that way exactly because Mom made me responsible for everyone. I have to pull myself together.

I try to be logical, the way Dad would. "Let's say Ruby's right. If I were Owen, I'd play some golf, then I'd look for a treat, and then I'd get tired, sit down, and fall asleep right where I was. So where would that be?"

We check the cantina. No Owen. We walk over to the store, barely more than a magazine stand with its awning down. I try the knob on the side door. It opens, and a whoosh of dust flies at me. I beat the air to clear it and find my brother lying on the dirty wood floor surrounded by cookie wrappers. At first, I think he's dead, and my heart sort of stops. Then I see he's breathing, and he's fast asleep, with chocolate cookie crumbs covering his lips, cheeks, and chin. He clutches a neon green golf ball in one little fist.

I lift him, and Owen wakes up talking, "I got a hole-in-one! The man gave me a ball."

The man. That chill hits me again. I try to call Mom on my cell, but there's no service. Carrying a forty-pound kid, I run as fast as I can back to our van. Owen clutches my neck, wraps his legs around my waist, and giggles. It's a game to him. Pam and Amina chase after me, yelling. "Mom, Aunt Jean, we found him, we found him!"

We get to the spot where we slept last night and find Mom standing by the fire pit, her hands out from her sides, a crazy wild look on her face. I stare at her and wonder for a second what's going on. And then I get it. The van's gone.

"They took it," she whispers. "They took everything."

Mom's whole body shakes. She lowers herself to the ground like she can't stand anymore. She talks so quietly, I have to lean over to hear her.

"My wallet was in there, my passport. All your birth certificates. They know everything about us. They can empty my bank account. We have no way to get to Dee's."

I squat next to her, trying to think of something to calm her, but I've got nothing. We've lost everything. No home, no vehicle, no clothes, no food, no money. All we have left are the clothes on our backs and the things in our pockets. My heart starts pounding, and my head buzzes; I can only breathe in short spurts. It's too big an idea. I look over at my sister and cousin and watch their eyes widen, close, and open as they get it. We have nothing.

Mom looks at me, sees Owen in my arms, and holds out her arms. I hand him over, and she buries her face in his shoulder and sobs. His face goes from glee to uncertainty to sad in a split second. He pats her head and says, "It's okay, Mama. It'll be okay."

Blood rushes to my face. "You shouldn't have left the van," I yell at Amina.

Her face crashes and tears run down her cheeks. She turns on Ruby and says, "You made me do it. It's your fault."

My hands clench, fingernails digging into my palms. I want to hit something or scream, but there's no one to blame. "Fuck!" I yell as loud as I can. "Fuck."

Mom doesn't say anything about my language. She clutches Owen and looks off into space.

My voice gets louder than I ever thought it could. "Why didn't you say something about it, Ruby?"

Ruby's lip quivers, and she shrugs, "I didn't . . ." She covers her face with her hands.

Pam wraps her arm around me. "We'll be okay, Ren. We'll figure it out. It's going to be okay."

"Good thoughts can't fix this. We need a plan."

I yank my body out of her hug and think about running away from them. I'd have a better chance on my own, but I can't leave Mom like this. I can't leave any of them. I pick up a branch lying at my feet and fling it as hard as I can across the campsite. Then I realize I lost the hammer. I must have dropped it when I picked up Owen. I'm such an idiot. There's a thief in the woods, and we're unarmed and pathetic.

"It's my fault we lost everything." My voice could crack at any second. I clutch my head and turn in circles. "I couldn't even stay awake for four hours."

My throat is raw from trying not to cry. I feel like I've been dragged across the ground behind a speeding car. Everything we try to do, every way we try to save ourselves gets turned upside down. "Why is this happening to us?"

Amina says, "I feel that way too, Ren." She leans her head on my shoulder; after a minute or two, my breath comes easier. My sister is the smart one. I must not be dumb if she feels the way I do.

Owen holds up his neon green golf ball. "I got a ball from the man!" He grins as if this is the good news.

"The man?" Mom asks.

"I told you. I told you," Mira says. "Nobody listens to me."

"What man, Mira?" Mom asks as if my baby cousin is thirty instead of four.

"The bad man with the glasses who took our van," the baby says.

"You saw him?"

"He looked at us when we were sleeping."

Ruby whispers, "He's still here."

15

Jean

SOMEONE is watching us, waiting to see what we'll do next. Whoever stole the van is hiding, going through our things, examining my license and passport and papers, pocketing my cash, and considering what else we might have that he wants. I picture him turning my things over in his dirty hands, sniffing our sleeping bags, fondling our clothes. I think of the girls and shudder.

I put Owen on his feet and turn in circles, peering into the woods, twitching at every flicker of leaf and shadow. I remember the groundskeeper, how he came out of nowhere. His hands on my body, how I couldn't scream—it comes back full force. At least then, the kids had a place to hide, to get away. Now we have no resources, no weapons, no way of escape.

I have to improvise, but my mind is blank, wiped clean by our losses. We can't stay here; any minute, he could come back. I have to keep it together. Closing my eyes, I hear the quiet shush of the waves lapping on the lakeshore.

Signaling with my hand for the kids to stand close to me, I whisper, "We're going to the beach. We're going to take the boat Pam found. That's the fastest way out of here."

At first, there's only fear on their faces, their eyes wide and mouths open, and then they brighten. They have such courage. Doing something, anything is better than doing nothing, and much better than standing in a circle waiting to be attacked. That's what I've learned from our first two days on the road: stop thinking and do something.

I can't linger on what we've lost. My fingers stray to the silver locket around my neck, the one thing I have from Ted, holding my only remaining photos of Caro and him.

"Walk like me," I say. They giggle at this family joke as I imitate Igor from *Young Frankenstein* for a few steps. My legs are stiff, my bones hurt, but the joke untangles us from our grief.

I can barely process what the theft of the minivan means. My identity—official proof that I am who I say I am—is gone. I can't provide any evidence that I'm me, or that I own the vehicle someone stole, or that I'm the children's mother and aunt. Yet I have to walk away from it and not look back. My stomach churns as a scream builds in my chest, but if I scream, the bad man who stole from us will know he won, and that satisfaction is the one thing I can keep from him.

Ren puts a hand on my shoulder. I startle, still not used to the idea that he's taller than I am. "They didn't get everything," he says. He looks up into the branches of the tree. Two backpacks hang from bungee cords above our camp. "They didn't notice them. We have food and water and whatever other stuff was in the bags."

I am so proud of him, I get the chills. "You are one ingenious guy, you know that?"

In two seconds, he's reclaimed the packs. He wears one, and Amina pulls on the other. Pam adjusts Mira on her hip. I hold Owen's hand, and Ruby takes my other hand, more to comfort me, I think, than for her own safety. I aim for jaunty as we move out—another day on vacation—but my face feels like the skin has been pulled under my chin and stapled down. The kids walk with their heads down as if concentrating on their feet.

It takes every ounce of my self-control not to look over my shoulder as we walk to the lake. I pray whoever owns the boat hasn't hauled it away, but if it's gone, we'll walk west and north along the shore until we find a way out. We are not going back through the campground. We step out from the underbrush onto the beach and walk to where I saw the boat this morning. I hold my breath. It's there. I'm unable to suppress a sigh of relief.

Ren walks around the boat and examines the motor. "It's just a rowboat with a small electric outboard motor." He sounds tired and sad. He doesn't deserve this.

"Yeah," Pam says, her voice thick with disappointment, "it looks smaller than I remembered, now that we're standing around it."

Mrs. Pittman's words come back to me. Something about fitting in a boat. I shrug the warning off. She couldn't have known anything about this, although I'm not sure we will fit into this boat or that the motor has enough power to pull our combined weight through the water. I'm relieved to see it has oars, but the idea of going some distance by rowing doesn't appeal to me.

It comes down to this: we either use the boat or walk. The road through the campground is out of the question. He could be waiting there, expecting us to walk out that way. Now that I've done the unspeakable, I know every human is capable of desperate acts. The man who stole our van could run us over with our own vehicle or shoot us. We're taking the boat.

"Pull it out into the water. We don't have time for a thorough test. Let's just see if it works before we all get into it." Every instruction I utter is dragged up from a deep well. Time speeds up. We might have only moments to leave before the next dreadful thing happens. If only I hadn't left the girls alone, but I don't have time for recriminations.

Ren and Amina drop the backpacks at my feet and drag the boat into the water until they're standing up to their knees. The boat rocks in the mild waves. They clamber over the side, and Ren figures out how to lower the motor into the lake. The look on Pam's face tells me that I should have let her do this since she found the boat. I tell her to test the motor. She splashes into the lake and climbs aboard.

I watch them figure out how to get the motor going. Even though time is slipping away, I marvel at them, at their teamwork, pointing, discussing, nodding. Then Pam adjusts her baseball cap, turns something, and pushes a button. The motor whirs, and the boat jerks forward. Amina and Ren lurch onto the bench seats.

"Don't go too far from the shore," I yell. "Take it a few yards and see if it sinks!"

They grin at me as if they're still innocent kids and this is a vacation. The boat putts off at a speed too slow to be measured in knots. Their faces make me think of every explorer who ever set out for a new world, hope and fear competing for dominance. I watch them make a turn. The boat doesn't tip or sink. Despite everything, Mira, Owen, Ruby, and I raise our fists above our heads and yell, "Yay!"

With the youngest kids sitting on the bottom in the center of the boat with the backpacks and Ruby, Pam at the tiller, Amina with Ren on one seat, and me on the other, the water is only two inches from the gunwale. One unexpected wave, and we're swamped.

"Stay close to the shore," I say to Pam. She engages the motor.

I look around us. Movement in the bushes ringing the beach catches my eye. My throat constricts. "Go far enough out that no one can walk in and grab the boat."

Pam's widened eyes follow my gaze. "I can do that," she says, slowly turning the boat toward deeper water.

I nod my approval. "If we tip, Pam, you swim to shore; Ren, you grab Owen. Amina, you get Mira. I'll get Ruby. You've both had the Red Cross water safety training. You remember it, right? Grab them from behind under their arms and swim on your backs to shore."

"I can swim on my own," Ruby says. "I'm good at it. I used to be on the swim team."

Dark clouds have materialized out on the horizon and loom toward us. If there's a strong wind, waves will rise on the lake. The kids stare at me, my fear on their faces. This isn't a fun adventure; it's serious business. No one knows what comes next, and someone could get hurt. The docent's warning whispers in my mind.

"Okay, let's go west and north as far as we can go."

As we watch the shoreline, people emerge from the trees and scowl at us. There's nothing odd about them. They're not monsters. *We* are the enemy they hid from. We're the ones bringing the virus or worse into their lives. We invaded *their* space. They took our van in retaliation. And now we've stolen a boat from them and think nothing of it. Mira waves to them before I can pull down her hand.

16

Ren

WE get ten miles from the campground when the electric motor stalls. Pam tries to restart it, but nothing happens. That feeling of being about to explode builds in my stomach.

"It must have run out of power, you know, like a phone." Pam looks like she wants to scream or cry, but she's not a high-drama kind of person. She has that in common with Amina.

We drift for a few minutes. Waves rock the boat. Mom watches the shoreline. I guess she's thinking about what to do, but I feel helpless. We're not in control of anything. The coastline is lined with resorts and campgrounds, but at least we don't see any other people. The storm that was out on the horizon is closer now, with big gray clouds starting to fill the sky. We can't stay on the water; a high wind will swamp us.

I try to put myself in Mom's mind to help her figure out what to do, but I feel annoyed too; like why couldn't she just handle this like she's supposed to? She's the one to blame for this whole mess. If we'd stayed home, none of this would've happened. My life could've been the way it's always been. I want to be a kid, along for the ride, playing my game, not responsible for anything, able to sleep at night because the adults are in charge. Now I think I'll never sleep again.

"Mom, we have to do something."

"We'll use the oars," Mom says. "We need to turn the boat toward shore and let the waves take us in."

The oars are tiny; they don't look big enough to stir coffee in a cup. She tells us how to rearrange ourselves in the boat so we can row. I scoot over, the boat rocks, and I hold my breath. All the while, my head fizzes over with NO. The first two times we try to turn the boat, it wobbles a little but keeps going in the same direction, just like I thought it would.

"Keep it up until the boat turns," Mom says. "Together now."

We rock in the water, going nowhere. Dark clouds come closer, moving fast. The wind whips around us.

"Oh, wait," Pam says. "I have to turn the tiller." She shifts the tiller until the front of the rowboat turns toward the beach.

"Good," Mom says. "Row together now. And now, and now."

We get a rhythm going, and eventually, the boat heads for the shore. Pam holds us in the right direction, and we glide toward the beach, pushed along by waves that are getting higher. When we can see the bottom, Pam pulls the propeller out of the water. Mom jumps out of the boat and drags it ashore. "Pull it up on the sand, guys, the way we found it. Maybe someone else will need it."

We get the little ones up on dry land, drag the boat onto the sand, and turn it upside down. Amina points to a path that leads through reeds away from the lake. No one's around now, but people have left trash everywhere like they don't care about anything. At the end of the path is an empty parking lot with a trash can and a picnic table.

Mom pulls her phone out of her back pocket and turns it on. "At least the phone works. That's something. Good thing Dad insisted on waterproof."

While Mom's studying the maps to find out where we are and where we're going next, Pam and I pull out crackers and peanut butter from the packs.

"No. I hate peanut butter," Mira says.

Sometimes my perfect little cousin is a bit too much of a princess. We've lost everything, but she can't let peanut butter touch her lips.

"I'll eat yours," Owen says, reaching out his hand for a cracker, and with his first bite, smears peanut butter across his chin.

Amina hands Mira an apple. Starving, I paw through the packs looking for the highest calorie item we've got and find hotdogs. I rip the package open with my teeth and offer Owen and the girls a dog before I stuff one into my mouth. Pam hands me a ball of cheese. I pack that in my other cheek and look for something else.

"I think we're near Sandusky, Ohio," Mom says. "It's a big city." She doesn't have to remind us that means danger.

"You know, Mom, if your phone is working, you can change the pin number on your bank card, so whoever stole it can't use it."

"Really?"

"Yeah, I'll show you. We can totally do your other passwords, too. And I can set you up to pay for stuff using your phone. But we have to get it charged soon."

Mom closes her eyes and runs her hand over her face. "My charger is in the van." Her lip quivers.

"I've got one in my pack. We just need an electric outlet."

She looks at me like I'm a hero and the best thing that ever happened to her. Before I can get cocky about it, I settle down beside her, and she hands me her phone. A few raindrops hit us, and we look up. That storm we spotted out on the lake is overhead. Mom's not even worrying about taking cover.

"You do it—change my passwords and stuff. Tell me what you did when you're done." She roots through a backpack and pulls out cheese and an apple. "God, I'm so hungry it's ridiculous." She crunches down on the apple, closing her eyes for a second.

The second after I set up her new passwords and her i-pay, we hear the *whap, whap, whap* of car tires approaching on the asphalt road leading to the parking lot. Too fast for us to figure out where to hide, a police car pulls into the lot, and a uniformed officer gets out of his vehicle. He ambles over to us, his palm on his holstered weapon. I totally freeze.

Eight feet from us, he stops and stares at Mom. "Morning, ma'am." He glances at Owen, staring back at him with his saucer eyes. "I see you're out early with your family."

I watch him take in our wet, dirty clothes and shoes, our small picnic. He looks around for the man of the family, I guess, and then at me, but he doesn't ask. Instead, he says, "You from around here?"

Mom shakes her head. "West Virginia."

"You need some help?"

Ruby's head goes up as if she's sniffing the air. Mira tilts her head and inspects the officer. Mom watches their faces and waits.

"He's okay, Aunt Jean," Mira says. "He's not a bad man."

Mom bursts into tears, her shoulders shaking. Looking at her makes my eyes feel heavy. Amina and Pam run to her and wrap their arms around her.

"We were at a campground on the lake. Our car was stolen," Mom says between gasps. "We're on our way to Michigan, to a relative's house.

Everything we had left was in the car." Mom chokes a little, coughs, and wipes her face with her hand. "Is it safe here? Is there a place we can stay for a day?"

She's not telling him everything, but she's saying too much, trusting him because Mira says he's okay. Mira's a baby; she doesn't know anything. He's only one of many. He could have bad friends. He could tell the virus police he saw us and where we were. We shouldn't let our guard down, but she's the adult, and I'm the one who screwed up my watch. If I'd stayed awake, Owen would never have wandered off, and we wouldn't have lost the van.

The officer takes down a description of the vehicle, the license plate number, and Mom's name and says he'll report it stolen. That makes me nervous. That information will go into the system, and the virus police will find it. I've seen it on TV. They can trace us from it. Why is Mom telling him this stuff? She knows better. She's too tired to think straight.

When he's done taking the report, he drives us in his car to a small motel outside town that has online check-in, where Mom pays with her phone. We open the door lock with a code they text to Mom's phone. He knows we don't want contact with other people.

They must have the virus here, and he must be one of those people who isn't susceptible, or he's a carrier and doesn't know it. He doesn't talk about the pandemic or about anything, but his helping us scares me as much as some monster gearing up to attack us. He knows exactly where we'll be when we're sleeping.

"You folks moving on tomorrow?" he asks like it's a random question.

There are no random questions. I'm not fooled anymore by kind-seeming people. Anyone could turn out to be a bad guy. Helping can be a trap. We already know that routine from the docent and the Elyrians; we need to stay alert.

Mom says, "Uh-huh," without giving him any other information.

"Do you use your gun?" Owen asks.

Mom says, "Owen!" but the officer laughs.

"Not very often," he says. "Only if I have to." He lowers his head and looks sternly at Owen.

My brother pouts a little and then laughs. "I'm a good guy." He lifts his chin and bats his eyelashes.

"I'm sure you are," the officer says. "I'll check back on you tomorrow," he says to Mom.

That sounds like a threat to me. We have to be out of here by the time he comes back.

She stands up straight to her full five-feet-four-inches height. "No need. We'll be fine, Officer. Thank you so much for helping us. It was very kind of you." She waves to him, and we scoot into the motel room.

The minute Mom opens the door, I spot the clean sheets folded over blankets, plump pillows on the beds, and an outlet to charge our phones. The smell of bleach makes me think of home on cleaning day. The first thing Mom does is plug in her phone. Then she gathers up our clothes and sneakers and announces she's going to do a wash. We take showers, and Mira and Owen get baths. Their faces shine. "Don't forget to brush your teeth," Mom reminds us. "Even if you have to use your finger."

Mom ordered extra cots, and six of us squeeze into one room: that's safer. We have food delivered to the door and eat like we haven't eaten in weeks, even though it's only been three days since we left home. Unhappiness makes people hungry.

Mom checks the window and door locks three times and gives us a new rule. "Nobody leaves the room." Then she checks her texts and groans. "Aunt Dee says the border is closed."

"What does that mean?"

Mom flops onto a cot and looks up at the ceiling. "It means we can't get across the river to Canada legally, so we have to find another way." Her voice is dreamy, like she's already drifting off.

She's asleep before I can ask how we do that. I look over at Pam, and she looks back at me, unsmiling. A new obstacle has been erected on the gameboard in our minds, and we don't know how to get around it.

I lie on my side with Owen sprawled diagonally across most of the bed and scroll through the GPS maps on Mom's phone while mine is charging. It's 444 miles from here to Sault Ste. Marie using the shortest route on a major highway. All the routes go over a bridge. It's six and a half hours straight north if we could drive. Big places, dangerous cities like Toledo, Ann Arbor, and Detroit are between us and our destination.

We have to find our way around the big cities. If we walk, the Google map says it will take 140 hours. But that estimate's for experienced adult hikers, not a four-year-old. Even if we could walk six hours a day, that's more than twenty-three days. Might as well be a century. There's no way Owen and Mira can walk that much, and we can't carry them that far. We need another solution. For two seconds, I consider an Uber and delete that thought. We don't need to be in contact with another stranger we can't trust.

I click on the bicycle icon. Thirty-nine hours, 481 miles. If we bike five hours a day, it'll take slightly more than a week. That seems doable, even if carrying Owen and Mira means it takes us twice as long to bike to Aunt Dee's than the directions say. Two weeks, then. We can do that. By the time we get there, the border will be open again.

A voice in my brain says, "Are you crazy? You'll be out in every kind of weather. People will see you. No way the girls can bike five hours a day." I ignore it. Google gives me turn-by-turn instructions on an actual bikeable path. The last thing left to do is convince Mom to get bikes with child carriers. If only bikes could fly, we could cross the river without touching the ground.

In my dream, I see Owen pedaling as fast as he can as his bike rises into the sky and crosses the full moon.

17

Sgt. D. Cooper, USVPD

A LONG twenty-four hours later, we're notified that Bennett's vehicle was spotted by drone surveillance in Breezewood, Pennsylvania when she stopped at a four-way intersection. The tech apologized for the delay in processing and forwarding the image. So much for relying on technology.

"If you'd listened to me about Pennsylvania being on Bennett's laptop map search, we might've saved a day and had our fugitive by now," I say to LT.

She gives me the same look my father always did, like there's snot dripping from my nose, and says, "Grow up, Cooper," which pisses me off.

LT is the poster child for why the police solve only sixty percent of murders and thirty percent of rapes, not to mention only about half of every other kind of crime. As a corps, we need to work smarter.

Riley verifies that the license number checks out, and we head for that town on a route that takes us through places I never would have seen otherwise. Truth be told, if it weren't for this no-holds-barred search for that Bennett woman, I never would've been out of Maryland. When this is over, if she's still alive when we detain her, I just might thank her. She's broadened my horizons.

This time, we don't suit up in advance. It'll take two hours to get to this hole in the wall, and who knows how many hours till we catch up with her from there, but the hair on the back of her neck should be standing up. We're coming.

Video from cameras outside the Breezewood Post Office confirms her van came this way without stopping at 6 A.M. two days ago. We talk to the postmaster, the gas station manager, and some guy walking his dog. I get the feeling they're the last three people alive here.

"We don't get many visitors out here," the postmaster says while we glance around the small brick building. "Anyway, if video from the camera outside says she went by here, she went by here." He shrugs and looks over his shoulder like he's expecting someone to walk in the back door any minute.

With her jump-start, she could be anywhere by now. It's a big country. We debate the likelihood of Bennett hoping onto Interstate 76 in Breezewood. Based on this being the first place her vehicle's been spotted, Manny bets she's using back roads and avoiding highways. We've got nothing better to go on, so LT agrees, and we take the local two-lane road heading northwest.

In half an hour, the road narrows to a one-lane bridge over some river's headwaters where an old guy, his head wrapped in a bandage and a rifle cradled in his arms, pretends to be the toll taker. He isn't impressed with our siren and doesn't budge out of his folding chair when Manny flashes the lights.

LT tells me to check him out. I mask up, put on my best police patrol persona, and amble over to him nice-like, so he doesn't spook and shoot me. The old guy squints at me like I'm hard to see. That would be a first. I'm not a tiny female. I can hold my own with any man in the entire Directorate.

"What're you s'posed to be?" His voice is raspy, and his face caves in where his teeth used to be. That's when I notice he's not wearing a mask, an infraction I ignore. I also refrain from referencing his firearm, which he is free to bear in this country.

I display my badge. "Seen a woman in a van drive through here?"

"Yeah," he says, then spits on the ground. I try not to take this as a provocation. "A van charged through here t'other day and knocked me clean over. Driver didn't pay and didn't stop to see if I was alive even after she sideswiped me. You gonna do some'ut about that?"

He's what LT calls querulous.

"When was that, exactly?" There can't be a lot of traffic through here, and he should remember precisely if Bennett's vehicle clipped him.

"Could be this week, could be last week," he says. "Mebbe it was yesterday."

The virus has gotten into his brain, or the fall he took out of his chair knocked a screw loose, but the gang of maskless dodos that walks up to me confirms that the vehicle went through yesterday, same day it passed through Breezewood. The key thing they agreed on was that a woman was driving. Good thing we don't have to take these witnesses into court. Their testimony would never hold up on the stand, not to mention that their occupation is highway robbery.

The old man moves his chair and waves us through. We already know Bennett is driving a van, so this sighting only confirms we're on the right track. With no other option, we stay on the one road that takes us out of here with no idea where she's headed. There must be a better way to track her. My suspicion grows that LT's not much of a leader. As much as I want to nab the fugitive, I hate going nowhere fast.

About fifteen miles up the road, the first non-residential site we come to after the bridge is a golf course in the middle of nowhere. LT tells Manny to pull in because Bennett might have stopped here. I think we'd do better if we used a crystal ball. We perform a cursory search through the clubhouse and a scan of the grounds, but there's no sign of her. The only thing we find is a size zero pink hoodie on the pool deck. No grown woman ever fit in that. As we return to the bus, a guy in one of those electric golf carts flags us down.

"You come to investigate the assault here?" he yells. He pulls a black mask with some kind of gold logo on it over his nose and doesn't get out of the golf cart.

We mask up; LT walks to within six feet of him and flashes her USVPD badge. "An assault?"

"Yes, the groundskeeper was stabbed through the eye right here just yesterday. No one else was around when it happened. There was blood everywhere. Club members arriving to play were shocked when they found him passed out in the parking lot. They thought he was dead."

The golfer removes his sunglasses and stares at LT, the insignia on her cap, the weapons on her hip.

"Huge inconvenience and we were worried about contamination," he says. "We had to pay for a cleaning crew to remove the mess, and now that he's blind, we have to find someone else to take care of the grounds."

In his black polo shirt and white pants, he reminds me of a snooty teacher I had in fifth grade. I want to let the air out of this guy's tires too.

"I called the police to report the attack," he says. "Frank had some problems, but no one we know would do something this barbaric." He puts his sunglasses back on like the interview is over, and he's dismissing us. "Whoever did this had to be a man. Frank was a big guy, six feet, strong, with a hair-trigger temper. It would have taken superhuman strength to overpower him."

LT gives the guy our standard "it's a local police problem" response and takes his business card with a nod and a thank you. Our informant makes me jittery, like we're an inconvenience too, seeing how we interrupted his idyllic afternoon. I'm itching for a reason to take him in, but I need to stay focused.

"I told you Bennett is dangerous," I say. "Not only is she a viral fugitive, but now she's attempted murder."

"Don't jump to conclusions," Lt says. "We have no way of knowing if Bennett attacked the groundskeeper. Highly unlikely with kids in tow." Like she knows anything about how adults act around kids.

That flat-out annoys me. LT could just use her imagination. It's obvious who did the deed. It kills me that rich people get away with everything; privilege is the virus that killed democracy.

"Evidence, Cooper, you need evidence." There's no proof, LT says, that Bennett even stopped at the golf course. If her plan were to stay off highways, LT says, we should stay on the same road until we get to a crossroads or a city where there might be cameras or witnesses.

Route 30 takes us straight into Wilbursburg, a place that looks like it's a blink away from being a ghost town. We check in at the local police station, and I learn from the lone intake clerk that the entire squad is either in quarantine or dead.

"Any recent reports of strangers in town, any homicides or break-ins in the last two days?" I ask.

The clerk smirks behind the bullet-proof glass separating us. "Like someone's going to come to this town during a pandemic. I don't think so. Residents are in lockdown except for doctor visits and food shopping. We're lucky to get food deliveries."

"Got video from street cameras or drone surveillance?"

The clerk hoots and then half strangles from a coughing fit. I back away and bolt out of the station as fast as possible.

Going door to door on the main street, we find only kids, no parents, which is freaky. None of them will talk to us; they slam doors in our faces or run away. We don't have orders to evacuate them, so we leave them to their own devices. There must be another virus squad working this town, and there are so many targets they can't keep up. I wonder how the children are feeding themselves and what they'll do when the food runs out, and I remember how it felt to go hungry for days when Dad was on a bender and forgot we existed.

We're about to give up on this town when Popova points to a historic mansion. "As long as we're here," she says, giving LT the side-eye, "we might as well see the main attraction." She holds up her phone screen, so LT can see the website.

LT only says "Humph" and waves her hand for Manny to pull into the visitor's parking. I guess she wants to use the facilities.

Inside, we find a little old lady who seems half off her beam. She should not be rattling around inside this mausoleum alone, but she doesn't appear sick. When Popova gently questions her about seeing a family in a van, she nods, and her cheeks get red. "I did."

"Do you know where they went?"

"The boy," she tells us, "the one who looks like Orpheus, he said they were going north." Like we'd know who that foreign perp is.

"Do you remember his name?" LT asks.

"He was named for a bird, but I don't know for sure. They didn't introduce themselves. Their manners were barbaric."

She swears up and down that the woman who came to the house kidnapped her granddaughter and stole valuables.

"You should do something," she says, wagging her gnarled finger. The accusation gets my blood pumping for a few seconds, till Popova docs some quick arithmetic.

"If Pittman has a granddaughter," Popova points out when we're out of the old lady's earshot, "she'd almost be old enough to be *my* grandma. I think she might be stretching the truth a little."

LT pulls us out of there when Pittman offers us tea. "We're wasting our time. She dreamed the whole thing up to have our company for a while. She'll just keep spinning out the yarns to keep us here as long as she can."

We end the day with nothing, having traveled three hundred miles with no fugitive in hand to show for it. We head out of Wilbursburg and go north, the old lady's claim clanging in our brains, and stop at the first open motel. LT makes her daily report, and we get take-out.

LT slaps me on the back on the way to our rooms. "Don't worry, Cooper; we'll get her tomorrow."

She thinks we're on some kind of holiday, but every day that we don't find Bennett is another twenty-four hours she's infecting others. We shouldn't be sleeping.

)(

"In 2002/2003, a novel coronavirus (CoV) caused a pandemic, infecting more than 8,000 people, of whom nearly 10 percent died. This virus, termed *severe acute respiratory syndrome*-CoV was linked to a zoonotic origin from rhinolophid bats in 2005."

—INSTITUTE OF VIROLOGY, UNIVERSITY OF BONN MEDICAL CENTRE, GERMANY 2013

)(

18

Dee

I SPRAY down the kitchen counters and bathrooms for the hundredth time with one of the twenty bottles of bleach I bought when this whole thing started and tell myself, *You're not sick. There are no germs here.*

But, of course, there are germs. The second I went outside with the trash, I was enmeshed in germs. Even after I wash my hands, viruses are in my hair, on my face, and on my clothes. I feel invaded and claustrophobic, beset by a microscopic enemy intent on killing me just for fun. The randomness of who gets sick and who doesn't makes me paranoid. How can I fight chance?

Experts keep claiming, "The virus is not airborne," but how the hell is it spreading, then? On my morning walk, I suddenly understand. They're not stupid; they're lying.

"What do you think of that, Picasso? Should I storm town hall with my pitchfork and demand the truth?"

Picasso looks at me sideways, sighs, and puts his head down on his paws. I guess that's a no.

In my desperation to find a way to communicate with Jean, I stumble upon a page on the town website that allows me to download a letter of exemption to the travel ban. The loophole to the lockdown rule! Georgia said there's always a way around rules. If I'm essential personnel for some company, with the appropriate papers to show officials at checkpoints, I can cross the bridge to the US side and come back. I need one for Canadian officials and one for Michigan. And, eureka, I can make the same documents for Jean to get her over the border.

In half a minute, I overcome my ethical qualms about doing this. This is war. Everything's fair. I invent a company, fill out the provincial forms to create it online, and name myself president. Costs a few hundred dollars, a small sum to avoid being trapped in one spot for the duration. At the end of the tax year, should I live that long, I can declare that my company earned zero and take a deduction from my taxes for the loss. It's a double win.

I've never been president of anything. I feel an unexpected surge of pride that I've accomplished so much. A day later, I'm ready to try out my wares on a government official. This isn't a foolproof scheme. The letter doesn't require certification from any public authority; a customs official might look at it sideways and arrest me. And if I can do it, anyone can do it, a thought that gives me pause. There are always bad guys ready to exploit any situation, and even the government must know that. I should be careful about over-zealous enforcement officials. I'm not at the top of my game when I'm under scrutiny.

Once, an officer stopped Georgia and me for driving thirty-five miles an hour in a twenty-five mph zone. My face froze; I could barely get my mouth to work, instantly forgetting where we lived and where we were going. Georgia winked at me and said, "Watch this." She did her whole crazy old lady thing, jiggling the white curls on her head and saying, "Oh my, I'm so sorry, officer, how terrible of me," batting her eyelashes and pouting as if she were going to cry, and the policeman apologized for scaring us. That would never have happened if I had been alone in the car.

As long as I'm making up a company—Food for Thought, an inspired name—I might as well design a logo and letterhead stationery that prints nicely on my laser printer. I didn't teach graphic arts for thirty years for nothing. A company website takes me another few hours using one of the platform's templates. It doesn't have to be gorgeous or win awards; it doesn't even have to attract any real eyeballs. My ingenuity and the freedom to create something from scratch spurs me to take other small risks.

The folded letter will fit into my passport holder, but I need one more prop for my deception. In half an hour, I upload my new company logo to a website that will print and send me magnetic signs for my vehicle. I buy four. Two for me and two for Jean. Superwoman that I am, I imagine meeting Jean stateside in an alley and giving her the documents and the sign for her vehicle. I see us caravanning back over the bridge to the Soo with the children stowed under tarps in our two vehicles. I feel like a French Resistance fighter saving children from the Nazis.

While I'm at it, I design a brochure to sell my non-existent product—special vitamins, shakes, cookies, and nutrient bars concocted with enzymes extracted from rare Canadian plants that support efficient brain function. It's a dietary supplement and never has to be tested or approved by any government entity. Stock photos of active old folks enliven the brochure.

I print a few copies in case a curious officer wants to know what my company does. The copy is so convincing that I almost think I should start taking the little green pills. These product assertions aren't any worse than claiming Ginkgo biloba helps with failing memory. I sprinkle in a few testimonials on the page from people I invented for relatability.

"Before I started taking Food for Thought," Joe from Montana tells us, *"I couldn't remember where I left my keys. But after six weeks on the pills, I find them every time."*

My phony company manufactures its products at a plant in Michigan, thus requiring me to cross the border occasionally for oversight and accounting purposes. I've become so adept at lying that I could almost be a politician; Georgia wouldn't recognize me.

In a few days, armed with a passport, a handful of brochures, the letter, and my new FOOD FOR THOUGHT magnetic signs mounted onto the car doors, I climb into my bright red Fiat 500e, ready to leap my first hurdle. Palpitations make my breath come in short spurts. My cheeks feel hot. I check myself in the mirror—the color on my face matches the vehicle—and take five deep breaths to calm myself. This is only an experiment, my life's not at stake.

Anyway, better to be detained when I'm alone than with a load of kids hidden under a tarp in the car. I have no record, the car is like new, and all my citizenship papers are in order. There's no reason for a police officer to stop me.

I look in every direction twice, alert for police cars, pull out of my driveway, and putt down Queen Street toward the bridge access. No police vehicle zooms out of a side street to hail me down. I don't know why I'm worried about this. My car moves at the speed of a souped-up lawnmower, but even so, I'm at the border in fifteen minutes. Access to the usual customs booths is fortified with a zigzag arrangement of cement barriers that require drivers to slow down. I hand the customs officer my letter and identification and hold my breath.

My car isn't the only one in a line of trucks of varying sizes. That surprises me; I thought I'd be alone in my deception, but many people are trying to subvert the government's intentions. Drivers wear an array of guises, from calm composure to frantic aggression. Masks dangle below chins to allow cameras to capture their faces for facial recognition tracking.

My thoughts run wild. I imagine them all as bank robbers on holiday.

The uniformed, gloved customs officer, whose mask makes him look like some kind of insect, reads my letter and opens the passport.

"It's been a while since you visited the States."

"Yes. I only need to do a quality control check twice a year." It's amazing how easily lies come to me, as if lying is a native ability I've tamped down for seventy years.

"You know, they'll check you for fever on the US side."

I nod. I didn't have one this morning.

The officer hands back my documents. "Have a good day."

In twenty minutes, I'm on the other side of the bridge going through the same drill with the American officer. No problem. Now I have to find a way to kill two hours before I can return, or I might get the same officers on my way back through customs. I don't want anyone to remember me or question my itinerary.

I have some old friends on the Michigan side, people I taught with who stayed with me once in a while for a summer vacation. Georgia loved to entertain. I pull into the empty Freighters Restaurant parking lot near the locks and check my phone. There's service! I can call people here. It must be the cell towers on the Canadian side that are down. I call Jean straight away. No answer. But my text has gone through. At least I told her the border is closed if she ever looks at her texts. God knows what she's going through.

I call Margaret, who shared my faculty office at Lake Superior State University. If she's not home, I can kill an hour at Krist Food Market. But Margaret is home, and now realizing I'd been missing it, I'm overjoyed to hear another human voice in my ear.

"Can you do me a favor?" I ask. "Can I leave something with you for my niece to pick up?"

Of course, Margaret says yes.

Before I forget, I text Jean my scheme. *If you can get to Margaret's, she has documents to get you across the bridge. Be safe.*

In my haste, I realize only when I'm back home that I forgot to include Margaret's address, last name, or any information allowing Jean to find her. There's no service when I try to send another text.

19

Jean

I DREAMED about poisonous plants and making deals with God that require sacrifices and woke up knowing we had to keep moving. Somehow, I have to figure out how to travel 500 miles without a car, but for a few minutes, I want to pretend everything's okay.

I order breakfast and watch the children eat as if this is just another vacation. The scrambled egg around Owen's mouth, the way Mira sucks on her bacon like it's a lollipop, Pam's dainty bites, and Ren wiping his mouth with the back of his hand—I want to memorize everything, even if one part of my mind is saying we have no future and I'll have no time to remember anything.

Ruby eats with her back to me as if she has to sneak the food. Her stealth makes me sad, and I pray my kids are never that afraid. They've already changed in small ways; they devour their breakfast tortillas as if they know this is the last time they'll get a treat like this. Maybe it is. It's a good thing they've come to expect nothing.

They live in the present; the future is something only adults bother with. We have clean clothes, a good night's sleep, the toilet works, and there's toilet paper. What more could any sane person want? All the things we had—the surfeit of luxury I imagined I couldn't live without—don't matter anymore.

And then the moment's over, and I have to think about what happens next. That's my job, but I have no idea what to do. Ted always said, "Fake it till you make it," about being an adult. I've been doing that since the day he died. Choose a destination, head for it, overcome the obstacles, deal with the consequences, pick myself up, and start over again. Each day it feels like I start from zero, like I've learned nothing that helps me deal with the next crisis. I keep making mistakes, but we're still alive and together. Together, that's the key thing.

"I figured it out, Mom," Ren says. "We can bike to Dee's."

I laugh, but given our circumstances, it's not a bad suggestion. "A car would be better." That's the adult solution, what Ted would do.

On the other hand, if I rent or buy a vehicle, I will announce our existence and location to a car dealer, my insurance company, and bank, and I'd need a driver's license that I don't have to complete the transaction. And who knows what government entity a dealership is required to tell about cash sales?

I think briefly about stealing a car. Could we do it? I have no idea how to break into and hotwire a vehicle. Could we carjack one with the keys in the ignition? I picture a nationwide manhunt for us. We're captured by goons dressed in spacesuits, separated, and locked in cells. I hear Owen calling, "Mommy, Mommy," as they drag him away from me. I hear Mira sobbing. Too risky.

"Mom?" Ren waves his hand in front of my face. "Earth to Mom." He waits a second for me to focus on his face. "We should get bikes."

His idea of how to proceed is no crazier than any I have. We can't take public transportation. Even if buses and trains are running, they're bound to be contaminated, and there are cameras in the terminals. The virus police will know exactly where we are. We'll be surrounded by strangers, trapped in the same space with them for hours. And anyway, the bus can't get us across the river. It's the same problem with hiring a driver. The border is closed.

Walking to Canada with the kids is absolutely out of the question. I can hear the bickering and whining before it even starts. It will take too long, increasing the chances of being hoodwinked by more bad people. At least bikes are off the radar, and no one would suspect us of being infected. Sick people don't ride bikes. From above, tracked by a drone, we'd look innocent, like a family on an outing.

No one knows we're here unless there's a warrant out for us and local police have been alerted, in which case, our friendly Sandusky officer knows exactly where we are. I banish the thought. He wasn't looking for us; he didn't call us in or check his onboard computer database. He just helped. That makes him kind, not a threat.

"Look, Mom. Google Maps shows a bicycle shop nearby," Ren says, nudging me to accept his idea.

No harm in checking it out. We don the masks the officer gave us, grab the backpacks, and troop over there to test the feasibility of Ren's idea. The shop looks empty—the door's locked, and the lights are off. I turn away, but Ren knocks anyway.

A man comes to the door and talks to us through the glass. "Yes?"

"I want to buy five bikes," I say, holding up five fingers.

He opens the door and waves his arm to indicate we should enter. Bikes hang from the ceiling and along the walls. Light comes in from the windows at the front of the darkened store and runs along a glass counter where small equipment is kept. For a second, I'm disoriented, as if I've been transported to the interior of the Earth, where small cogs turn wheels large and small.

The owner has a goatee and a bald spot that reminds me of my husband. He says he hasn't had any customers for months. He goes around to the other side of the counter, keeping as far away as possible from us, puts on a mask, and flips on the lights.

"I'm surprised you're open," I say.

"People need exercise," he says. "Business was brisk at the beginning of this thing because biking is something you can do without talking to anyone. You never know when the exercise bug is going to hit someone. I come in every day for four hours and fiddle around in the shop because, well, you never know."

I can't argue with that logic.

He shrugs. "Anyway, what else am I gonna do? I've owned this shop for thirty years. We live in the apartment upstairs. My wife is used to having it to herself during the day. If I sit around, she nags me to fix things, and I hate fixing things."

I laugh because that's what's expected of me. "Well, I'm glad you're here."

"You from around here?" he asks like he's just making casual conversation.

We must look foreign. I glance at the kids. They look normal to me—jeans, sneakers, t-shirts, hoodies tied by the sleeves around their waists. I must be the one who flags us as alien, even though I'm American-born and bred. My fingertips stray to my locket as if the images of Caro and Ted could prove I'm an acceptable human. Except they're both dead.

"We're going on a trip. I want to buy five bikes that are already assembled. And two kiddie seats. Do you want to sell them?"

He sizes me up. "You been tested?"

"Tested?"

"Yeah. They're giving out certificates now if you've been tested. They text them to you on your phone."

"Oh, I got tested before they had that." How would he know if I'm telling the truth? And he's not asking if I tested positive or negative. Anyway, I could test fine one day and be sick the next.

"Take your pick," he says and gestures toward the hundreds of bikes in the shop.

Ren and I try out riding with an extra kid onboard. We bike on the sidewalk outside the shop with Owen in the kid seat on the back. The store owner stands in the doorway, his arms crossed, keeping the other kids in the shop for collateral. No cars or people are on the street. We're in a ghost town.

Owen shouts his glee at the ride. I sweat. After a few times up and down the block, it's clear I might have to walk the bike up hills, but at least Owen and Mira won't have to walk hundreds of miles. Anyway, if it doesn't kill me, I'll get stronger. I need to be stronger. Who knows what's coming? Pam and Amina will take the backpacks. They find bikes that are right for them, their faces as serious as if they're buying firearms.

"I can ride a bike," Ruby announces.

"Of course, you can. Pick one." I notice the look of gratitude on her face, even though she doesn't say thank you.

She chooses a purple one with sparkly streamers hanging from the handlebars. Unexpectedly, I feel a surge of fondness for her because somehow, in this moment of desperation, a young girl caring that streamers have sparkles matters.

I wave my phone over the reader and close my eyes as the bike store owner processes the transaction. I miss the van. It was our makeshift home. I can smell it—the stale fast food, bubble gum, kid sweat—and feel the press of the driver's seat against my back. Buying it was Ted's idea. An ache opens in my chest.

"That's some trip you're taking," the owner says, interrupting my reverie. "I haven't had as good a day as this in years." He smiles effusively as the credit okay comes through and throws in saddle packs, bike locks, tire repair kits, and water bottles for free.

The bike locks give me pause. It hadn't hit me that someone might steal the bikes while we slept by the side of the road. They might take our food, kidnap Mira, kill us. We'll have to find places to hide to sleep. We've just increased the degree of difficulty by two more weeks. I take deep breaths to slow my heart rate. Thinking will stop me in my tracks.

We consult the GPS on our phones, and before we mount up, heading toward Mackinaw City, I try to call Aunt Dee to tell her it will take us longer than I expected, but I can't get through. "Rats," I say, then glance at the little ones to see if they heard me. No worry there; they're arguing a fine point of the Twenty Questions rules.

Dee's is a long way away. At a pace of twenty-five miles a day, it'll take us sixteen days. But Ren is convinced we can do it, and the girls are happy. Sun shines on their faces, and the wind blows through their hair. They sing as they pedal, and for a while, I agree with Ren.

Until we reach the bridge over Sandusky Bay, the shortest way north on a paved road across Lake Erie. The bridge entrance is blocked by police cars. Across the water, yachts bob on the inlet, and big houses front the lake. The guards are protecting rich folks from us, the refugees, the ones most likely to be diseased, the ones who require sympathy and assistance.

We dismount and nonchalantly try to walk our bikes past the police and onto the bridge as if we live there and are returning from a day trip. A cop in a black uniform with what looks like fifty pounds of gear on his belt and a riot helmet waves his arm at me.

"Residents only," he yells from a safe distance. Two other officers move closer to us, hands on their weapons. How can they see a woman and six kids as a threat?

"We're just biking through," I say, but stay ten feet from him. He's got one of those tasers.

"Move along, lady," he yells. "No crossing here." He waves his arm again and points in the other direction.

I have zero ID and can't prove who I am, much less argue that we belong in that privileged enclave. There's no point in confronting him. I don't want him calling for our IDs or reporting this as an incident. We're no threat to anyone, but logic doesn't matter. Without the right address and the right license, we're not going to cross this bridge. He has the weapons and authority, and we're automatically dangerous because we're out here and not over there. In my old neighborhood, we did the same thing.

There's another way to go north, but it will be longer. Ren and I huddle to consult the map on his screen. The cops stand shoulder to shoulder as if preparing for us to blitz by them. I wonder if that severe look on their faces is tiring.

We decide to go west on Route 6 and then north toward Toledo. An extra twenty-five miles. It'll take us another day. Ren shrugs the way his father would have. In my head, I hear Ted say, "Gotta do what you gotta do."

"Once we get to Toledo, there's a side road next to Route 75 that takes up right to Sault Ste. Marie," Ren says, a grin on his face like it's totally doable and fun to boot. "From Toledo, it's just three-hundred-seventy-six miles."

Just three-hundred-seventy-six miles. Like that's nothing. Anything could happen. If we were driving in a car, it would be a cinch. Only five and a half hours. One day's driving. We could sing all the way. How I miss our freedom—the freedom from fear, the freedom that feeling immortal gave us. That was so long ago. We keep acting like the virus won't get us, like we're immune, but we already know that's not true. The more places we go, the more people we interact with, the stronger the possibility. I'm not prepared for any of us to be sick.

I can't say this to the kids. I have to appear strong and sure, like Ted said. I long for Caro. Even when she was pissy and stubborn, I could confide in her, and she would tell me what was true, even if I didn't want to hear her. I can't put that on Ren. I'm the mother; he's the kid.

"Let's go," I say, faking it the best I can, and our traveling circus mounts up again.

We have to bike twenty-five miles, eat, and find a safe place to sleep. *Stay in the moment,* I repeat to myself. *Stick to what keeps us alive,* but what I need to do is lie down and never get up again. The whir of my wheels going around and around and the whoosh of the tires on pavement carries me forward hypnotically.

20

Ren

A SIGN says *Welcome to Henry County, Ohio*. My breath stops in my throat. We missed a turn somewhere onto the road that takes us north. Easy to do where the country is a whole lot of flat, and every mile looks the same. Owen is getting heavy, and my legs are tired. And I look back and see Ruby's fading. Mom's on automatic, scanning the horizon, looking over her shoulder, singing nonsense songs with Mira. Pam and Amina have that look of the last ten minutes of the last class of the week, when every second more of the teacher's voice makes you want to puke.

"I have to pee," Owen whines.

I put up my hand and stop. Everyone pulls up next to me.

I steady the bike, and Owen hops off to pee in someone's field. What-ever modesty my five-year-old brother learned in our original life has evaporated.

"I'm bored," Ruby says. "We should play a game."

Everyone looks at her but doesn't say anything. Mom runs her palm over her face.

Mira perks up. "I know a game. Let's tell stories."

Mom exchanges a look with me, and I'm sure she knows everything I'm thinking in a blink. She points to a farmhouse in the distance. "Might as well try that one. Be nice if they let us sleep in the barn. We should get off the road before dark."

She doesn't look hopeful. I think the van being stolen yesterday and then the border being closed put the kybosh on every plan she had. We're like those bugs that scatter when you pick up a big rock off the ground. She acted brave, but driving to Canada was her best idea, and when that blew up, she couldn't think of what to do next. She's just going from one minute to the next now. That's as bad as doing nothing—and way more dangerous. In my game, when everything's stacked against me, and I can't figure my way out, that's when I'm most likely to do stupid things. You can die that way. I get it now that we won't make it if we try to bike it to Canada. We need a new strategy to win this game.

Corn is already starting to come up in the fields. We find an aisle between the plants and walk the bikes through it with the little kids between us so we don't lose them. Since we lost Owen at the campground, my fear of it happening again is like a plank jammed through my chest. Half a mile through the field, we reach a cleared space around the house.

Nothing's moving. The windows in the house are shut. No dogs are in the yard. Farm equipment isn't lined up by the barn, in the lane, or even left in the middle of a field. There's no sound of a tractor or any animals, but a weird humming comes from the slowly turning wind turbines I spot on the other side of the barn. Mom hands me her bike to hold.

"Stay here," she says. "Be ready to ride out in a hurry."

We huddle together at the cornfield's edge as she strides across the overgrown lawn to the front door.

She's an easy target. "Wait, Mom! It could be dangerous." I watch the window for light flashing off a rifle barrel.

She turns to look at me and smiles a little. "I know. That's why I'm going to check it out first."

"But you, someone could get *you* . . . and then we're . . ."

"Wait ten minutes. If I don't come out, leave." Now she's not smiling.

Anything could happen in ten minutes. "Everybody squat down," I tell the kids. "Be ready to hide in the cornfield." Mom's idea of riding away on our bikes is ridiculous. There's no way we could outrun a speeding bullet. Pam adjusts her baseball cap; she's ready.

We hunker down in the cornfield and watch as Mom knocks, waits, then knocks again. She turns the doorknob and slowly opens the door. Over her shoulder, she looks back at me, signals for us to wait, and goes inside. I turn in a circle trying to spot any activity on the periphery. I watch the windows for movement.

Amina's breath comes fast. Pam wraps an arm around Mira. Ruby has a hand on Owen's shoulder to restrain him. Mom is gone for a minute by my watch, but the minute goes on for a long time. She used to joke that she could wash the breakfast dishes and take out the trash in one minute. In two minutes, she returns to the front porch and signals to us. "Come on."

We run with the bikes to the house. The pedals on Mom's bike whap against my leg, but I don't stop till we get to the porch. Mom meets us at the front door like we just got home from school.

"No one's here, but the water is on," she says. "The toilet flushes. We can lock the doors and bed down in the living room. We'll be out of sight of anyone who's after us. And maybe there's canned food we can eat."

I try to remember when we stopped thinking that taking other people's stuff was stealing or when we decided that entering people's houses without permission was our right. Nobody else in my family seems to care. We line up to hit the john while the little kids explore the house. Nobody's lived here for a while. Spiders have made webs in every corner of the ceiling. An inch of dust covers the surfaces, the furniture must be from the last century, and the dishes in the drain are dry. Everything looks like props on a movie set. The worst news is there's no food in the refrigerator. Thinking about food makes my stomach gnaw on itself. We open the cupboards. Nothing.

"I'm going to see if there's anything to eat in the basement," Mom says as she turns the tarnished brass knob on the old wooden pantry door in the kitchen. The door creaks open; instead of shelves, behind the door is a double stainless-steel door. Next to the door is a panel on a wall with one button. Mom stares at it, and in the next second, before I can say anything, she pushes the black button.

"Mom, you don't know what—"

The doors woosh open and reveal a sparkling clean elevator compartment. She steps back and shakes her head. "That's . . . eerie."

"It's way past eerie, Mom. Let's get out of here."

We're in the middle of nowhere, in an old farmhouse that needs fixing up, and there's a modern elevator in the kitchen. I try to convince myself that someone in a wheelchair lived here until recently, but I don't believe that. The elevator is way cleaner than the rest of the house. Someone's using it. I look out of the kitchen window toward the barn. No one's in sight. If the people who lived here died recently, where are the bodies?

"Do they have tornados here?"

Mom shrugs. "Pretty fancy tornado shelter for an old farmhouse no one lives in. And with electricity."

I step into the car. "I'll check it out." It's dangerous but tempting, like a new game I'm itching to play.

Mom grabs my wrist. "Not without me, you won't—which means not without all of us because I'm not leaving them alone here." She gestures to the kids, who have gathered in the kitchen.

Mom hesitates for another second and then steps inside the elevator car. Everyone piles in after her. She pushes the only button on the panel, and the door whooshes shut. I close my eyes. Either we're going to die, or we'll be fine. Can't get more binary than that. The sensation in my stomach tells me we're going down, fast, and way farther than where a basement would be. My knees bend.

Owen and Mira say, "Ooh," at the same time and grab my shirt.

The door slides open onto a long corridor with lights on the ceiling every ten feet. The polished tile floor and walls remind me of a hospital. Three black doors are spaced out along the hallway, one at the end and one on each side. I could be in one of my games—unknown enemies behind every door. All my senses are alert. There's no smell, and the only sound is a whoosh from the HVAC system, like in school.

We walk in a bunch toward the door closest to us. Mom pushes the doorbell. She knocks. No one answers. She calls out, "Hello." Nothing.

On the keypad near the doorknob, I type *Open Sesame*. Nothing happens. I try "12345678910." That's not it either. No one would be dumb enough to use that for their passcode. If I were running away from a world-ending disaster, what would I have time to type? My fingers tap 9-1-1 onto the keypad on the wall, and the door lock opens with a *plunk*.

"How did you know to do that?" Pam asks.

"I don't know. Just seemed logical."

We push the door open carefully, Mom in front, me behind her. There's no sound in here either except the air conditioning system huffing. The heat from the other kids' bodies warms me. I turn and put my finger on my lips to warn them to be quiet.

The lights go on automatically when Mom steps inside the apartment. She looks in both directions. "It's like something out of the *Architectural Digest* website."

"What do you mean?" The place is fancy and way neater than our house, but it's bizarre that the lights go on like someone was expecting us.

"Wood floors, sleek furniture, wall lighting," Mom says as she wanders in. "The kitchen has a stainless-steel French-door refrigerator, stove, sink, wood cabinets, and granite countertops. This is the kind of place Dad would say we could never afford for vacation."

Like that ever mattered to us when we could hear the ocean. Will I ever see the ocean again? I close my eyes and see it in my head.

"Hello," Mom calls out as if she's a friend making a normal afternoon visit for coffee and cupcakes like we used to do when I was Owen's age.

I grit my teeth, expecting men to burst out of other rooms, guns drawn. Why isn't Mom afraid?

"Hello," a woman's voice says. "Welcome."

I jump back and put my arms out to stop the other kids from walking in.

Mom giggles. "I know that voice. It's Alexa. This is a smart house."

I'm sure now she's lost it. The 'Dora has gotten to her brain, and losing the van was the last straw. All the trouble we've been in has overloaded her circuits, and she's not normal anymore; she doesn't know how to sense danger. She's totally numb.

She walks down the hall, opening every door like she's inspecting it to decide whether to take the place or not. No one leaps out of any of the rooms to stop her. She turns around and goes in the other direction.

"There's a stocked pantry and a laundry room. With detergent!" She checks the bathrooms. "There's body lotion and shampoo. God, a hot bath. What a luxury."

When she comes back to us, she looks tired but happy.

"No one's here but us. Get the bikes inside so the virus police don't figure out we're here. We're going to stay overnight, at least. Give my aching muscles a chance to recover from biking thirty miles." She tries to call Aunt Dee and says, "Well, there's no service down here." Then, she throws herself down on the couch, and Owen and Mira climb onto her lap. Mom flips on the television and finds a kid's movie. Amina, Pam, Ruby, and I go back up in the elevator to get our bikes.

"There are two other apartments," Pam says, pointing to the other doors in the corridor.

"Maybe there are people in them," Amina says. "People who can help us." My sister always sees the bright side.

"They're not coming out to talk to us," Ruby says. "We're too dangerous. We could be infected. They'll wait until we're out of quarantine."

The girls look at her and squinch up their faces.

"Anyway, we're not supposed to ask strangers for help," I say, trying to head off a fight. "And they might not be friendly."

I'm also tired of Ruby acting like she knows everything. She's just a kid who doesn't know any more than I do, pretending she knows stuff to make herself feel better. I'm not mad at her, though, because, in a way, I'm doing the same thing. Anyway, I owe her. She helped save Mom from the groundskeeper.

"Let's get the bikes like Mom said."

When we zoom back up to the farmhouse kitchen on the elevator, the bikes are neatly stacked inside the kitchen by the elevator door. We left them lying wherever they fell outside on the porch. Slowly my mind pieces these facts together. Someone else did this; someone beside us is here, in the house. They know we went down in the elevator and went into the apartment. They can see what we're doing; they can hear what we're saying.

When that thought hits me, my chest tightens, and a lightning bolt crashes through my bones. We look around, grab the bikes, and take the elevator down. I've got to tell Mom we've got trouble.

By their faces, I can tell the girls are as freaked out as I am. Pam is so scared, she has her hand over her mouth, holding in giggles. I feel the same way, like fear causes the same sensation as being tickled, and I'm going to burst out laughing and won't be able to stop. Right underneath the laughter, like a shark under a surfboard on a wave, is terror. What kind of crap are we in now? We barrel into the apartment, and I push the door closed fast, lean against it, and secure the four locks.

"Mom. Someone's here with us. They know we're here. They put our bikes by the elevator."

"A caretaker who anticipates our needs," Mom says. "How interesting."

"Mom! We're in danger, don't you get it? This is a trap. There are other people here. They can see and hear us."

"I think we're safe in here for a while. There are locks on the doors. And I need to sleep."

Mom's so calm, I'm sure, now, that she's lost her mind.

She gets up off the couch and starts opening kitchen cabinets. "What's for dinner?"

"There's pasta," the house says.

Mom opens the refrigerator. "And sauce. And salad stuff and fresh fruit." She opens the freezer. "There are steaks! And chicken. We can have feasts for days."

"Mom," I say, about to tell her something's wrong with this picture, that someone must have been in the apartment right before we entered the house, that they knew we were coming, but she's so relieved, I can't bring myself to do it.

She smiles at me, and I can't help but smile back, but inside, I'm a mess. Who put that food there, and why haven't they asked us if we belong here? It feels like an experiment, and we're the mice. But Mom's so happy and tired, I can't say anything. After she gets a good night's sleep, I'll tell her we have to leave. She'll have to listen to me.

21

Jean

B Y the end of three days, Ren and I are locked in silent combat. "Mom, we have to leave," he says through clenched teeth. He looks at me with such intensity that I think he's trying to send me a message telepathically. His eyes are yelling, "Danger, danger, danger."

He's worried that this is a set-up, that we've been enticed to stay here for someone else's benefit. I can't imagine what that would be, or who. How would they have known we were coming? I scramble up a bunch of eggs and put English Muffins in the toaster oven.

"Why do you want to leave? We could stay here until the pandemic is over. The virus police will never find us here. It'll be like we disappeared off the face of the Earth."

"Exactly. We could die, and no one would ever find us." Ren puts his hands in his hair like he's trying to hold his head down.

I don't let myself think about why no one's asked for money for rent or food. If someone wants to help us, why shouldn't I accept it? But then I remind myself, there's no free lunch. Someone is going to demand payment of some kind. If only I could delay negotiating that until I figure out what to do next.

"All things run their course, Honey."

"How can you think it'll ever be over, Mom? It's been a year. Before we left home, it was only getting worse. Are you saying when seven billion people have gotten the virus and either died or not, that's when it'll be safe to go out again? I'll be a thousand years old!"

"Right. You're right," I say, although I think that at the rate the virus is killing people, it won't take that long. It could take three years, though. And God knows what the world will be like then or who will be in charge. What's wrong with staying here where it's safe?

I yank the muffins from the toaster and singe the tip of my finger because I'm not paying attention.

"But it's safer here than wandering across the continent on bicycles. There's food." I gesture to the pile of eggs. "I do wish we had oranges." It hits me that I may never see another tropical fruit. "We have beds, toilets. It's comfortable."

"Mom, you're being deliberately dense. We're stuck underground with only one way out. We have no windows. We don't know what's coming. What if the electricity goes out, and we can't escape? We don't know why this place is here or who's giving us food. We had a plan, and you're changing it, for no reason. We're supposed to go to Aunt Dee's. Don't you know she'll worry if we don't show up?" He sighs, shakes his head, and walks away.

Ren's right. I've forgotten why we're on the road. I think of Caro and feel that absence in my heart I haven't become accustomed to. We fled so the kids could stay alive and free; that's the point of this journey. Is this the life I imagined for them, cooped up here, hiding underground? That's the opposite of free.

I need to know more, what we used to call news, those breadcrumbs of facts my brain assembled into something useful, a map to plot my life along. I'm as confused and detached from my body as if I have a fever. The kids are edgy, sometimes manically laughing, sometimes fighting with each other. If there are people in the other two apartments, they might know something. We're in the same boat; it can't hurt to ask them.

After two games of Monopoly, two rounds of multi-player Solitaire, three movies, and a bowl of popcorn, I put on my mask and walk out into the hall while the kids are napping and knock on the door opposite us. My watch says it's 6 P.M., but time is irrelevant without the daily cycle of light to dark.

I don't know whether anyone will be there and if they'll be friendly or afraid of me, sick or healthy, but it doesn't feel like a greater risk than not knowing whose guests we are. It's as if we'd been shipwrecked on an island that had been prepared for our arrival, and our hosts on the other side of the mountain are waiting to introduce themselves until we're sufficiently plump.

An unmasked old man opens the door and studies my eyes. "I wondered when you'd get around to calling on me," he says.

"Oh. Sorry, I . . ." I turn away.

"No." He puts his hand on my arm. "It's okay; I can see you're cautious. I'm not angry. Come in."

Inside, his apartment is the same as ours, down to the abstract oil painting above the fake fireplace. I hadn't expected that. "What is this place? Are you the owner?"

His face wrinkles slightly, his forehead rippling up into his hairline. "Have a seat." He gestures to the sofa.

I detect the telltale scars of previous plastic surgery. His eyes are the color of bleached denim. How old is he, anyway? He strokes his long gray ponytail.

"We built these apartments a decade ago when we thought the end of the world would be caused by nuclear weapons. You know, the previous lunatic president . . ."

I look at him more closely. He's famous. His name is on the tip of my tongue. He used to be a country music icon. What age-defying wonder drug is he on?

"I bought the property from the farmer for a song, literally. He gets the royalties."

He winks, and I feel squeamish.

"I had these underground bunkers designed for me and my family—an apartment for me and my wife, one for my daughter and her kid—that's the one you're in—and one for my sons, so we wouldn't crowd each other. The walls are nine-inch-thick concrete."

I nod, acknowledging his rightful pride in the design.

"We make our own electricity. There's an air purification system. We capture fresh water from an underground aquifer, and our waste is recycled into harmless runoff. Our cars and the jet are parked in the barn, so we can leave in a hurry if we need to."

As he boasts, I keep trying to place him. "You're that singer." I almost have his name. The casual way he says, "the jet" makes my shoulders twitch.

"Yeah." He's pleased that I remember and pretends to be appropriately humble. "I came out here the first day news of the virus hit. The minute they shut down DC, I knew it would be bad. Felt it in my bones. My kids wouldn't come with me. Can you imagine that? I offered to send the jet for them, but they thought I was nuts."

He runs a gnarled hand over his face, and I wonder if he still plays the guitar.

"When I asked them a second time, my son said, 'It's gonna be over in a second.' My daughter confessed she couldn't abide spending eternity with me. 'You know we'll fight, Pop,' she said. My other son gave me some cock and bull story about herd immunity. He said he was gonna take his chances."

He sits on the edge of the couch, pours some bourbon from an expensive-looking bottle on the coffee table, and scratches his white-bearded cheek.

"That was six months ago. I don't go up on top a lot. Last I checked, my sons had died, and my son-in-law was sick. When you arrived, I thought at first my daughter had reconsidered. But she only has one kid, and she would never ride a bike, not if the devil were chasing her."

He saw us from a distance. An alert crashes through my chest and makes me shiver. "Sorry about your sons," I manage to say.

"Yeah. Me too. My caretaker told me the World Health Organization experts said the infection rate is up to ninety percent of adults. Half of everyone who gets it dies."

I shrug like these statistics don't mean anything. The coldness of my reaction stuns me. Half the world's adult population will die. Everyone is as desperate as I am, and no one knows who's next. When anyone can be a carrier, everyone is the enemy. I'm the enemy. He's the enemy.

"I'm grateful for the accommodation, but why did you let us in?"

He shrugs. "I wanted company."

"How did you know we wouldn't make you sick?"

He smiles with the side of his mouth. "At my age, would it make any difference?"

He has his own solution to the problem of the pandemic. The only difference between us is that he had the foresight and money to build this bunker for his family, and I didn't. He doesn't ask what brought me here.

"Where does the food come from?"

"The caretaker. He has an underground apartment in the barn with an office at ground level to communicate with the world. He gets the food from somewhere; it gets dropped off by helicopter. We don't ask any questions. We just pay the monthly amount he asks for and thank our lucky stars we planned ahead."

"You keep saying we."

"My wife and me. No way I could be here alone. It would be like being the last person on Earth. I'd go out of my mind."

"Where is your wife?"

"She's sleeping." He looks at his watch. "She takes a nap every day. Your kids are asleep. What are you doing awake?"

"How do you know that? That my kids are asleep?"

"I can watch you."

A chill starts on the back of my neck. This is what Ren has been warning me about. "What do you mean?" Then I get it. Mr. Famous is not harmless, the whole place makes me claustrophobic, and there's not enough air. My mouth dries, and my skin crawls.

He points to the ceiling.

When I look up, I see the small cameras for the first time.

He watches me noticing them for the first time. "Security," he says. "In case someone breaks in here. I can see who's prowling around the grounds a mile away or what's happening in the house. I get a ping on my watch and see the intruders on the screen. Like I saw you."

No wonder his daughter didn't want to be with him. He must have told security to let us in. Was that an act of kindness, curiosity, or something more like what Ren's thinking?

"I think it's time for us to leave but thank you for your hospitality." I stand and move toward the door.

"Where would you go? There's no place the virus hasn't invaded. It won't be safe out there for years."

"We need fresh air, and we need exercise; we have to get going," I manage to say even though my throat is closing. "Family is expecting us."

"I don't think I can allow you to leave, now that you know where I live," he says.

"What do you mean? Why would you stop me, and how?" I edge toward the door, my eyes darting around the apartment, looking for a weapon aimed at me. I think of poison darts, toxic fumes, how we have to get into the elevator to get out of here. How there's no other way out.

He rolls his eyes upward to the ceiling and smiles. "I have help," he says like it's the obvious answer.

All my nerves jump. "Who?"

"The security guys I hired. Ex-Special Forces."

"Why would they . . . ?" I can't take another second of this conversation. His apartment is organized like the one we're in. Four steps to the hall lead to the bedrooms; five more steps get me out the door; a dash across the corridor, and I'll be behind a bolted door before he can get off the couch.

In his hallway, while he's recounting the exploits of his security force, my curiosity gets the better of me. I nudge open one of the bedroom doors. The smell of rotting meat leaks out of the room. A woman lies on the bed, her white hair spread across the pillow. Her skin is gray. Her chest doesn't rise and fall with her breath. I edge a few steps closer. A bug creeps out of her nose.

I rush out of his apartment. Behind me, I hear him call out, "Hey, wait."

But I'm faster than he is. Inside the apartment where my kids sleep, I lean against the door taking heaving breaths and think for a minute about what an idiot I am. On the kitchen counter is a bowl full of oranges. Someone came in here while I was with him, while the kids were asleep. I blink as if I'm waking from a trance.

I rouse Ren. "We're leaving," I whisper. "Get ready." I point to the tiny cameras in the space between the wall and the ceiling and put my finger on my lips.

"Thank you," he says, giving me a quick hug before bolting to the bathroom. He smells like brown sugar cooking. I can barely let go of him.

22

Ren

WE take all the packaged food and dry cereal that will fit into our
packs. Mom grabs rolls of toilet paper and the oranges and shoves
them into a pillowcase she takes off the bed.

Amina looks at her in disbelief. "Why are you taking those?"

"One small luxury. Is that too much to ask?"

Pam rolls her eyes and puts on her cap. She's ready to leave.

"I want to take the Monopoly game," Owen says on the brink of
bawling. "If Mommy can take toilet paper, I can take a game."

I look at Amina for help.

"How are you going to carry it, Owen?" she asks him. Her voice is as
gentle as the way she runs her hand over his head.

His lip shakes. Tears balance on the rim of his eyelids. "Can't you
carry it for me?"

"We have hundreds of miles to go, and we'll be on bikes," Amina
says. "We can only carry what fits in our backpacks, and we have to take
food and water."

I'm not sure logic works with a five-year-old, but Owen listens and
puts the game on the table. He looks at it sadly.

"You're a big boy, Owen," Amina says, clinching the deal. Owen
grins and takes her hand.

"Are we ready?" Mom calls from the door. "Everybody got all their
clothes on?" She surveys us.

She's washed her face, and her cheeks shine. In another life, she would
get married again. She's pretty in a mom way.

"Huddle up," she whispers, and we shove in as close to her as possible.
She puts her head down so she's looking straight at Mira and whoever's
monitoring the surveillance cameras can't see her lips moving. "We're
going to steal one of their vehicles."

Everyone's mouths drop open. Mira laughs. She has no idea what stealing a vehicle means.

"But," Amina and I start to say simultaneously, look at each other, and stop. Because why not? We blinded a guy, stole a boat, broke into someone's home, took their food, and slept in their beds. Why not take a car?

"You guys are going to walk the bikes out to the lane on the side of the house." She points to Amina, Pam, Ruby, Owen, and Mira. "They'll be watching us and will think we're going to ride bikes.

"But Ren and I are going into the barn and coming out with the largest car they've got in there. We'll meet you in the lane. All the supplies go into the trunk. We're leaving the bikes. You scramble into the car seats and buckle up. It has to happen fast so we can get away. Can you do it?"

Everyone nods. We go up in the elevator and out to the front porch. The full moon lights up the whole place. For a second, it looks to me like the farm and the land around it are exactly like a photo I saw on Google Maps, and I'm confused about which came first—the original farm, the photo of a farm on a map screen, or the stage set of what was once a farm but is now camouflage for the bunker under us. Our life feels like this, too, like a game I'm playing, only in three dimensions, and the consequences are very real.

"Okay, go," Mom says. The kids bounce the bikes down the stairs, and we walk as fast as we can without running to the barn. "Walk like you own the place," Mom says. I straighten my shoulders, lift my chin, and pretend I'm Spiderman. Mom glances at me and giggles, and I feel like me again.

It's two-hundred-fifty yards to the barn in the open. The walk there takes forever. We could be shot from a hundred different spots. It takes every ounce of my self-control not to keep looking over my shoulder. A drone could get us; the ground could be mined. Someone could lob a grenade. It feels like my skin is on high alert. I listen for the blast of a bullet leaving a gun.

When we push open the doors, the barn turns out to be way bigger than it looked from a distance. Inside are a small jet and three cars, one of them a tank-sized graphite-colored vehicle. "How did you know about the cars, Mom?"

"Mr. Famous, the guy who owns them, mentioned them when I talked to him." Mom points to the biggest car. "Let's try the Hummer first. Remember, act like you own it."

She yanks open the driver's door, pulls down the visor, checks the glove box, flips up the floor mat, and quickly runs her hand along the underside of the dash.

"No key," she murmurs.

We both scan the barn looking for a bulletin board or set of cubbies. Nothing. Then we notice the man, who must be the one Mom calls Mr. Famous, standing in the open doorway. With moonlight behind him, he looks like a shadow. Mom stops moving.

"We need the key to the Hummer," she calls out as if it's the most normal thing in the world to take his car. Her voice echoes in the barn.

"I need you to stay." His voice rumbles like gravel tumbling down a steep hill.

She shakes her head. "We have to go."

"I want you here. I told you my daughter isn't coming. I need company."

"I'm sorry. I can't stay here. I understand what you're going through. That grief . . . I know it. My husband died, and I didn't get to bury him. And my sister. I . . . You lost your kids, your wife. It's horrible. But we, me and the kids, have to keep going. I need to get them away." She shudders. "You should leave too."

He shakes his head. "I'm staying here," he says. "There's nothing out there for me. I have to insist that you stay." He's so polite, and then he pulls a rifle out from behind his back and points it at Mom.

My mouth goes dry. In my head, I scream, "No," but I can't make a sound. I scan the barn for a weapon, a board, a shovel, but it's spotless. There's nothing I can use. I picture Mom running at the groundskeeper, her wildness, that fierce look on her face. No-holds-barred ferocity, that's how to win. I don't know if I'm brave enough.

We're about the same height, the old guy and I, and I'm younger. That should give me an edge. While he's talking to Mom, I step into the shadow, thinking I'll sneak up behind him. I'm not sure what happens after that.

"Shooting me doesn't get you what you want," Mom says. Her voice shakes a little. "My kids will hate you. They'll find a way to escape, and you'll be alone here. You should go be with your daughter and grand-child. They're what's out there for you."

His face crumbles. I step on something that makes a crackling sound. He pivots suddenly and aims the rifle right at me. I freeze.

"You will not kill my kid," Mom says, her voice deep like she's the elven queen Galadriel just materialized in this barn. She seems bigger as she walks toward him directly in front of the gun barrel. "Put the gun down." Her voice booms in the barn. "This isn't who you are."

While he stares at Mom, I think about the fifty steps between us, how fast I can go, and how hard I can strike him. The thought makes my bones weak inside.

"Would you shoot your grandchild?" Mom says. "Shooting my son won't help you."

He trains the rifle on her and holds out his hand with the key fob dangling from his fingers, taunting her.

"Throw it to me," Mom says. He has the power, but she has guts.

He grins at her and says, "Come and get it."

She takes two more steps.

"You won't get far," he says to her. "They'll track the vehicle and catch you."

I summon my power and bolt toward him while he's looking at her, slamming into him with my shoulder. He grunts and drops to the ground; his head smacks against the cement floor. I fall on top of him. He lets go of the rifle, and the key fob lands a foot away. His body goes slack. I scramble to my feet.

Mom dashes to get the key and runs to the Hummer. "C'mon!" she yells. She has the motor going before I close the passenger door. "Pray that's bulletproof glass on the windows in case he's still alive." She does a k-turn and barrels out of the barn, swerving around his body.

I adjust my idea about my mother again—and about me. We've changed. Nothing's going to stop us from getting somewhere safe.

She pulls the vehicle up to where the kids are waiting. "Get in!" she yells. The kids pile in, taking their usual places—Mira and Owen in the built-in car seats with Ruby between them—as if this were a perfectly natural thing to do. Pam and Amina sprawl on the seats behind them.

"It smells funny in here," Mira says.

"That's the smell of money," Pam says. "Leather," she clarifies.

Amina and Ruby tilt their heads and stare at her. Has everyone changed while we slept in the bunker? Did that man pump something into the air, or was it just being cooped up and feeling like we would never escape that made us different?

Mom rams her foot down on the gas pedal, throws her head back, and whoops, "Woohoo! We're free!"

After half a second of shock, the kids cheer along with her. I twist around in my seat to join in and see a different man in blue overalls sprint out of the barn with the rifle fitted to his shoulder. "Mom."

"I see him." She goes faster. "He's the whole special forces security. What a hoot."

In the next second, a bullet flies by the vehicle. I shrink down in my seat and watch him in the side mirror. Another shot pings off the rear window. Mom jumps each time but keeps driving, her head hunched between her shoulders. The man stops, shrugs, and lowers the gun. It's easier to let us go than to shoot us and have to clean up the mess. Anyway, more food for him if we're not here. Every way we ever calculated consequences has changed. Dad would be stunned.

"Where are we going?" Amina asks.

"Same place," Mom says. "Aunt Dee's. But in this tank, I think we can risk going on the highway. It'll be faster, and no one's looking for us in this vehicle. We'll save days. The less time we spend out here in the world, the better off we'll be. The virus is in the air." Mom looks at me over her shoulder. "Agreed?"

Her face tells me we're partners now. I have a say in what happens. "Agreed."

"Good. Figure out how we get back to Route 75. Next stop Mackinaw City Bridge." Her lips press against each other, and she stares straight ahead. She makes me believe we'll make it.

23

Sgt. D. Cooper, USVPD

THE next morning, when LT checks the daily regional reports on her computer, she pulls up a notice about a stolen vehicle. She puts her face close to the screen, like that will make the words clearer.

"Hey," she yells, waving her hand for us to come over. "We're close. This stolen vehicle, it's hers, Bennett's van. Same description and plates. It's on the report."

The report says the vehicle was stolen from the A-OK campgrounds on Lake Erie—and to be on the lookout for it. Takes some special kind of chutzpah for a fugitive to tell the police her vehicle has been taken.

Popova jumps up and down, and Riley grins like a split pig as if we already got Bennett. A wave of satisfaction flows through me, but then a slew of other thoughts pop into my mind. Bennett must have arrived at a destination she thinks is safe and ditched her vehicle on purpose so she wouldn't be spotted. Her tactics are wrong. Reporting the theft draws attention to her, puts a pin in the map; it makes her visible when she's succeeded in staying off the radar for so long. She's made a mistake, like every perp, and that's how we'll nail her.

We head directly to the A-OK campground to begin our inquiries and find the van with Bennett's ID and keys in it sitting in the middle of the lane at the gate, doors ajar like she planted it. Finding the vehicle here makes me worry that local policing is not everything it should be, but now, I'm sure she deliberately abandoned it and took on another identity to fool us.

I can't help but take this personally, like she knows I'm after her, and she's doing everything she can to thwart me. That gnawing feeling in my stomach, like I'm hungry even though we ate breakfast burritos on the way over, is telling me something.

We search the van, and while I'm bagging and tagging her purse and its contents and Manny's arranging for the impound tow, I go through her wallet, looking for an address or note about where she's going and find her passport. I put that clue together with the old lady telling us the boy said they were going north. How far north? We've already traveled 500 miles from Maryland. The Canadian border is closed, but Bennett might not know that. She won't get farther than Michigan.

I allow myself a small spurt of glee. "We've got her now," I call out. "She's trapped."

"Yeah, trapped in an area of three million some odd square miles," Riley says. "We're on it now."

Manny laughs, Popova smiles, and LT turns away. I don't like the idea that they're laughing at me.

We find plenty of other folks at the campgrounds to interrogate for information about where Bennett went. Six families appear to be living in camping vehicles and tents, not one of them masked. Of course, they don't line up to talk to us like civilized witnesses would. Instead, they scatter into the woods like wild animals, and we have to chase and subdue them. The tasers work just fine.

Right as we force what we think is the last adult to kneel on the ground, hands behind their heads, LT loses her patience with the whining, forgets her warning not to make a Waco out of it, and says we're taking them to the nearest isolation camp.

"LT, we don't know if they're sick or not," Popova says.

LT puts up her hand to stop Popova's mouth from motoring on. The rookie gets this look like she's been hit with a stun gun, but LT ignores her and calls HQ to report the unanticipated find of half a dozen infected adults.

We're in the process of handcuffing and loading them into the isolation section of the bus when a woman bolts out of a camper with a rifle aimed at LT, yelling, "You're not taking my kids!"

Riley shouts, "Gun!" He zips out his weapon and shoots the woman before she can get off a round. She drops, and amid all manner of screeching and wailing from the campers, someone—we never figure out who—shoots LT in the gut and wounds her pretty badly.

LT's face goes blank; she collapses onto the ground, groaning. After which, we lose any restraint, pull out our guns, and let 'em have it.

I make a split-second decision to leave the bodies where they dropped and get LT to the nearest emergency room. We wrap up her wound the best we can with what's in our first aid kit and take her to the hospital, lights and sirens going the whole way.

Popova calls in the injury to headquarters and puts me on the line.

"With LT gone, you're in charge of the squad for the remainder of this mission, if you want to continue," the chief says. "It's your choice; no harm done to your record if you call off the search. It won't go against you in your review."

He sounds like he means it, but this is my opportunity to show off my supervisory skills. I put all the starch I've got into my voice. "Thanks, Chief, but we'll pick up the search tomorrow. I'll file my report about today's riot after I know LT's stable."

The chief thanks me and signs off. I look out of the window and notice a storm is headed in. We're not going anywhere tonight.

Mostly to be polite, we check in with the local police to let them know we're in their area and ask for motel recommendations. The place they suggest is clean, which is a relief, and I catch a good night's sleep despite Riley's raucous snoring I hear through the wall between our rooms.

The next morning, we interview the officer who took the stolen vehicle report. He says he didn't know the woman he talked to was a fugitive because he didn't check the BOLOs before he met her and would never have suspected her of anything.

He says this with a completely innocent face like he's been practicing in the mirror, and he couldn't have known from looking at her that she was a fugitive. I find that hard to believe. She's been on the run for days; she'd have been pretty grody, not to mention the kids.

"She didn't behave like a felon," he says. "Just looked like any other mother in trouble trying to find a safe place for her kids."

What an idiot. He finds a woman in a roadside picnic area accompanied by a passel of children and doesn't interrogate her or ask where she's going. We don't need softies on the force. We have to be bold to get the job done and keep the country safe. I want to cite him for negligence, but I refrain in the name of good inter-departmental relations.

Of course, Bennett might have been cagey about her plans. She told him she was going to a relative's house. I ask the officer every way I can figure out where that relative lives, and when I run out of patience, I count to ten twice and try to maintain professional courtesy. He keeps shaking his head, shrugging, saying he doesn't know. Bennett must be sneakier than I give her credit for, her being a housewife and mother, and so on. I mean, I'm the professional, the one with the federal badge. That should give me some kind of advantage, and it's infuriating that it doesn't.

We check with the motel he took her to, and the reception clerk confirms Bennett was the name on the i-pay account she used to pay for the room. From there, the squad splits up and goes door to door in the neighborhood. Most places are closed. We find a taco stand open for delivery, but the owner says they don't keep any records. Every other store is shut down. Some have windows boarded over, and others have signs like CLOSED FOR THE DURATION.

I get the uneasy feeling that the few people we find are deliberately lying to me. Bennett has vanished, and a police officer helped her do it. I should recommend that the feds set up a national hotline for reporting officers who let viral fugitives slip away. Innovative ideas for new practices are another way to get noticed for promotion. Pretty sure I got this wired now.

I'm getting a clear picture of Bennett as a dissident, the kind of person who stirs up trouble, a lawbreaker. Anti-authority. Divergent. She's out there spreading the virus with complete disregard for other people. We're going to find her and put her where she belongs. Whatever it takes.

We follow our customary approach of staying on back roads as we head north, particularly around a big town like Sandusky, thinking that's what she would do, but now, we have no idea what kind of vehicle she's in, or even if she's in one. She might as well have taken a helicopter or holed up in another one of those campgrounds along Lake Erie.

At the first bridge that would take us north, the rent-a-cops stationed at the entrance tell us it's residential owners-only transit. Pedestrians and drivers need the correct ID, including us. I explain that we're looking for a family who might appear to be on vacation.

"No way," the officer says. "No one like that came through here. We know our people." He's pretty proud of that. "You can tell by how they dress, what they drive." Like guarding the rich makes him one of them. He's in for a shock one day. Those rich bitches would sooner push him off the bridge than let him onto their island.

We stay on the road we're on and wind up in nowhere, USA. No sign of anyone. Just thousand-acre farms as far as the eye can see and corn up to our knees. I'm a city girl, so I wouldn't know about corn-growing season, but it seems a little early to me. Must be from that global warming thing. We knock on a few doors, but they're far apart, and no one's answering. We're wasting time.

When we hit the Indiana line, the team wants to give up. "We're done, Cooper," Manny says. "LT's not getting out of the hospital soon and, no offense, but you just ain't a leader, even if you're the Sarge. You don't have it in you."

His comment makes me feel helpless and stupid. That heat I used to feel when my father sneered at me climbs up my legs and makes my belly shake inside. I grit my teeth to keep my face from quivering and tell them quietly, "We have to keep going for LT. This is her mission."

"Bull hockey," Riley says. "She didn't give a rat's ass about capturing Bennett. Time to turn around."

Don't take the bait, I remind myself. *You're in charge.* I bat away the memory of my father throwing a bowl of soup at me, the sting of the hot liquid through my shirt, how the dish broke apart on the floor, how he yelled, "Now look what you made me do. Clean that up!"

While wracking my brain for something that will recommit the team to our mission, I get a text from the hospital saying that in addition to her gunshot wound, LT has tested positive for the virus. The text says the whole team could be infected, and we should quarantine ourselves in separate quarters for fourteen days.

We might be infected. That thought clangs against my bones like I'm a xylophone. We've been interacting with strangers and then sitting in the bus together for hours, unmasked. We stopped checking temps two days ago. Statistically, three of us have it already, but we can't spare fourteen days. In that time, Bennett will be long gone.

It takes me two seconds to decide to keep this latest information from the squad, but I scrutinize each one to see who's sweating or has the chills. Everyone looks fine. We don't need to panic; besides, if I told them they'd been tagged, that would be their excuse to go home.

Way I see it, if we're going to die, might as well be in the service of something bigger than us, like our duty. I'm focused and prepared—everything my daddy said I'd never be. If I get Bennett, I'm definitely in line for lieutenant, and it won't be far from there to captain and then chief. My future's laid out in front of me like a shining path. I just have to convince the squad to keep going. I ignore the sound in my head of my father sniggering.

"We're going north," I tell the team, "like the old lady said. That's where they're headed."

When all else fails, be authoritative. I read that in a book.

)(

"[A] giant virus, named *Pithovirus sibericum*, was isolated from a >30,000-year-old radiocarbon-dated sample when we initiated a survey of the virome of Siberian permafrost. The revival of such an ancestral amoeba-infecting virus used as a safe indicator of the possible presence of pathogenic DNA viruses, suggests that the thawing of permafrost either from global warming or industrial exploitation of circumpolar regions might not be exempt from future threats to human or animal health."

—PNAS MARCH 18, 2014

)(

24

Jean

THE three-lane asphalt highway is an obstacle course of stopped vehicles, moldering bodies strewn where they fell, and abandoned suitcases split open like clamshells as a wave of scavengers pawed through whatever was left behind for anything that might save them. The viral tidal wave dragged them here and dropped them as it moved out. Local governments must not have anyone left to take the bodies away.

If these people had stayed home, would death have skipped over them? I scan my kids' faces. They're wearing that blank look of horror: mouths open, eyes wide; they're speechless. I need to refocus on something I can control.

I glance at the dashboard and realize I didn't check the power reserve when I floored the Hummer out of the barn. The gauge on this electric vehicle shows I have three-quarters of whatever full is. How far can we go before I have to charge the battery?

Ren notices me staring at the dash. "Mom?"

"Assume this car goes three-hundred-fifty miles on a full charge. How far will three-quarters of that take us? Then find where that is on the map."

"Around two-hundred sixty miles, if we're counting every last ion," Ren says without having to think about it. I start to compliment him on his math genius, and he points to the notation on the dash. "I'd like to take credit for being a whiz," he says, "but . . ."

"Oh. Right." He laughs at me, but that's okay. I'm fallible. It's better if we both know it.

He runs his finger along the map. "That puts us in Sweetpine. It's a small town in Michigan." He enlarges the image. "There's a charging station. Maybe it's open." He glances out his window as we pass a stopped car on the shoulder where the passengers are dead—a mother and three older teenagers. The windows are closed, but the driver's door is open. As we pass, the kids turn their heads to peer into the vehicle.

"He left them, Mom," Amina says. Her voice shakes. "The driver left them, and they died."

I know what she's asking. Will I abandon them? *Never*, I tell myself. *Never*. I'm with them to the end. "Maybe they were dead when he left the car." I don't know if that answer eases her pain. Probably not.

I feel Pam staring at the back of my head, almost hear her saying, "If we'd never left home, that couldn't ever be us."

We don't say anything for a while. It's worse here than where we came from. Here, people thought they had time to escape, like us, time to run to somewhere safer, and they died on the way. *We aren't going to die that way*, I promise myself. We're not sick. No one has a fever. No one is vomiting.

I have so many doubts. I long for home, for my room, for the light that flows through the front windowpanes and slides along the wood floor in the morning. At least we would have been comfortable. We could have had our funerals. I shudder and zip away from picturing myself laying Mira and Owen on a pyre. I flash on the kids burning my corpse. I can't go there either. There has to be another solution. That can't be our future; I won't let it be.

"I must be a silent carrier," I whisper to Ren. The words come out without my wanting them to.

He nods; he's been thinking about this also.

"So, when you're older . . ."

"Yeah," my son says. "We were around Aunt Caro before we knew she was sick. Do we carry the virus? How long can it ride around inside humans and not kill us?"

The thought of human extinction on the planet infects us both. We're silent for miles.

"Maybe if everyone has it, we won't die of it," Ren says. "We just change."

I stare at his profile. My love for him fills me from head to toe, the way it did when he was born and the doctor laid his shiny body on my bare skin, the way it does now when I catch him doing something unexpected and he's unaware of me. This is everything I ever wanted—to know what love was, to feel it radiate from me. To feel it now as a contrast to the fear I have every second both rips me apart and heals me.

"Watch out for that man!" Ruby yells from the back seat.

I look up to see a man darting across the highway right in front of me. He waves his arms and jumps up and down. He wants me to stop. Thousands of years of civilization and acculturation flash through my mind. I jam on the brake; tires screech on the asphalt; the vehicle shimmies. If we don't help each other, who are we?

"Don't stop, Mom," Ren says. "He could have a weapon. He could be sick or kill us. He could take the car, and we'd be stranded on the road with nothing." He puts his hand on the steering wheel. "We could die here." He gestures to the bodies littering the road. "Like them."

My son has already made the leap to the next version of human society, where altruism means certain death. I swerve around the man. In my rearview mirror, I watch him hold up his arms in the universal "What the hell" gesture, and then he flips me off.

Shaking, I leave the highway at the next exit as grief overtakes me. I've abandoned being human, left behind thousands of years of exhortations to care for the stranger, to be my brother's keeper. Fear scours out every instinct toward kinship, each impulse to establish clans. The other is my enemy. I have never felt so alone in the universe before.

I take a side road that parallels the highway. Slower is safer, I decide. Fewer cars. Fewer dead people. "Find another route," I say to Ren, who's already on it, charting a path away from here, away from the dead and what passes for the living.

25

Ren

WE switch up driving after seventy miles so Mom can rest. She says she's so tired her bones are melting.

I take the turn where GPS tells me, and the whole Sweetpine Alpine Village thing spooks me. I'm in the opening frames of another new game. Bad guys could be anywhere behind this happy ski-town façade. I have to remind myself I chose this way because it was the fastest backroad route to Sault Ste. Marie.

The welcome sign says the town's population is 3,687. Speed limit signs say twenty-five miles an hour, but I would have slowed anyway because there's snow on the ground. I haven't seen snow in years. The street is slippery, and it's already dusk. I flip on the headlights, and we swerve sharply.

"Don't use the brake," Mom says. "Take your foot off the gas and let the car's momentum slow on its own. You'll have more control." She stares out her window. "We should charge the car if they have a station and buy some warm clothes."

"Maybe get some food, like real food?"

"You must be starving."

"Yeah. Well. Growing boy, and stuff."

"I'm hungry too," Mira says. "I'm not a boy."

Mom turns in her seat and blows Mira a kiss. "We're going to eat, Sweetie. We just have to figure out a few things first. If we can't find anything else, we have food from the apartment."

A digital sign in front of a bank that used to show the time and temperature lists the number of people infected, 2,932, and the number dead: 1,375. The date is six months ago. Whoever was keeping track stopped.

"Tap the brake a few times," Mom says, her voice working too hard to be calm.

161

My eyes jump to the road in front of us. Six wolves are standing in the middle of the street. They stare at us with slanted yellow eyes; their heads are the size of half of my body. They're amazing, and this is their town; we're the invaders. The car swerves to the left as I try to brake. The gas station is behind them. It's like they're protecting it. I'm not stopping there.

"It's okay," Mom says, her voice under control but shaking a little. "They must have expanded their territory when humans stopped going outside." She consults the map. "Pull in there." She points to a shopping mall entrance. "Maybe we'll find what we need."

The Alpine decorations are intense and freakish outside boarded-up shop windows. Someone spray-painted *Stay Home* in red on the wall of one store. A single car sits in the parking lot. All the stores are dark. Everyone alive in this town is safe in their houses like we used to be. I wish we were back home, safe from the cold and the snow and the wolves. We avoid looking in the parked car. In this game, whatever strategy that guy was using didn't work. He ran out of lives.

"We have to get warm clothes," Mom says. She presses her lips together. "It's colder up here. If we can't buy them . . ."

"I'm good with locks," Pam says from the back seat.

"How do you know that?" Sometimes my cousin ticks me off. She likes to pretend she knows everything. All girls are like that; well, except Amina, who never pretends to be anything but herself.

Pam raises her chin and eyebrows and turns to stare out the window like a princess waving to the peons. "Because I do."

"Me too," Owen yells. "I'm good on locks too."

Amina riffles his hair and laughs. "I can break windows, so there's that. I mean, if we have to."

"There's a sheriff," Ruby whispers. "She might not like it if we steal stuff."

I scan the parking lot, trying to see what Ruby sees. Nothing's moving but us. The sheriff is another one of her guesses. I'm not listening to her anymore.

"Hard to believe anyone cares about law and order in a town where most people are dead," Mom says.

It's the second time she's been so blunt. She's also had it with Ruby's predictions.

"Drive behind the stores, Ren, back where the loading docks are. Let's get warm clothes first. Then we'll see if there's food and a charging station anywhere."

I park the Hummer where a sign says Snow Gear Loading Dock and pocket the key fob. Nobody's taking this vehicle from us. "Now what?"

Mom gets out and stretches like this is some casual vacation, and we're just taking a break. I turn in a circle to see if anyone is watching or if the wolves followed us. It's cold out here. Amina shivers and puts her arm around Owen. The dash temperature indicator says thirty-nine degrees, but it feels colder. We haven't been anywhere this cold in years.

It's so quiet here, the air hums. We could be the last people alive on the planet. Pam hops out of the car and heads straight for the steel door next to the pull-down loading gate.

"I don't think so," I yell.

"Watch me," she says and turns her back to me. Her elbows twitch. Ruby's watching her also. In the next minute, Pam throws the door open. "Ta-dah!" she yells, her arms in the "goal" position. Her voice echoes.

"How did you . . . ?"

"It was already broken open," Ruby says, so only I can hear. "They used crowbars."

"Everybody inside the store." Mom picks up Mira, and Owen runs inside. For a second, I wonder how Mom is keeping track of us, and then I let it go. It's not my job.

It takes a minute for our eyes to adjust to the darkness. Plywood-covered windows make it gloomy, and the lights don't work, but daylight sneaks in around the spaces between the wood planks. The store has been ransacked. Racks are overturned, glass cases smashed, and stuff is scattered across the floor.

I get that clutch feeling in my chest, like I do when I can't find something and I'm in a hurry. "Why break things if you can take whatever you want for free?" My voice sounds strange to me.

The mess makes me feel stressed. There's no logic to it, no purpose. I get people taking what they need, but why wreck stuff? For a second, everything goes blurry, and I can't see. All the rules my parents taught me have been turned upside down by people who cheated, who hacked a game to win because they didn't want to risk losing. Where's the cred in that?

If we can't trust folks to behave how they're supposed to, if they freak out and destroy things because they're impatient, then there are no safe spaces. Anyone can blow at any time. We always have to be alert, and that makes me tired.

"Anger." Mom shrugs. "They have no other way to express their frustration and hopelessness. Their fury gets away from them. At least they beat up things and not people."

I understand anger. It boils up in me when I don't expect it. Sometimes the smallest thing makes me want to put my fist through a wall and curse. I want to yell in Mom's face and cry so hard my skin will peel. My anger gets big enough to make something burst into flames. I can't let it out, or my family won't be safe, so I stuff it down inside me. At least my games chill me out, but on this trip, we're losing every round.

Mom sighs. "Okay. We need warm boots, pants, long-sleeve shirts, sweaters, jackets, and it wouldn't hurt to get hats and gloves. See if you can find anything that fits you." She turns to the girls. "It doesn't have to match."

Amina and Pam roll their eyes. Mira pats Mom's back the way she's seen her mother do. "It'll be okay."

"Do it as fast as you can. Ten minutes. I'll take care of finding things for Mira and Owen. Put the clothes on as you find them."

In no time, Ruby and I are dressed for the slopes, from hats to boots. Our new hats have headlamps on the brims. We switch them on, and the lights careen across the store as we move our heads. We spotlight Amina and Pam arguing about who found the pink woolen gloves first. Mom and Owen wear jackets and ski caps, and she's pawing through clothes for Mira.

"Turn those off," Mom yells. "The light's in my eyes." In the next second, she finds a jacket in Mira's size and slips it on her.

"I'll check the stockroom," Pam says, disappearing into an even darker room.

"Stop right there," a woman's stern voice says. "Hands where I can see 'em."

I turn toward the sound with my hands in the air. My headlight shines on her. She's in a brown uniform, with a brown jacket, wearing a hat with a badge on it. Her gun is pointed at me. She's squinting. Her hand is around Mira's neck. My throat tightens.

"Turn that damn light off!"

"The sheriff," Ruby says. Her voice sounds like her tongue is stuck to the roof of her mouth.

The sheriff motions with her gun for us to group together. Mom puts her hand out in front of her and shields me with her body. "That's my niece you have there, ma'am. She's only four years old."

"You got proof of that? For all I know, you kidnapped these kids."

We have no proof of anything.

"She's Aunt Jean," Mira says, looking up at the sheriff. No one could question her innocence. "She's taking care of me because my mommy died from the sickness."

The sheriff barks. Must be her way of laughing. "So, you're turning these kids into liars and thieves? That's your idea of taking care of them?"

Mom steps forward to just beyond an arm's length of Mira. The sheriff aims her gun at Mom's chest. "I know how this looks, Officer, but we're desperate. We're from a town similar to this, only not so pretty. We're going to Sault Ste. Marie."

The sheriff's gun wobbles. "You sick?" She backs up a step, dragging Mira along.

"No, no. We're fine. We left home because the neighborhood was infected. The snow reminded me it's not warm in the North." Mom waves her arm toward the windows. "We never see snow anymore where we come from." She laughs like she's saying what a dummy she is.

The sheriff doesn't laugh.

Mom takes another step toward the gun. "We had to leave quickly, so we don't have any warm clothes."

The sheriff waves her gun around. "Don't talk at me like I'm some second-class idiot. You should have thought of that before you left." She takes a step backward, away from Mom.

"I know. I know." Mom shakes her head. "There wasn't time."

The sheriff's not buying the helpless, batty woman routine. Her face twitches; her gun wobbles. I wonder if she's sick. Can't be easy being one of only a handful of people left alive in this town.

Mom waves her phone like a wand. "I'm happy to pay for this stuff."

"Don't pretend you don't know the store's closed. You put that merchandise back. I'm taking you in on a charge of breaking and entering and burglary." The sheriff's voice is tight, like she's losing it.

"Does court still convene?" Mom asks.

I groan. Mom plans to talk the woman into a coma.

The sheriff rears back. "You a lawyer?"

Mom snorts and shakes her head. "In my state, we no longer hold trials. Too dangerous."

"Shut up and let me think." The sheriff grips the collar on Mira's jacket and pulls her closer. "Don't try any of your lawyer tricks on me."

Mira wriggles free of the jacket and runs toward Mom. The sheriff goes rigid for a second, then takes her weapon in two hands, bends her knees, and levels it at Mira. The gun clicks as a bullet enters the chamber.

In the next second, the sheriff sprawls on the floor as a booming sound bounces off the walls. The gun skitters across the floor to my feet. Pam stands above the sheriff, holding a snowboard.

"You don't shoot little kids," Pam says to the prone sheriff. She looks at Mom, her eyes huge, her face so pale, it radiates light. "I didn't mean to kill her, but she was going to shoot Mira."

Mom runs her hands over Mira and lifts her into her arms. She scrutinizes each kid. "Are you shot?"

Everybody shakes their heads. "No," we say at the same time.

"Maybe she's not dead," Amina says. "You only hit her with the board once."

Mom inhales loudly. "Let's get out of here."

Mira wraps her arms around Mom's neck and puts her face on her shoulder. Mom closes her eyes for a split second; then, she picks up the small jacket off the floor, grabs Owen's hand, and runs for the back door. Amina and Ruby dash to hold it open for her. I pick up the gun, find the safety, flip it on, and jam the gun into the pocket of my new parka.

Pam runs into the backroom. "Wait for me. I saw something we need. I'll be there in a sec," she yells over her shoulder.

Wolves stare at us from the edge of the parking lot. They *did* follow us. My guts freeze. I drag my eyes away from theirs. "Hurry up," I yell.

She comes out of the store dragging a box four times larger than she is. "Help me. It's heavy. Pop the trunk." On the box is a photo of an inflatable boat.

"What are you . . . ?"

"We need it to cross a river."

"Where?"

"On the map. When we were home, I saw the river on the map. We have to cross it to get to Canada."

The wolves pad a few steps closer. I take Pam's word for it that we need a boat. The box won't fit when we try to slide it in the back. It's too tall. We turn it on its side, but it doesn't fit flat either. I could take the boat out of the box, but that would take too long. When I look at the wolves again, I see them circling.

"Come on, you two," Mom yells. She starts the engine.

I look at Pam. Without a word, we lift the box onto the rack on the roof. She runs back into the store and comes out waving bungy cords to tie it down. She throws me the ends of two cords. "Hurry," she whispers. "The sheriff moved."

My fingers are stiff and won't work right. Even in my parka, I shiver. I pull my side of the cords down over the box, attach them to the rails, and test them to make sure they're secure. We throw ourselves into the car.

"Drive, Mom."

She backs the Hummer up, and the wolves howl.

26

Dee

THE day after I stocked up on toilet paper and mass quantities of food and other necessities for my guests, I woke up with a fever, feeling drained. It figures, but where did I get it from? I thought I was being so careful.

I picture the American customs official. He examined my papers without wearing a mask and gloves when I came back into Canada. Breath. The virus is carried on breath. He breathed on my papers, then gave them back to me. I held them in my hand. I rubbed my eyes. That had to be it. The very thought terrifies me.

My body aches. An indescribable pain radiates from inside my bones, through my muscles, and outward to my skin. The touch of my flannel pajamas is too much to bear. Even though I don't want to get out of bed, I drag myself into the shower, hoping steam releases the chainmail wrapped around my chest.

How many people did I infect in the market yesterday? Water streams out of the showerhead. I feel every ping on my body. I got it from Margaret. I should never have sat in her kitchen. Damn Americans. The last thing I need is to be sick. But if I'm going to die, I might as well be clean.

Between drying off and dressing, intense chills force me to sit down. My hands shake. My face in the bathroom mirror is mottled. I rub the mirror with the towel. It isn't steam on the mirror that makes me look that way. I don't recognize my face. It's worse than I thought.

I stick out my tongue and see it's coated with a thick, white film. I gargle with Listerine. I can't die; I have things to do. The kids are coming.

I take vitamin C, echinacea, hot tea with honey, and a decongestant; I pull on warm socks and an extra sweater. Half an hour later, I'm sweating so profusely, I have to pull off the sweater and socks and open the kitchen window. I need something to break the fever, handle the aches. Two ibuprofen tablets later, I drop, exhausted, onto the couch.

Picasso whimpers and I take that as sympathy. I remember how Georgia gave herself to death, almost smiling at the end as if she were surrendering to a lover she'd been expecting for a long time. That won't be me; surrender isn't in my DNA.

Bleeping wakes me from a coma-like sleep, and I grope for my phone, blink a few times to clear my eyes, and stare at the screen, trying to understand what I see. It's a text from Jean. The cell towers must have recovered.

Got your message. We're in Michigan. We'll find a way around. It's rough out here.

My fingers tremble as they find the keys. The letters on the screen blur. *Phone coverage is spotty. Be safe. Leaving the door unlocked.*

All thoughts of telling Jean to stop at Margaret's and get the papers I created fly out of my mind. In a flash, I see my niece stopped at the border, dragged out of her car, the children separated from her and each other by ages, put into cages, the littlest ones dazed and weeping, hearts in their mouths, clinging to the metal rungs of their prisons. I hear Owen calling out, "Mama, Mama."

It would be better if they didn't try to cross the border in the usual way. But how would they do it? I can't think clearly enough to invent a solution. Jean will have to rely on her ingenuity. At least, that runs in the family.

I toddle to the back door and unlock it. It's insane to leave the door open with that gang of boys hanging around, but if I die, I don't want Jean to have to break into the house. After Georgia passed, I often thought about how to handle medical emergencies now that I was alone, picturing myself lurching to the door to unlock it as I was having a stroke or heart attack, so the emergency medical techs could get inside without any problem.

I keep my health card and driver's license in an obvious place on the kitchen desk, so authorities can identify me even if I slip into unconsciousness. Imagining myself in a pile of broken bones at the bottom of the stairs, I mentally rehearse how to drag my body on my elbows to the phone. I assume other old people think about this.

Another wave of exhaustion hits. This stupid virus is battering my internal organs, looking for a way to defeat me. I refuse to let this illness get me. I crash on the sofa and pull up the comforter.

For no discernible reason, I remember a T-shirt I bought in my thirties. It's like I'm holding it up right before my eyes. The words, "I know I'm efficient," are written in glittering letters across the chest. "Call me beautiful." It made Georgia laugh when she saw it. She always called me beautiful after that.

I hear Picasso whining, but there's nothing I can do about it. He licks my face.

27

Sgt. D. Cooper, USVPD

WE'VE driven twenty miles on every northern route in Ohio, zigzagging across the state without luck. No Bennett sightings, no pops on the original BOLO. When I sent in my report yesterday, HQ sent a nasty message asking what in hell we were doing burning fuel across four states with nothing to show for it. They ordered me to turn around and return home if we don't find the subject in the next twenty-four hours. If the target were sick, she'd be dead by now, the message said.

The big shots don't know how tricky she is.

Word from the hospital is that LT isn't getting better; she's not returning to work. After days of this, there's lots of chatter from my squad, standing together, whispering, shooting me looks. When we break for dinner, they take their burgers and fries into Popova's motel room and close the door. They're close to full-blown mutiny. I need a sign that we're on the right track and tangible proof that Bennett's out there to keep them in line. HQ is right; she's probably dead by now. Even I'm beginning to wonder why I care so much about nabbing her.

I picture my father sitting in his chair, picking on a whisker, his toothless mouth in a grin about my most recent failure, like he enjoys it, like this was exactly what he expected, and no one should be surprised it happened. I hated the way he gloated when I got divorced.

"Who could love you?" he asked. I wish he'd lived long enough to die from the virus, but liver cancer killed him a year before this bad boy showed up.

Then Riley checks this morning's BOLOs and finds the sign we need. A Hummer was stolen from a farm in Henry County. The perp is a woman; she's got children with her. That's got to be Bennett. I knew it. I knew she was tricky. She's taunting us, waving her lawlessness in our faces, daring us to catch her. Popova jots down the description of

171

the stolen vehicle with the license number and VIN. Last seen headed northeast on Rt. 24, the BOLO says. What's weird is I could swear we passed that vehicle yesterday.

"Riley, map out a route north from where we are. The border with Canada will stop her. She can't get across. She'll have to find a place to hide. That'll give us time to catch up."

He eyes me. "Sarge, you got any idea how big this state is, not to mention Michigan? We're not in Maryland anymore. They got lots of land out here. What road do you want to go north on? It's hundreds of miles to the Canadian border, and there are ten ways to get there."

Popova lines herself up with him, shoulder to shoulder. "You know it doesn't make any sense that she's the one who stole the vehicle. The last known location for her was outside Sandusky. Henry County is miles away from there. How would she have gotten that far without a vehicle?"

This is it; they're making their stand. They wouldn't oppose me like this if I were a man; it would be "yessir, no sir," no questions asked. This is the mutiny I've been expecting.

"Locate route twenty-four and follow it northeast," I say like every word is a piece of wash pushed out on a clothesline stretched between tenement buildings. "We're going to find her and detain her." Restraint makes me sweat when I want to scream.

"We've been on every road she could have driven on," Manny says. "We've spent four nights in motels, plus meals. HQ isn't going to like the bill. We're not going to find her. Anyway, you don't know it's her. Someone else could've taken that Hummer. Or the guy could just be mad at his wife for running out on him."

That last jab triggers me. "I'm the one giving the orders, Manny. We didn't know what we were looking for before. Now we do. Figure out a route and stop your squalling."

Manny looks like he might display a little aggression, but instead, he gets this smile on his face, like he just got a Christmas gift he didn't expect. "Hey, wait a minute. I got an idea. Don't those fancy cars have some kind of onboard tracking device, in case they're stolen?" We turn to watch him as he nods and punches keys on the onboard computer. "Yeah," he says and points to the screen. "I type the VIN number in on this nationwide database, and I can see where the vehicle is on a map."

We wait. The air in my lungs bunches up in a ball. Popova puts her hands on Manny's shoulders, and her perfume drifts over to me. Are they a thing, or is she doing it with each of them?

"There she is!" Manny says. "We got her. She's moving north on a side road that parallels I-75. She's in Michigan. That's why we can't find her in Ohio."

The light comes back on in everyone's eyes. We've got the scent; the hunt is on. Popova pulls up a map on her phone, and she and Riley pick a route that gets us to some town called Sweetpine, where the Hummer appears to have stopped. We need to get on the road fast before Bennett's vehicle moves again. She's got a couple of hours lead on us.

Two hours later, we exit the highway and stop at the nearest sheriff's office to check for any updates on the vehicle and its occupants. We've lost the uplink somehow; it's possible another officer already caught up with Bennett, and they've got her locked up somewhere.

That thought takes the wind out of my sails a bit. I have to be the one who apprehends her, the one who puts her in an isolation camp where she belongs. She's my collar, and I want her to see those turquoise earrings in my ears as the camp guards drag her away. That'll even us up, somehow, make her no better than I am. After this level of effort, that's only fair.

In Sweetpine, the one remaining officer in the county appears to be going a little stir-crazy by herself. Her face is pale and sweaty, she has trouble focusing her eyes, and she can't seem to stay on topic. She might be suffering from the neurologic effects of the virus. When I describe Bennett and the vehicle, though, she sits up straighter.

"Yeah, that woman and her gang came through here," she says. "They broke into a store in Sweetpine, stole a passel of goods, and assaulted me. They need catching."

My blood boils when she tells me that.

"They're criminals, for sure. One of them whacked me in the head with a ski board. I lay on the cement floor with a head wound for an hour before I came to enough to crawl out to my car. Wolves howling woke me. I drove twenty-five miles with blurred vision, a headache, and dizziness to the closest urgent care and had to pull over twice to vomit. The doctor diagnosed a concussion and gave me fourteen stitches. They had to shave my head right here." She turns her head to show me.

I debate taking her to a hospital because, as far as I can tell—and I've seen a bunch of folks who're close—she's a goner, but why bother. Pretty soon, everyone in this town will be dead. It'll be another contaminated ghost town and years before anyone can live here.

"Don't worry," I say. "I'll get them. The Bennetts will be locked up till they die. There are no court proceedings for our cases. We round 'em up and lock 'em down. The paperwork is simple. Whoever we say goes into the camps."

She smiles, but I can't tell if that's because she believes me and is genuinely relieved, or she thinks Bennett will outsmart me. I hate being underrated; it sets the edges of my skin on fire.

Before we set out to hunt them, the sheriff gives me one more valuable piece of information. They stole her gun.

)(

"In a Mexican cave system so beautiful and hot that it is called both Fairyland and hell, scientists have discovered life. It is trapped in crystals. The evidence of life could be 50,000 years old.

"The bizarre and ancient microbes were found dormant in caves in Naica, Mexico. They were able to exist by living on minerals, such as iron and manganese.

"The life forms—40 different strains of microbes and even some viruses—are so weird that their nearest relatives are still 10 percent different genetically."

—ASSOCIATED PRESS, MARCH 03, 2017

)(

28

Jean

BACKROADS will work until we get to Mackinaw Bridge, but Route 75 is the only way to get across. It's the major highway north. I wish there were another way. We'll be too exposed. Everyone I love, my whole world, is in this vehicle. The thought makes me gasp. We're easy to pick off. Bored police officers or random vandals might stop us on a major road in broad daylight, but we can't stay in one place, either. We've already learned that lesson. We have to make it to Dee's.

"There, Mom." Ren points. "Charge up there. It looks open."

The gas and charging station has twelve bays and a large convenience store right before the bridge entrance. It's unpeopled. I wave my phone at the card reader, and the automated system behaves the way it's supposed to. The irony of this doesn't escape me. People might be quarantined, but money moves freely around the planet. Someone is getting rich from this pandemic.

I yield to the constant urge to look over my shoulder while the vehicle charges. If we didn't kill her, the sheriff from Sweetpine could be after us. Even sitting in the Hummer with the doors locked, my skin prickles. Someone is chasing us; I know it, even if I don't see anyone.

My fear seems irrational. We're so far from home that the local virus police must have lost track of us by now, but the last time I slept, I dreamed we were followed by a van with the infinity symbol. Of course, in that dream, Caro is a librarian telling me to look for clues in a book, and Ted smells like a clean white cotton shirt dried on a line outside in the sun. I woke up aching for the feel of him.

"I have this uncomfortable feeling we're being followed." I look over my shoulder at Ruby, who's dozing in a third-row seat.

Ren touches my arm. "I checked, Mom. No one's around."

I scan the highway and try to convince myself that we're safe in this semi-armored car. No one knows this is our vehicle. That gives us some cover from the virus patrol, but anyone can come at us from too many directions while we're tethered to a pump.

I lean toward Ren and whisper, "People out here have weapons. We haven't encountered any gangs yet, but they're lurking."

"Mom." Ren puts his hand on my arm to calm me down like his father used to. Heat from his hand leaks into my skin. "We have a weapon, too." He touches his jacket pocket. "We're a gang."

His words clang in my head. He's right; we're a gang. We're losing our humanity. I feel nothing about the people we've harmed, and I'm not even surprised by that. I can't blame the virus for my loss of compassion; this hardening of my soul is on me. From the moment I decided to run, I began shedding commandments. The five-millennia-old "thou shalt nots" intended to keep peace across twelve tribes, to subdue man's baser nature in support of the collective good were easy to let go; they were in the way.

Survival has its own ethics. It doesn't rely on accepted morality. What's right is anything that keeps us alive. Finding a dry place to sleep, getting enough food for the kids to eat, protecting our meager resources—*that* is the good. Whatever puts us in danger or leads to death is evil. My job is to protect us from evil. I can't be soft and succeed. Caro entrusted her children to me; those children and mine are the only tribe that matters. All others are the enemy.

"Mom." Ren points to the gauge. "We're fully charged."

"Oh, thanks, babe." He disengages the nozzle. I twist my head to work the knots out of my neck and pull back onto the highway.

The four lanes are empty, with only occasional trucks lumbering by like ancient wooly mammoths. How much courage it must have taken for humans to run on foot next to giant animals and spear them when they knew they would be crushed if the animal veered into their path. I could never do it; I have no real courage. I'm only pretending, hoping no one will notice.

"What are you thinking, Mom?" Amina asks.

"About hunting wooly mammoths."

Pam laughs. "What?"

Ren gives me a strange look.

"Why are you thinking about wooly mammoths?" Amina's voice has a tinge of terror as if this is the sign her mother's gone around the bend.

"It's okay, guys. I'm not a hunter. I don't have a clue about how to throw a spear."

The kids exchange looks. My answer doesn't make them feel better.

I don't tell them I'm afraid we're the hunted, easy to cut out of the herd and pick off. Out on this open road, there might as well be a target on the roof of this vehicle.

In the rearview mirror, I spot a white bus about half a mile behind us. My breath catches in my throat; my temperature goes to zero. I can't tell if it's the virus police or not, but I can't speak; I can barely breathe. Watching the van come closer and closer, I run through my options. Have they found us?

Get off the road! Caro roars at me. *Get off the road.*

I veer off the highway at the next exit onto South Mackinac Trail. Trembling, I pull onto the shoulder. My hands shake on the wheel.

"What is it, Mom?" Ren asks, looking around to see what spooked me.

"I saw them."

"Saw who?"

"The virus police. I saw that white truck that came to take our neighbors."

"Mom, that can't be them. We left them in West Virginia. No way it's the same vehicle way out here. Even if it's one of the directorate's, it's a different crew."

I wait for my heart to stop hammering. "Find another way to get there."

The border is closed. We can't use the bridge or ferry to cross into Canada. They won't let US vehicles through. We need to be clever, and none of my little brain cells are connecting.

"This side road, the one we're on, H63, goes north from here through Sault Ste. Marie on the US side toward St. Mary's River," Ren says. "We could try that."

When we're on the road again, the children play a word game that erupts into yelling and tears. I'm learning to ignore the outbursts. It's easier for everyone if I don't react. Amina is now the arbiter of squabbles. She is the queen of calm, kind discernment. In my next life, I want to be like my daughter.

Ren concentrates on his cell phone screen. Good thing we can charge the devices when the vehicle is running. We've lost our printed maps; finding our way depends on the GPS.

"There's a road that goes to a campground along the river east of town," he says. He's excited, like an explorer spotting uncharted land. "From there, we take a causeway to Sugar Island. And then we take Pam's boat to cross the river."

Just like that, as if the real world were as navigable as the one in his games, he's identified a route. I pull over on the shoulder to see what he's talking about. He's right. It's an easy drive. Halfway across the island, about three miles, a road takes us north to Cook Island preserve. From there, Canada is less than a mile across the river—the narrowest point downstream from the Soo locks and rapids—but too far to swim, too deep to walk, and way too cold.

I switch the GPS map to satellite view. Mansions and a few docks dot the opposite shore. The Sault Ste. Marie golf club is just beyond Queen Street. The area looks civilized, unlike the uncharted territory in my nightmares. Hopefully, the people who live along the river are so involved in their own lives that they don't stand on their porches scanning for desperate refugees crossing the water.

"Pam," I call out, so she hears me over the vehicle noise and the kids bickering. "We'll use that inflatable boat you found."

"Like I thought," she says. She's watching out her side window. "We can all be clairvoyant," she mutters so softly, I almost don't catch it. Ruby throws her a look but doesn't take the bait.

Crossing a freezing river in an inflatable boat seems so logical, I know it must be crazy. A month ago, I would have considered this entire expedition impossible. Now, this is our only hope; I need to believe it will work. At some point, I lost parental authority. I'm only the camp counselor. The kids have their own ways of dealing with each new problem. They're thinking ahead, unlike me. I'm always behind the event, reacting.

I watched Pam drag that huge box out of the outfitter store and wondered what she had in mind, what she was preparing for, but I didn't stop her, and I didn't question her motives, even though she's only twelve. I assumed she knew what she was doing. Our roles have flipped. Do the kids know I can barely muster the energy to tackle each new hurdle right in front of me? They must feel like they have to fill in the gaps.

Next to a campground, we spot Clyde's Drive-in, and the kids chant, "Food, food, food." Our stomachs growl; we've already eaten everything in the backpacks. The place needs a paint job, and in another universe, I would have worried about food poisoning, but it reminds me of the Dairy Queen we used to go to at the beach every night after playing miniature golf. The taste of soft vanilla ice cream coated with a thin chocolate shell that breaks off on my tongue fills my mouth.

"Are you cooking?" I ask the server at the outdoor window.

"Yep," Clyde says. "Only restaurant open on this side of the Soo. Not exactly making a bundle, but I'm not here for the view either. What's your pleasure?"

Noticing the three-day stubble on his face, I realize he's not wearing a mask. I smile behind mine out of habit and back up a step. The kids order the greasiest stuff he has. I would pay him a thousand dollars and smile until my face breaks to have the kids feel good for five minutes.

Even though it's forty-five degrees outside, we plunk ourselves down at a weathered wooden table with a view of the river. Grease covers the kids' chins and cheeks as they chew. They grin. I snap a photo of them to preserve this moment when, despite everything, they are happy. We're so close to our destination, so close to this nightmare being over. We bump water bottles to celebrate.

After we clean up, we drive out to the campground on Cook Island, a sandy spit of land right on the river. The small boathouse looks deserted, and when we pull on the door, it's locked. I thank our lucky stars that no one else is here and think of Caro. She was right. We do have an angel watching over us.

It's an odd way to think when I've lost my husband and sister. I'll never see them again, never hold them, and never hear their voices. My husband will never look at me with his eyebrows raised when I comment about how dark the sky is and say, "Here on Earth, we call that night," so that I laugh for fifteen minutes and then whenever I remember, which will be forever.

The ache of missing him rocks me for a second, and then I look at the kids. They're alive, exploring their environment, taking in everything.

Pam points to a spot across the river, and Ren nods—they've pinpointed our destination. The kids will make it; they'll get to safety. So, you win that argument, Caro. I believe in them.

It takes us a while to figure out how to inflate the boat. I get myself out of the way while Ren, Amina, and Pam work on it. My questions and suggestions only impede their progress. I'm glad the boat has an electric motor and oars, as advertised on the box. We test its seating capacity on land to see if we'll fit in it. We do, barely. But no one can move once they've taken a seat. I remember Mrs. Pittman's prediction and point out the handholds to the kids.

"Everybody holds on the whole time we're on the water. Understand?"

The little ones nod, serious and attentive.

"If we tip, grab hold of the boat. Understand?"

They nod again.

"If you fall out—"

"Grab hold of the boat!" They yell in unison.

The river current is slow. A giant barge glides past as we watch. The kids wave their arms as it takes forever to move out of our view. Even if we saw one coming in the distance, we'd make it to the other shore at the five miles per hour the electric motor is supposed to propel us before the ship was close enough for its wake to swamp us. It should take less than fifteen minutes to travel the one mile across the river. At least I hope that's true.

Ren figures out that he can power up the boat motor by plugging it into the Hummer's electrical system while we nap inside the car. We'll cross when it's dark to lessen the probability of the Coast Guard catching us. I cancel the thought of someone standing on their porch with binoculars watching us, calling the Mounties as we make the shore. Don't add levels of difficulty, I school myself. It's hard enough.

There's no room for supplies in the boat, even our backpacks. We'll have to abandon everything we can't carry in our pockets, but if we make it, it's less than a mile from where we land to Dee's. One mile. Even the little ones can walk that far without a problem. To be so close to safety, to see it over there just out of reach. I'm like a pilgrim sick from two months at sea, spotting the rocky coast of an unknown continent on the horizon. Salt wind beats against my face. Elation and fear battle for dominance inside me.

I notice Ren studying my original instructions. "Only two miles to go, honey."

He nods and shoves the paper back into his jacket pocket. "I was checking the address, to see if I had it right."

"We'll leave the keys to the Hummer," I say. "Maybe someone else will need it." I try to keep the worry out of my voice.

Ren shrugs. He doesn't care about the car. He's focused on the next task. "We'll make it, Mom."

Keep hold of the boy, Caro whispers as I fall asleep.

29

Ren

WITH my eyes closed, I hear a man's voice say, "Well, what have we here?"

His voice sounds like a sharp-edged can opener teasing off a metal lid. I can tell he's a bully from his voice—they all have the same way of sneering at people they want to hurt. I imagine him white, short, skinny, with a sharp chin, gray teeth, a scruffy goatee, and long, greasy hair. I already hate him.

When I open my eyes, he looks nothing like that. He's a hulk with a full blond beard and a shaved head. He's wearing a ripped, puffy jacket over a dirty sweatshirt. Maskless, his face presses against the glass of my window. His breath makes a cloud shape.

Mom squeezes my arm. "It's dusk," she says. "Time to set out."

The tone of her voice says "danger, danger" and doesn't match her words, but I understand her. She stares at the men outside the Hummer and doesn't say what she means because they might read her lips. There are four of them, and they look like they've been living rough for a while, from before the virus. They have nothing to lose. They surround the car, one at each door. The minute we're out of the car, they've got us.

"Who is that man, Mom?" Owen asks.

"Bad guys," Mira tells him in her soft, high voice. "They're the bad guys."

"Whyncha get yerselves outta there," the pack leader says to me through the window. He might as well be speaking another language. His gang stares at us like we're creatures from another planet. They remind me of the wolves, their yellow eyes following our every move without blinking.

I hooked the boat's electric motor into the car battery; we can't drive away without unhooking it. Also, I'd have to get out of the car to do that. The boat itself is tied to the tow rack on the back of the Hummer, so it wouldn't blow away while we napped. Maybe they'll just take the boat and the motor. I doubt it, though. We're not that lucky. I see the greed on their faces in the deepening dark. A car, boat—worth real money. They've hit it big, and they're going to take everything.

Pam and Amina stare at them, their eyes giant, without speaking. "They want to hurt us," Mira says. Ruby nods, finally speechless.

We know what Mira knows. Evil has a smell. Even through the car windows, they reek. Mom's not saying anything. Her face is frozen.

"C'mon," the bad guy says, his tone soft like he won't hurt us. "We can make a trade." His pack snickers as they circle around the car and punch each other. They're warming up. The trade will be they get what they want, and we get nothing.

"Maybe I can trade them the Hummer for the boat," Mom says, her head down so her lips are hidden, her voice low. "We're not going to use it again anyway. I'll distract them. You get the boat and motor unhooked while I talk to them. What do you think?"

First, I don't know what to think. Then I realize that Mom doesn't get it. For her, some of the old rules still apply. She's going to try to reason with them, to bargain. She thinks there's a way to win. Talk distracted the bunker guy and the sheriff until we could get away, so she expects these punks will be polite and listen to her. It's not the same this time. Those other guys were old; they used to play by the same rules Mom did.

These scumbags are like the troll at the bridge. They have the power, and rules don't matter anymore. They're ruthless. We're the outsiders with no allies. I don't need a demonstration to prove that. We don't mean anything to them; we've got nothing to bargain with. They can take what they want, and we'll be lucky to walk away with our lives.

"It's not going to work," Ruby says, like we need her advice.

"Shut up," I say. "I don't want to know what you see."

Ruby sits back, stunned, and even Mom looks surprised at my reaction. My chest tightens. I'm sorry I said that, but I don't want to tell Ruby I'm sorry. I twist around in my seat and look at her.

"It's okay. I know you're scared," Ruby says.

I feel worse about it now. Pam reaches over the seat and squeezes Ruby's shoulder.

"Get out, bitch!" the bad guy yells. Times up on his patience. "Get out of the car, or we'll tip it."

"Mom?" Owen says. His voice shakes. Mira takes his hand.

"Yes, everyone out of the car," Mom says.

We open the doors slowly and exit the vehicle like the police have stopped us for speeding or a broken taillight. Mom signals with her hand, and we bunch up together behind her. For the first time in my life, Mom seems small to me, too weak to protect us.

"I'm Jean," she says to the leader and holds out her hand to shake his. My stomach turns over. When was the last time he washed? If ever there were a viral carrier, he's it. I'm glad when he doesn't shake her hand.

"Yeah," he says. He looks over at his boys and winks.

"Look, we'd be willing to let you have the Hummer and everything in it as long as we get the boat and the motor," Mom says.

Ruby stares at the ground. Pam and Amina stare at the men as if they're an exhibit of Neanderthals in a museum.

"Lady, looking at the odds here, a little woman and six kids against . . ." He gestures to his boys. "We get to take whatever we want. Right, boys?" He grins, and they cackle. I want to kick him in his crooked teeth.

One of his boys slides up to Amina and yanks her jacket open. "Hey, lookee here. Look at these cute itty, bitty titties." He jerks up Amina's shirt.

She shrieks and leaps backward.

He grabs her braid. "Be quiet, little girl, or this is gonna hurt." The men laugh.

Pam and Ruby throw themselves onto him, beating him with their fists and kicking him. He flicks them off and hoists Amina into the air with his hand between her legs.

A wildness comes over me so fast, it almost cracks me open. My face heats, my teeth clench, and my body feels like it's expanding. "Get away from her!" I yell in a voice that's bigger than me. I see myself ripping his body apart and stomping on it. The men ignore me like I'm not even here. My head's going to explode.

The ringleader grabs Mom by the arms. "I know what I want."

"Cut it out," I yell, my face close to his. His breath reeks.

"Whatcha gonna do, little boy?"

My whole body shakes, and my fist flies toward his head. He ducks and pushes me. I stumble backward and fall. Mom slams her fists against his back. He turns and drags her toward the reeds. She struggles, flailing her arms around, kicking him. He doesn't feel it. Nothing stops him.

The other guy tosses Amina on the ground. She scrambles away on her hands and knees. Pam jumps on his back, pounding his head with her fists. He flings Pam away with one arm while he seizes Amina's ankle with his other hand and pulls her back toward him. The men waiting for their turns laugh and clutch Pam's arms. She squirms and screams. Ruby scoops up Owen and Mira and runs behind the car where they can't see what's happening. They're wailing.

I yank the sheriff's gun from my jacket pocket. It's heavy in my hand. I release the safety and aim for the man who has Mom. His back is to me. I tell myself it's just another game. These aren't real people, and anyway, that burning in my chest and the buzzing in my ears makes it impossible to think. My avatar is doing this: aim and squeeze the trigger. I've done it virtually a million times.

The bullet goes wild, and the recoil from the gun jerks my hand up. I grip the gun in both hands this time and aim. The bullet catches Mom's attacker in the butt. He brays like a donkey and twitches. I shoot him again in the back. He slumps onto Mom. She pushes him away from her and struggles to her feet.

I shoot the man attacking Amina. The bullet hits him in the shoulder. His body jerks, he screams, and he falls to the ground. The surprise on his face almost makes me smile. Glee bubbles in my chest. Amina runs to Mom and burrows into her. They cling to each other, rocking and murmuring.

The remaining two men turn to rush me. I face them, the gun steady on my targets. "Run, you assholes. Run as fast as you can before I shoot you too."

I want to kill them, to keep firing until the bullets are gone. My finger twitches on the trigger. I picture them dead on the ground, blood leaking from their bodies. They would have killed us without a thought. I imagine the last breath that makes their chests shudder, how their legs would jerk and stop.

But I don't shoot them. That's not who I am. I keep the gun trained on the two scared rabbits as they hop through the reeds until I can't see them anymore.

30

Jean

THE man is on top of me, his smell making me gag, his sweat dripping onto my cheek. His fingers scrabble at my breasts, at the button on my jeans. A bang, and then another. Then he slumps against me, heavier than before. I push him off and scramble to my feet, my eyes frantic for Amina. Another bang, and she's in my arms. Our shaking synchronizes. I kiss her face and head and anywhere my lips can reach. We're both alive.

Over her shoulder, I see two of the scumbags scampering away like their joints have separated, puppets detached from strings, knees high, arms flopping. Images register in my brain one by one; their meanings come a second later. Ren is holding a gun. Two men are lying on the ground like discarded trash, moaning. There's blood. Ren shot them, the gun in his hand still trained on the receding attackers. His body is rigid, his face wet with tears. He trembles. The weapon might accidentally discharge. Where are the little ones?

I walk up alongside him. "Ren, sweetheart."

He doesn't seem to hear me. The roaring must be in his ears, the sound of his blood raging through his veins. I know the sound. I heard it in my head when that scumbag threw me down and climbed on top of me.

"Ren, honey, I need you to hear me." I slide my hand onto his shoulder. He jumps. "It's okay, honey. It's okay."

His head jerks up, and he collapses against me. His arm falls to his side. I put my hand over his gun hand and take the weapon from him. It's hot. I slip on the safety and stow it in my pocket, in case we need it again.

My son wraps me in his arms, puts his head on my shoulder. His whole body quakes as I pull him close enough to feel his heartbeat. The children run over and wrap their arms around him. We rock together, one small colony of souls too close to the edge of dissolution. My boy saved us. *He* is my angel.

We can't stay like this for long. We have to move. Those assholes could come back for their friends or the Hummer. They might bring cops or reinforcements. We don't belong here. No one will believe us.

"Pam, figure out how to unhook the motor from the car. Amina, untie the boat. We're leaving everything else."

Ren lifts his head and stares at the river, then back over his shoulder. With his mouth pulled tight over his teeth, he shudders. "I couldn't let them . . ."

My heart squeezes tight in my chest. "I know, Sweetheart. You stopped them. You're so brave. We're going to go now. A storm is moving in, and those monsters could come back."

We don't have time for more comfort than that. While the girls drag the boat into the water, I check that I have my phone, turn off the car, and leave the keys on the driver's seat. Someone else will need a vehicle, and it's not mine, anyway. Mr. Famous can track it and send someone to collect it.

I make one final sweep to find anything we accidentally dropped and spot Pam's baseball cap on the ground. I pick it up and stuff it in my pocket. The man lying near it moans and reaches up a hand. I stare at him for a second, astonished he thinks I would care or even consider helping him, and mull a million small acts of revenge. But I don't give a fig about him. Revenge takes investment and time; he's just slowing me down.

Pam steadies the boat while I deposit Mira and Owen in the middle section. I tug her cap onto her head. She smiles at me. This child trusts me, and I don't deserve it.

Ruby squishes between the little ones and wraps her arms around them. "Hold the grips on the boat," I tell them, guiding their little hands to the attached rubber-encased loops. "Don't let go until I tell you to."

They nod their heads, faces serious.

"Pam, you've got the tiller. Ren, sit on your knees in front of Pam. Rowing will be easiest from there if we need it."

My son lets me guide him into the craft. It's hard to remove my hands from his body. I want to hold him in my arms for hours and hours, but we can never get back what we lost.

I rip my thoughts away from regret and focus on what we need to do. "Amina, you're the lookout at the front. We're headed for the long dock on the other side. There's a light at the end of it. See it?"

She nods even though she's shaking.

"Call out any obstacles you spot. When we get to the shore, you'll tie us up."

"Where are *you* sitting, Mom?" Her voice cracks.

She's afraid I'm leaving them. I didn't protect her when she needed me; I promised to always be there for her, but I wasn't. A man violated her, tore her spirit, and ripped away her trust in everything. Ragged edges of that loss scrape my heart.

"I'll be right behind you. Right here."

My back will be to the babies, but Ruby is with them, and Ren is right behind them. I need to see where we're going, to be able to spot problems before they happen. I remember Caro's warning—*keep hold of the boy*—but I don't know what it means.

The wind picks up, and the boat sways as I climb in. With so many of us packed in here, there's barely room to raise our arms. This is another insane act, yet there's no other way. We have to cross. The first raindrops splash our faces as Pam lowers the motor into the water and starts it. She maneuvers the boat away from the shore into the river. A light goes on in a house on the other shore. I pray it's dark enough to hide us from anyone's observation.

Pam heads straight across, her face a study in concentration. Far in the distance, I spot a cargo ship heading west for the locks. We have time to get across before it's close, even if we're moving at a speed that feels like a sloth crossing the road. The wind kicks up white caps, and the boat rocks continually.

Owen coughs and gags. "Mama, I'm gonna throw up."

Amina yells, "Mom!"

Before I can grab him, Owen stands. Ruby cries out, "Owen!" She reaches for him. The boat lurches, and Owen tumbles over the side, into the river.

I freeze, unable to think or speak or move. Ren flicks on the light on his hat. In a blur of movement, Ruby hands her headlight to Pam, yells, "Cut the motor and keep us steady," and pulls off her jacket. "I can do this," she says, jumping over the side.

"Ruby!" Ren yells. Pam throws off her cap, pulls the light over her head, and switches it on. Segments of the river light up as Ren and Pam scan the water.

"Owen!" I hear a woman shrieking and realize it's me.

"There!" Pam yells and points. "He's there!" She points downstream.

Owen's jacket has filled with air, and he's floating away. His head submerges. Ruby bobs up and looks in the direction of Ren's light. She takes a breath and dives again. The rain pelts us now. Another scream hovers in my chest. Caro's warning rings over and over in my ears.

Ren and Pam find the sound of splashing with their headlights. Ruby surfaces with Owen in her arms. He splutters and coughs, but he's alive. She struggles against the current to swim to the side of the boat with Owen under her arm and holds him up. He's almost as big as she is.

Ren pulls my baby into the boat. I grab Owen, peel off his wet jacket, wrap him inside mine, and crush him to me. He vomits on my shoulder and starts to cry. He's alive.

Ren reaches over the side to pull Ruby into the rubber boat, but he can't catch her hand.

"I . . . I didn't," she says. "I didn't know . . ." The boat shifts in the current. Her head slips into the water.

"Wait! No! Ruby!" Ren yells.

Amina yells, "Grab her! Grab her."

Ren reaches for Ruby's hair. She slips away from his grasp. Half out of the boat, he stretches out his arms. "Ruby! God, Ruby give me your hand," he calls out. "Pam, turn your light here." He holds out an oar for Ruby. "Grab the oar. Grab it!"

Her hand reaches for the oar and misses it.

Pam leans over the side where we last saw Ruby's face. "What happened to her? What happened? What did you do?" There's only darkness and swirling water.

"I was trying to get her. She slipped out of my hands. She should have been right here." He points, his face twisted, his voice strangled.

"Turn in a circle," I say. "Keep your eyes peeled. The current pushed her downstream."

Ren shrugs off his jacket and dives over the side of the boat. "Ren!" I scream. He disappears below the surface. Desperate, I look at Pam. She grabs the oars and pulls the boat in a circle.

"Ruby, Ren," we all yell at the same time.

Ren surfaces and clings to the side of our boat. "I can't find her." He sobs. "She's not there. There's nothing, nothing. It's so dark." He looks downstream. "Ruby, Ruby," he calls again, his voice raw.

The cargo ship is closer and no longer seems to be moving slowly. Ren clambers over the side and, sobbing, crumples into a ball. Pam throws his jacket over him. She rubs his head.

He groans. "I didn't save her."

The ship emits a long, low moan. Water shushes off its sides. We turn in circles, looking for Ruby. The freighter moves faster than I thought it could, and the wind picks up.

Every person I've loved and lost, every last bit of that sorrow folds itself into a howl that tears out of my throat so hard and fast that I have to lift my face to the sky to give it space, and in the next instant, I hear my wail echoed by each child, their faces also raised, calling for their lost friend, the missing member of our pack.

Empty, we look at each other, our faces slick with tears and raindrops, and I make the only decision possible. We have to move on, we have to save ourselves, or Ruby's sacrifice was for nothing. In all this time, I have never felt so helpless.

"Do you think she . . . knew . . . before?" Amina asks, her face a mirror of my sorrow.

"I don't know, but we're making too much noise; we'll be spotted. We have to go."

The children gape at me, astonished.

"Mom, Ruby's out there, in the water," Amina says. "We have to find her."

"Pam, turn on the motor."

"Mom, no," Amina whispers. "We can't just leave her."

Pam starts the engine. Ren sobs, his shoulders bucking. It's come down to saving one child or all the others. The kids' faces are blank with shock. Amina covers her eyes with her hands; her body judders as the boat lurches forward.

I want to go back to where we came from, at the start, back to our safe home, where things were orderly and made sense, away from the mess I made of our lives. We were fine there; we had our routines and knew what we were doing. I can't take any more hurdles; I'm barely holding myself together. I want to scream at the sky, "It's enough. I've had enough," but I swallow the thought. The kids can't see me defeated.

I glance at Ren, but he's staring straight ahead at our objective—the opposite shore.

"Will we . . . ?"

"We'll make it," he says tonelessly. "It's about half a mile. Close your eyes so you don't watch the ship." Pam revs the engine and steers the boat toward the Canadian shore. Owen whimpers against my shoulder, his little body shivering.

The bottom of the boat scrapes against something. I open my eyes; the beach is five feet away. Behind us, the cargo ship creeps through the river, its wake rocking our boat. Pam cuts the motor, pulls it out of the water, and we glide onto the narrow strand.

"We might need this boat again," Pam says.

Ren nods. "We'll carry it to Aunt Dee's." He glances at me. "Mom, you take the babies and lead the way. We'll deal with the boat."

The river chills my feet when I step into it to pull the children out. Owen was in that water. Ren. Ruby. I think about hypothermia; I won't think of Ruby drowned or it will cripple me.

When we're safely on dry land, we stand for a few seconds, hoping to spot her swimming up to the nearest dock. No one but us reaches the riverbank.

"She's not coming," Mira says.

Unable to say anything comforting, I lift her into my arms. She wraps her arm around my neck and kisses my cheek.

"I'm sorry," the child says. "She was a friend."

The older kids share a look and hoist the boat above their heads. A resident comes out of the nearby house with a flashlight. We freeze. Light strobes the area but doesn't find us.

A man calls out, "Hello. Is anyone there? Are you okay?"

"Sorry to disturb you," I call out. "We're fine. We're on our way."

We scuttle off his beach as quickly as we can and hope he doesn't call the police. On the GPS map, I type in Dee's address, select turn-by-turn commands, and take Owen's hand. Our little parade stumbles onto Queen Street, heading west.

After the darkness of the golf course, lights are on in houses along the way, tiny squares of light beaming out across the darkness—so normal and logical it feels surreal. When I spot the address of Dee's house, 112 Leo Street, written on the small marker near the sidewalk, and see the lights on in her house, I can barely keep from sobbing in relief.

31

Sgt. D. Cooper, USVPD

I SPOT a Hummer for a minute on I-75 and get a flash of adrenaline, my heart whamming against my ribs. *We got her!* But before I can point it out to Manny or say, "Follow that car," the vehicle disappears, vanishing completely like a mirage or a dream. It wasn't in my sights long enough to read the license number and could be any overpriced, oversized vehicle seen from behind for a few seconds.

For a second, I marinate in the envy the Hummer stirs in my gut, and then I imagine one well-aimed grenade fired from my shoulder. I picture the white-yellow-orange flash, the vehicle's backend lifting high as it flips. Doors blow away from the body, and shrapnel flies. I hear the ka-boom and can almost taste the burned marshmallow smell of the explosion. The image is so vivid, I expect to pass the smoking wreck of the car in the road.

No such luck, though. We drive until we're stopped by the border control blockade at the foot of a bridge that spans the St. Mary's River, according to the highway sign. The whole squad gives me the stink eye.

"Sarge," Popova says as we wait our turn to be interrogated by the border control officer, "we don't have the papers we need for extradition. We don't even have verbal authorization from headquarters to go ahead."

The others must have nominated her to do this intervention. Of the three of them, she's the only one with balls.

"It's time to call this search a day and turn around. We've done everything we can."

"Give me a minute to consider our options," I say, stalling for time. I've known this moment would come since Ohio, but sometimes, when you're on the hunt, you forget stuff on purpose because thinking slows you down.

Beyond the guardhouse, the river sounds like a light freight train running smoothly over railroad tracks. From where I'm sitting, Canada looks like America, which is a little jarring. There's another town over there with ordinary people in it, barely foreigners. I expected it to be different, but it's a continuation of what we've already driven through, only one mile across a narrow body of water. I could almost swim there.

Suddenly the US seems vulnerable. The enemy could invade with a flotilla of rafts. We share five-thousand miles of border with Canada. Bennett could have gone across anywhere. Why here? Someone must be waiting for her in that town, someone who's abetting her.

I wonder if the Canadian authorities know there's a possible coyote enterprise built around sneaking infected Americans into Canada. If I exposed that, captured a few of their leaders, I'd get a big promotion. It would be on national news. I'd be famous. What would you think of that, Dad, huh? I'd be a hero, more than you ever expected. You didn't think I'd make it to thirty. For a second, I bask in the imagined adulation as if it were real.

And then, out of the blue, my brain wakes up like it's morning, and the light is streaming through the window, illuminating a painting I'd never noticed. I could be free in a new country. I could get lost in all that space, shuck off my old skin, invent another history, and be someone completely different.

I don't have to be some mother-abandoned, snot-nosed kid with filthy hair and fuzz between her toes, wearing ragged clothes and hiding from her drunken father or picking up guys who turn out to be him, but a whole woman proud to be who she is, living her own life. It's like seeing what you never knew you wanted, but when you do, you know you've been secretly jonesing for it all along. The revelation makes me feel like my clothes are too tight.

Manny pulls the bus up to the gatehouse in front of the bridge. Dismounting from the bus with my mask and gloves on so I don't spook the guards, I flash my badge and ask if they've seen Bennett and her tribe. I describe the family and the vehicle and give them the license number. The border patrol guards check the list on their clipboards and shake their heads.

"Haven't seen a Hummer go through here, Sarge," the bulkiest one says, his hands on his hips. "Only essential vehicles are allowed to cross."

He pulls his mask below his chin so I can see his face. Must be some kind of signal that he's telling the truth because I can hear him fine through it.

"We'll be on the lookout, though. Leave your contact info. If she tries to come through here, we'll hold her and give you a call."

"Any other way she could get over to Canada?"

The big guy shrugs. "Ferry's closed. Small boat traffic is nil. The US Coast Guard patrols the river. So, I doubt it."

I hand him a paper copy of the BOLO with all the necessary information and climb back onto the bus. All the virus that might have spewed out between us in that minute hits me as I get back on the bus and makes me sneeze. I don't like feeling vulnerable. It's one of the reasons I joined the police force in the first place—that I'd be the one with authority, the one holding the weapon. This nasty virus makes everyone equal.

"Pull out and turn around," I tell Manny. "They're bulky and armed. No one's getting past them. She didn't go this way."

We get off the highway onto a side road and grid-search the town. No people on the street. Barely any traffic. Most places are closed. We don't spot the Hummer. Nothing pops up on that tracking website. We check the ferry crossing in case the guard was wrong, but it stopped running the day after we got the assignment to seize Bennett.

"No way she got over the border," Riley says. "Too many obstacles."

I don't trust his confidence. We consult our maps for other ways she might have crossed, but if she's not driving over the bridge or crossing by ferry, she's not going anywhere.

"Unless she got someone with a boat to take her across the river," Popova says. "That could happen, right?"

Her question feels like another failure someone's blaming me for. "Look," I say to tamp down her insolence, "she's got to be on the US side."

"Sarge." Manny puts a hand on my shoulder in some lame attempt to calm me down. I shrug it off. "We haven't found her. We're at the border, and we haven't found her. She made it over, and we've got no legal way to take her back."

"Time to head home," Popova says.

They've been colluding. I ignore her. "We're chasing a fugitive," I say, "someone who's spreading virus everywhere she goes. She's got kids with her who should be in protective custody. They assaulted a police officer. The family needs to be detained. We've got paper on her. Rules are rules."

"We're way out of our jurisdiction," Riley mumbles. He's an old guy, looking kind of peaky. LT getting shot took the last bit of stuffing out of him. This mission is way more dangerous than he signed up for. "It's time to pack it in."

Searching for the words to rally them, I say, "C'mon, guys. This isn't the time to give up. We leave no stone unturned. This is for LT!" I give them my raised fist.

They stare at their feet. They're not buying it, but I'm in charge. They have to do what I say. This weird feeling builds in my stomach, like something's cooking under pressure in there. I call HQ and ask for authorization to follow the fugitive into Canada, but the chief is dead, and most of the higher-ups are in quarantine.

Takes fifteen minutes to find a supervisor with the authority to give me the go-ahead, and she says, "Who gives a crap? Let Canada have her. She's their problem. We've got enough to worry about."

My face flames. I say, "Yes, ma'am," and swallow the curses. The pressure in my gut builds. I give a damn, I want to tell her; this is my mission, the task entrusted to me. It matters whether I catch her because if we don't care anymore, the entire world will go to hell, and there'll be chaos everywhere.

Bennett is every privileged bitch I've ever met, everyone who ever turned her nose up at me. She has to be riddled with the virus by now. She belongs in a camp, end of story. And those kids of hers, from what I heard from that sheriff in Sweetpine, reform school would be too good for them; they need a little law and ordering. The more I think about this, the faster my breath comes. My face is so hot, people could warm their hands near me on a frosty day.

Act now and apologize later—that's the maxim of successful generals. After I catch Bennett and her crew, HQ will forgive me for not informing my squad of the order to abort the mission.

"Mount up," I tell them, acting as if HQ gave me the go-ahead. "We're going to catch her. We'll do another grid search through the whole town from border to border."

Three hours later, there's still no trace of Bennett and her gang. Well after dark, we find the only open fast-food joint near a campground

198 × Ginny Fite

along the river. Reminds me of the places I used to skateboard to when I was young. Window service, wobbly outdoor tables, pretzel dogs with mustard. While waiting for our food, I tell the owner who we're looking for. A light goes on in his face.

"Sure, I saw her. I talked to her. You're saying she's a fugitive? She didn't act like no fugitive."

"Yeah. She's running from us. We got to bring her back."

"Yeah? Who are you guys, anyway? Never saw a vehicle with markings like those."

"We're USVPD, the virus protection patrol." I flash him the badge. "We remove the dead and infected."

He shrugs and cocks an eyebrow. "The cleaners, huh? She didn't look infected. Had a mess of kids with her. You sure we're talking about the same lady? She had a green mask with a multi-colored bicycle logo on it. Ponytail and a sense of humor. She took photos of her kids like they were on vacation."

"That's her, all right." I mean, how do I know if she has a sense of humor and a green mask, but the rest of his description fits. "Which way did she head off to?"

He didn't know where they went from his place. Bennett didn't tell him anything, but he saw the vehicle head east toward the causeway out to Cook Island like they were going camping.

We drive across the island until we reach an intersection with the only other road. Stopped at the crossroads, motor running, our headlights like white stripes through the pitch black, we consider our options. North, we wind up in the river. South leads to God knows where. Beats me why there are even roads out here. No one lives here. That's why she came in this direction; they're hiding out here somewhere, where no one would ever check. We might get lucky and surprise them. No one around to see what we're doing, nowhere for her to run.

We flip a coin and go north. At the end of the road, a small, weathered boathouse sits near the riverbank. We check the perimeter and then enter it, but no one's been in there for a long time. In the beam of Riley's flashlight, we find tire tracks but no vehicle. Without a forensics team, there's no way to know if the tracks are from a Hummer. Anyway, it could be any vehicle that uses those same tires.

Bennett could've been out here, turned around, and gone back the other way, disappearing into Michigan. She might never have been here. I'm dizzy with possibilities.

We spread out, search through the reeds, and find what might be blood but no bodies. It's too dark to tell what we're seeing, but something sizeable was dragged across the sand into the river. Suddenly I see the whole thing play out like a movie in my mind.

"So, here's how it went," I say. "Bennett found guys camping out here and killed them. Her gang dragged the bodies into the river, and they floated downstream. Then she and her gang got across the river somehow. So she's a killer, infected, and she's teaching those kids bad habits."

Popova rolls her eyes at me like nothing I say makes sense. "How'd she disappear the Hummer?" she asks. "She had to have driven away from the scene. But, if she could drive away, why kill the people who were here?"

My face puckers; I hate Popova. She always defies my authority. "Keep looking for evidence," I say.

Manny holds up a flattened cardboard box big enough for a few people to shelter in. Riley reads the marketing crap on the outside. "Says here there was an inflatable boat inside." He looks at me like he's trying to send me a message but doesn't want to say it out loud.

I blink, and the lights go on in my head like a pinball machine turned on. Bennett crossed the river to the other side in a rubber boat. That sneaky bitch. She thinks we can't get to her in Canada; my blood starts to boil again.

I kick the dirt around for a while to see if any other proof of the Bennetts being here turns up when Manny says, "Hey, what's this?" He holds up a piece of folded notebook paper. Now I know we're grasping at straws. I watch him unfold it. "Jesus H.!" he says. "Sarge, look at this."

I worry he's mocking me, but I go look over his shoulder at a hand-written list. It's grimy and tattered, and most of the writing's been washed away, but it looks like instructions. It must've fallen out of someone's pocket. In the first part, some of the writing is legible, and I can read something, something, *Aunt Dee's* and then *Leo Street* and *Canada*.

A surge of what has to be triumph fills me up. "See! You see. We're close. She's on the other side of the river on Leo Street."

The squad gives each other a look, and Riley bumps into Manny on purpose. "You don't know she has an Aunt Dee," Popova points out. I resist slugging her. They look anywhere but at me. I can feel their hatred coming at me in waves.

"We're crossing the border into Canada to arrest Bennett," I say. "We're on essential business for the US of A."

Their heads wag in rhythm. "You don't even know if that scrap of paper comes from one of them," Manny says. "Could be anybody's trash."

They cross their arms. "We're done, Sarge," Riley says. Standing there, shoulder to shoulder, they agree that this mission is over, and they want to go home.

It's an insurrection. Behind my eyes, my brain sizzles. I'm almost blind I'm so mad at them.

"It's time, Sarge," Riley says. "We got no authorization to follow a fugitive into another country."

"But we've got proof where she's gone." I wave the piece of paper at them.

"That won't get us an extradition warrant," Popova says. "It's worthless in court. You've got no way to know Bennett wrote it or any of them had it in their possession and no witness to validate where it came from."

"You gonna be a lawyer now?"

My irritation with her makes spots dance in front of my eyes. The hell with them. I don't need them; they're extra baggage I've got to drag along with me, weighing me down. I can nab the Bennetts on my own and keep the glory for myself.

"Okay," I say, pretending to appease them. My head's going to explode, but I keep my calm. "Let's head home."

They eye each other and hop aboard. They huddle over the onboard computer, check GPS directions for the fastest route home to DC, and debate whether they can drive a thousand miles, stopping only for pee breaks.

When they're fully engrossed with their backs to me, I pull out my taser and hit Manny, the biggest of the three of them, so fast and hard, that he falls out of the seat and convulses on the floor of the bus. Before Popova can get her weapon out of the holster, I tase her until she's unconscious. Riley practically has a heart attack before I hit him. When they stop moving, I shove their inert bodies out of the vehicle. They want to go home so bad, they can walk back. I'm going across.

)(

"For the past 15,000 years, a glacier on the northwestern Tibetan Plateau of China has hosted a party for some unusual guests: an ensemble of frozen viruses, many of them unknown to modern science.

"Scientists recently [took] a look at two ice cores from this Tibetan glacier, revealing the existence of 28 never-before-seen virus groups."

—LIVESCIENCE.COM, JANUARY 22, 2020

)(

32

Dee

I OPEN my eyes to a hullabaloo, lights flicking on, the door pushing open and then closed, Picasso barking and snuffling, shuffling feet, whispering, and then a woman's masked face leaning over me, saying, "Dee, Dee, Aunt Dee, are you okay?"

They've arrived! And when I least expected it. The fever broke this morning, but I was spent, my clothes soaked in sweat. I had enough energy to shower, change my clothes, and fall back asleep on the couch. I had been dreaming about the sun braiding itself through Georgia's hair when we were young. How she used to kiss my fingertips. I didn't want to wake up.

"How? How did you get here?" I croak. My normal voice is gone. Must be one of the long-term effects of the virus. "I was so worried about you."

"Long story," Jean says. "We've been knocking. Finally, we just walked around the house and found the open door. That was dangerous. Your house could have been invaded."

Children crowd around me, from tiny to towering. I feel like Frodo Baggins waking in Rivendell to the marvel of elves. They're dirty, wet, and noisy, but their eyes glow. I've never seen anything as glorious.

"I didn't want you to have to break in."

Although that seemed logical when I originally thought it, I can see leaving the door unlocked will take a fair amount of explanation. I don't even have the energy to push myself off the couch. "You must be starved. I should cook you something."

Jean gently nudges me back onto the couch pillows. "You're pale, and your eyes are bloodshot. I can see you've been sick. Stay put. What we need are warm showers and clean clothes. We'll scrounge food for ourselves. And then we need to sleep. We're just so glad to be here, to be safe."

She kneels on the floor and lays her head on my shoulder. I forget about germs, viruses, infectious droplets, and death and wrap my arms around her. Jean's shoulders shake as if so much pain has accumulated in her body that it needs to be released in waves before it blows her apart.

I stroke her head. I never had a daughter, never felt needed this way, as if I had the power to comfort, to make everything better with a touch. What my heart is doing stuns me. "My poor girl, my dear, sweet girl, I'm so glad you made it."

"Okay, guys," says a tall girl with a long braid. "Boys shower first cuz you're faster." She shoots a look at the older boy, who nods. "Pam, you're next."

A younger girl tilts her head but doesn't object.

"I'll take care of Mira's bath," the tall girl says. "Put your wet, dirty clothes in a pile by the washer." She points to the laundry room off the kitchen.

Jean, surprised, looks up and asks the girl, "Are you okay?"

"This is what comes next, right?"

Jean's face looks disheveled by pride. "Right."

"Then it's my turn to tell people what to do. Finally." The girl almost smiles at Jean. "Aunt Dee, could you spare some sweatpants and stuff?"

"In the bureau in my room," I say. "There's Georgia's things too. I never cleared them out. What's your name?"

"I'm Amina, Jean's daughter."

"Wow. You're the spitting image of my sister, your grandmother."

"Is that a good thing? Mom never talks about her."

"She was beautiful."

The girl blushes and manages to be even more wonderful-looking.

I look down and see the tiniest girl staring at me with the same intensity I usually fix on people. I realize at that moment how unnerving it is. Picasso licks the child's hand, and she giggles. "My name is Mira," the child says.

"Mira, what an amazing name."

"My mommy died. Aunt Jean is taking care of me."

I close my eyes and hold my breath. The quiet, matter-of-factness about death in the child's voice. So many are dying; this is the new world speaking.

I glance at Amina, who is apparently in charge. "I don't have anything for the little one to wear."

"I'll figure something out," Amina says.

"Who is that tall, handsome fella by the door?"

"That's my brother, Ren."

Ren grimaces. "Hi, Aunt Dee." He waves.

Amina wraps her arm around the shoulders of the girl beside her, who is nearly as tall as she is. "This is my cousin Pam, Caro's daughter, Mira's sister. She's not normally shy."

Pam giggles. "Your house is in Christmas colors," she says, her eyes wide. "All red and green, everywhere." She grins at me. "It's like you live inside a holiday all the time."

I have to laugh. "That's what your mother said about it."

"I like the books and pictures you have," Pam says. "We had books at our house." Her voice sounds wistful.

Amina reaches around Pam and pulls a little curly-headed boy forward to introduce him to me. "This is Owen, my younger brother. He looks more human when he's dry."

"Oh my gosh. I've already lost track of who's who. You'll have to keep reminding me. How on earth do you manage all of them?"

Jean sits up and wipes her face with her hands. "Oh, they manage me." She smiles a little. "I'm grateful for them. I wouldn't have made it without them; I wouldn't have even tried. There would have been no point."

Owen kneels on the floor and puts his arms around Picasso's neck. The dog licks his cheek. A huge grin lights Owen's face. "We never had a dog before. But we had a 'venture. Somebody stole our car, and then Mom stole somebody else's car, and we stayed in an underground house, and, and Pam killed a sheriff, and men 'tacked Mom and Amina, and Ren shot them, and I fell in the river and was real afraid, and Ruby rescued me—"

"Ruby? Who's Ruby?" I scan the room for this person Amina failed to introduce.

"She was someone we met on the road," Jean says. "She . . . she—"

"Come on, Owen," Ren says. "Let's find the shower. Big boys who have adventures take showers." Owen kisses the dog's head and trots off behind Ren.

Pam studies the colorful rug on the floor. "Did my mom like it here?" A dozen different emotions flit across the girl's face. No one answers my question about this Ruby.

"Yes, she did. We had a wonderful time with her. Good grief, I just realized I don't have beds for all of you," I say to Jean. "I didn't even think about it."

"Don't worry," Amina says. "We're used to figuring stuff out." She takes Mira's hand and walks off to find the bathroom with a tub. "I'll do the wash when we're done with showers, Mom," she says over her shoulder.

Jean drops her jacket and wet clothes on the floor, wraps herself in a comforter, snuggles into a corner of the couch, and hugs a pillow. I stroke her hand because I don't know what else to do. "I'm not going to give you the virus, am I?"

"I already had it, or some version. But I've been so drained, I think it might be coming back. It does that, right?"

For a while, we sit without saying anything. Later, when the kids are sleeping, Jean says she's sorry about Georgia dying. Her eyes fill, and I know she's thinking of her husband. And then my whole life together with Georgia comes rushing at me at warp speed, and I'm folded in brilliantly colored memories.

"She was my diva, right out of Hollywood. I'm so plain, I couldn't believe my luck that such a glamorous woman fell in love with me."

"The way she walked, the clothes she wore!" Jean says. "All those necklaces, the things she said, how she walked the Earth as if it belonged to her. I was so gaga over her."

When Jean laughs, I see the girl I know. Now she says it, I see Georgia from the girls' perspective. All the so-called adults in my family shunned me when I came out—no harsh words, just no words at all, no time for me, a mild shudder if I touched my mother, and my father couldn't look at me as if his disappointment would kill him. When Jean and Caro visited us, they saw between us what was missing between their parents, why they couldn't stay married, and knowing that made it a little easier for them.

"We were so happy together. The last thing she said to me was, 'I love you.' Then she took three deep breaths and just stopped. I sat there a long time with her, thinking about the grit it must have taken to say those three words."

"I guess that's what matters, right?" Jean says. "That you loved each other." She puts her head down on the pillow and falls instantly asleep.

My great-niece, Pam, wearing Georgia's pajamas with the cuffs rolled up, tells me she'll take over and I should go to bed. She kisses me on the forehead as if I were the child. I stagger upstairs, thinking Caro did a great job with her, and this pandemic has given me something I would otherwise never have had at this point in my life—a family.

33

Ren

I dream that a window is breaking. My mind tumbles around like an astronaut spinning loose in space. I grab onto the smell of warm buttered popcorn and apple juice—Owen curled up next to me. When I open my eyes, I remember we're in Dee's house in Canada, where it's supposed to be safe. Ruby's face appears in my mind like a warning signal and then blinks out. I don't know if coming here was the right thing to do, but for Mom, it was the only thing. She never asked us what we thought; she simply said this was what we were doing. That we might have an opinion didn't even occur to her.

The room is dark except where light sneaks in between the blinds from the outside streetlight. Another crash and pieces of glass falling onto the tile floor in the kitchen wake me completely. My body freezes for a second. I turn my face toward the sound as if I hear with my nose or I can see in the dark. When my eyes adjust, I make out the bedroom door, the dresser, a rug on the floor. Holding my breath, I hear thumps, the click of the backdoor lock, whispering, footsteps across the floor.

I run over in my mind where everyone landed after we ate. Mom was so exhausted that after her shower, she didn't make it off the couch in the living room. Pam's on the floor next to her. Amina and Mira are in the other guest room. We didn't set a watch because we thought we were safe. My huge mistake; I won't make it again. But right now, there's no time to feel guilty.

"Owen, wake up. Get under the bed." I swing my feet to the floor and shake him.

His eyes pop open, and he pulls the cover over his head.

"Now," I whisper. "Don't make a sound. I mean it."

He nods, slides over the side of the mattress to the floor, and squiggles under the bed. I adjust the cover, so he can't be seen from the doorway.

"Don't say anything. Stay here no matter what. I'll come and get you when it's okay."

The intruders open and shut the cabinets in the kitchen, obviously without trying to muffle the sound. They don't care if anyone is here or if anyone hears them. That could be us, taking food from the golf club or searching the farmhouse. The refrigerator door opens with a sucking sound. More whispers. Something heavy falls on the floor. They're hungry. Eating will slow them down.

Thunder rackets outside. Rain—the other sound I heard—rain on the roof, running through the gutters. I tiptoe into the guest room with the twin beds and shake Amina's shoulder. She opens her eyes. I put my finger on her lips. She gets stiff, her eyes wide. I notice she cut off her braid.

"Hide," I whisper.

She throws off the covers and looks around the room. I point to the closet. In three strides, she opens the door and scans the space. There's a hatch in the wall to a crawl space. She points. I nod. As I leave the room, she's waking Mira.

The floor creaks as I step down on the top stair. I look over my shoulder at the sound of Aunt Dee opening the door of her room. "There's a gun taped under the tabletop by the front door," she says, not whispering. She's holding a rifle. "I'll take care of the girls."

I hurl myself down the steps without worrying about the thump I make as I land. Under the tabletop, my hand feels for and finds the gun she taped there. I rip it away and move to the archway from the hall into the living room. It's dark in the hall. None of them notices me. They're focused on Mom.

Standing near the couch, Mom points the sheriff's gun at the intruders. It wobbles in her hands. Pam sticks close to her, glaring at them. Her look alone would stop me.

Six kids of assorted sizes wearing masks of one kind or another are lined up, facing my mother. Two of them have trash bags over their clothes, but their jeans aren't torn. They can't have been out there longer than we've been. Their parents must have died recently. Two of them are bigger than me.

Mom's face is pale. Pam is calm, the kind of calm that makes me nervous. She's planning something; I know it. She glances sideways at me. Her hands clench, open, clench, and open again. In twenty seconds, she's telling me. What does she want me to do? My mind whirls through options.

"Look." Mom keeps her voice quiet, but I hear her trembling under it. "I see you're hungry and scared. I know what that's like. Take the food you need and move on. This house is full. You can't be here. This isn't your place. You have to find somewhere else."

The tallest boy hoots. Above the mask, his eyes are blue. By height, he's a year older than me. He puts his hands on his skinny hips. "Lady, you don't have control of this situation. Don't try none of those fake Jedi tricks on me."

Mom thinks talking to them will work. Doesn't she remember? Dialogue is done. From some long-ago cops and robber game with my grandpa, I hear him say, "Shoot first and ask questions later." I remember laughing and yelling, "*Pow, pow, pow!*" Good guys, bad guys, it doesn't matter. You have to be tough. That's the rule for survival.

Mom waves the gun. I cringe. She tries for stern, but her voice shakes. "This is our house. You don't belong here. You need to leave now." She makes a terrible tough guy.

"Was," the kid says. He slinks over to her and grabs the gun right out of her hand like she's offering it to him. "This *was* your house."

Mom gasps and steps back.

He looks around, sizing up the room like he's going to buy it. "Looks like a good place to stay. You're the ones who need to leave. I'll give you ten minutes to clear out before I start shooting."

I admire his guts and hate his bullying.

The rest of his gang hangs back, clumped together. I don't see any other weapons unless someone's got a knife. They haven't been at this breaking and entering for long. They haven't encountered an opponent before. He's not ruthless yet; he's making it up as he goes.

Mom's body vibrates from her stomach outward. Pam puts an arm around her. "Leave her alone," Pam says to the kid with a low growl. "Get out of here now."

The gang leader squints at her. "Adult time is over, girl. They're dying. Haven't you heard? You got some grit. You should join us."

"No thanks," Pam says. "I have my own gang." Her eyes don't leave his face.

He shrugs. "Hey, it's your funeral. One way or another." He looks at his gang, and they laugh.

That's the thing about bad guys. They always laugh about someone else's pain. That's what gives them away, their laughing, how they eat up the fear they're causing. That's what makes me want to kill them. It's what I remember about those guys on Cook Island. The laughter, the snicker, the open-mouthed jeer. How they don't give a damn about anyone else.

I step into the room, my weapon aimed at the leader. That rage that began at the riverbank now rises in my throat. I clench my teeth. "Get out. Get out, now. You've got until I count to three."

"Whoa, hey, another country heard from," the asshole says. He smirks. "Better take you guys seriously now, eh."

He mugs for his gang and waves the gun around. "But hey, you got this backward. This is a good place for us to settle down for a while, but you can stay. Plenty of room here." His followers laugh again, but they're nervous and back up toward the kitchen, stumbling over each other. They didn't come for a gunfight. They were counting on sheer numbers to intimidate an old woman. Instead, they stumbled into a house full of people with guns.

While he's looking at me, Pam steps in front of Mom and lunges for the gun in the kid's hand. Mom shrieks. The kid pulls his arm back. Pam grabs his hand and tugs. He tries to yank away and trips backward. The gun goes off. He drops it and scrambles away on all fours.

Pam groans and falls backward. Mom catches Pam in her arms. Blood leaks between her fingers.

I aim for him. A young boy's voice yells, "Watch out, Jack!" Now he has a name. My finger won't squeeze the trigger. I can't shoot him. He's just a dumb kid with brothers to protect and no idea what he's getting into. He's pretending to be tough and in charge. If he doesn't pretend, he's got nothing. I see the whole picture now.

"Get out!" I shout.

He beats it out of the kitchen door with his boys. They screech as they scramble out to the street. Their feet pound on the asphalt, and their cries fade. I hate myself for feeling sorry for them.

Seeing both sides slows down my reaction and causes me to think twice, making me an easy target. If I were really brave, nothing would touch me; I would just know what was necessary and do that, whatever it took. I wouldn't care about other people having rights or worries of their own, or even feelings—that empathy stuff Mom taught me is in the way. To survive, I have to be tough on the inside. I hope I never see these guys again because next time, I *will* shoot first.

Amina barrels down the stairs and runs to Pam. She drops to her knees, grabs a pillow off the couch, and presses it to Pam's shoulder. "We have to take her to the hospital."

Mom looks dazed. "Your hair."

"Mom, focus!" Amina yells even though tears soak her face. "Pam has to go to the hospital. Aunt Dee has a car. Ask her where the hospital is."

"We have no papers," Mom says, "We don't belong here. The hospital . . . The virus. We can't . . ."

"Mom!" Amina glares at her through her tears.

Aunt Dee stands in the archway from the front hall, her rifle pointed to the floor. "I called the ambulance," she says. "They won't care about your papers. They'll patch her up. This isn't the States. Keep your hand on the wound. Apply pressure."

Mom's face looks like a bombed-out city in one of my games, like she's got nothing left.

Dee puts her rifle on top of the bookcase. "The boy. Was he hurt?" She takes the gun from my hands and wipes the grip with her pajama top. "You didn't shoot?" she asks. Her voice is neutral.

I shake my head.

"It's okay, Ren. You did right." She hides the revolver behind the books on the top shelf of the bookcase in the living room. She picks up the sheriff's gun from the floor and wipes that down, also. "That kid invades my house, steals stuff, pulls a weapon, and shoots my niece. Maybe cops can find him and put him away." Her voice quivers, but her face is set.

"But we're the ones who are illegal here," Mom says.

Dee shakes her head. "You're my guests, even if you are Americans. Trapped here by the border closing. Those boys broke into my house and stole your ID and money. Who's to know any different?"

Pam groans. A loud knock on the front door startles us. Aunt Dee opens the door and points the emergency medical techs to Pam. Wearing full protection gear, they rush in and do the stuff to stabilize Pam. They carry her out on a gurney. Amina and Mom follow the ambulance in Dee's car. When they're gone, half of me goes missing.

The police officer arrives right as the ambulance leaves. He's wearing one of those transparent plastic shields in front of his face and a mask under that. Dee tells him about the kid and the shooting. She says the boy accidentally shot Pam, but he intentionally invaded the house. She can't describe him; he was wearing a mask.

The cop looks at me. My breath comes so fast I can barely speak. I can tell he takes that for fear. He doesn't need to know what I feel.

"They were wearing masks, six of them, kids maybe seven to fourteen by size, anyway." I could be describing us.

Dee shows the officer the broken window in the kitchen and tells him what's been taken. In addition to food, they took the cash she had in an old flour tin she kept in the cupboard. "They took my niece's wallet and ID, her passport, and everything."

The officer makes notes on his pad, but I don't think he'll do anything. These kids can't be the only gang wandering around the province without parents. This can't be the only house broken into. The police department must be overloaded.

"Might be the same gang breaking in all over town," the officer says. "Officer ranks are down," he explains to my aunt. "Everyone's out with the virus. But we'll find them."

Dee nods like she takes him at his word and hands over the sheriff's gun. She holds the weapon the wrong way, getting her fingerprints on it. "The gang leader used this," she says.

The officer calls in forensics, takes photos, and doesn't notice that she's messed with his evidence.

"I need you guys to hurry up," she says to him. "I've got young nieces and nephews here. They've had a shock." Aunt Dee is calm as if she lies for a living. That makes me like her.

If they find him, the boy might say it was our gun, but I don't think so. He won't tell them he wrestled a gun away from a woman and shot an unarmed girl. Even if he does, why would the police believe him? I don't want to think about what will happen to him if they catch him. I could be him. I imagine the cops locking him up and leaving him in jail forever. I hope he gets away, even if that means we have another run-in. We all need to be free.

I remember Owen and run upstairs to get him out from under the bed. He crawls over to me and puts his arms around my neck. His face is wet.

"I thought you were never coming back . . . like Ruby." He puts his cheek next to mine and just breathes.

Mira runs into the room. She throws her arms around Owen's neck and snuggles against us.

That's when I know we can't stay here. It's no safer than home. Mom's run out of juice. She's sicker every day, even if she doesn't know it. Last night, I saw her double over and grab the arm of a chair to keep from falling when she thought no one was looking. Her skin is almost transparent; I can see the tiny veins in her cheeks, and her eyes are bloodshot. She keeps saying she's just tired, but it's more than that.

I think about what that Elyria scientist said and know what we have to do. We have to leave. Without her. We have to go where there are no adults because they're the carriers. I sit on the floor, hugging the babies, feeling like I've just had the crap kicked out of me.

34

Jean

PAM doesn't whimper before or after the surgery. When the anesthesia wears off, she opens her eyes and blinks a few times. For a minute, she looks exactly like Caro when she was that age.

"Mom?" she whispers and breaks my heart.

"No, baby." I take her hand. "It's Aunt Jean."

"Oh." Tears leak down her cheeks. "For a second . . ."

"I know, Sweetheart. I wish it were true." I don't have to say anymore. Like my own kids, Pam can read my mind.

"I wish we never left home," she says. "My real home."

It's like I've been thrown off a tall building. My regrets tumble around me, and I flail. If I could find a justification to cling to, I would. The handholds slip by: we're here now. We made it this far. She's alive. But . . .

I hold a glass of water for her and don't say anything. Everyone in the hospital has been so kind. They asked no questions, swathed me in plastic, and let me stay with her.

She sips from the straw and pulls her face away. "I was mad at you. For a long time. Because *my* mom died, and you're alive."

Stung by her honesty, I sigh. Must be the pain meds that let her speak this way. She's earned this moment—if it had to be earned—if I couldn't have simply given it to her at the beginning of our journey. I ignored her grief because I didn't know what to do with it, or my own. There wasn't time to mourn; we couldn't wait to recover from Caro's death. But actually, I have no excuse. I just did what I always do—decided something and went ahead and did it, whether it was right or wrong.

"We left Momma in the backyard," Pam whispers. "We left her. You didn't give us time to say goodbye. Or talk about it. You didn't ask us if we wanted to leave. I couldn't even take anything of hers to remember her by."

214

My niece is a truth-teller. Admiration fills my throat, and I can't speak. All the guilt and regret—the recriminations for everything I did wrong, for the danger I put them in—comes at me like a mile-high wave.

She tugs my hand. "Aunt Jean? Did you hear me?"

I take a breath for courage. "Sweetheart, you're my hero. You saved us from the sheriff. You protected me from a kid with a gun, even though you're angry at me."

Pam studies my face. She reminds me of Caro when she was twelve and I was sixteen, and we stayed with Dee that summer when our parents divorced. Away from the drama, Mom had said, as if pain were as contagious as chickenpox. Although she was just getting the hassle of us out of the way, she might have been right about that. Children catch their parents' emotional chills.

That summer, Georgia taught us we could be any way we wanted to be, that we were allowed to be happy too. We could bend the world to our will, at least to a certain degree. Somehow, I need to tell Pam that in a way she can hear. Are there enough right words in the right order to make okay what should never have happened? I have to try.

"You're right. I should have discussed what to do with you and explained my reasons. You should have had a chance to say what you had to say. I should have listened."

The child sighs and looks away. "Would it have made any difference?"

She means I'm still not listening to her, that I don't get it. Why is this so hard? I unclench my hands. "I'm sorry."

And in that second, I'm also sorry for all those times I didn't listen to Caro, didn't give her time to say what was on her mind, to hear her objections and observations, accept her differences. To just take her as she was. God, how I miss my sister.

I'm sorry I didn't simply say, "I see you," without trying to change her. An entire world of sorrow passes through me as if I'm a gateway, and then it's gone, and I'm an empty landscape at dusk.

Pam closes her eyes. "I'm not mad anymore. I forgave you."

Instantly I'm delirious with relief. I didn't fail Caro. Her children are alive, and we're together. "I have something for you to remember your mother by."

I unhook the chain from around my neck, open the locket, and slip Ted's photo into my pocket. "This is for you, Sweetheart." I hold out the locket with the photo of her mother tucked into the silver heart—my favorite image of Caro, her smile wide, her eyes alight. The only thing I took with me. It's her daughter's now.

Pam touches the heart with her fingertips and presses her lips together.

"So you'll know she's always with you." I fasten the chain around her neck. Her lips tremble, but she doesn't say anything.

As I busy myself fussing around her bed, tucking in the sheet, smoothing the covers, pouring more water into her glass, a thought I can't quite snatch from its crevice in my brain nags me. I dig for it, catching it by the edge. The virus is still spreading, and I'm its transportation device. I brought it here. Adults everywhere are spreading it, even if they don't appear to be sick.

I follow this thought down a long, dark corridor and come to the idea that's been lurking there like my worst enemy. It wasn't that Ted didn't come home because he couldn't find a way through the blockade. He deliberately didn't come home because he knew he was infected; he sacrificed the comfort of being with us at the end of his life to save us.

I am depleted by grief. Broken. And now the final challenge in this horrible journey looms up in front of me, the last wall I have to scale, the one that overcoming will leave me baying in my sleep. I turn away from completing the thought. It's too soon; I can't face it.

"Aunt Jean?"

"What, Sweetie?"

"You're crying." Pam wipes my cheeks with her fingers.

)(

In the morning, Amina and Dee pick us up. Dee looks like she's been wrung out in an old ringer washing machine, but she stands outside the automatic door of hospital reception, leaning on her walker, wearing her mask. Her eyes are fiercer than yesterday. Amina, as always, looks like a Wagnerian goddess, but with her hair shorn off and dark shadows under her eyes. That quiet endurance costs her something.

I roll Pam out in the hospital wheelchair. Dee and I get in the backseat; Amina helps her cousin into the front passenger seat and connects her seatbelt. When she reaches her hand out to adjust her braid, her fingers graze her cropped hair. She shakes her head and drives us away from the hospital. This should shock me, but it doesn't. My cautious thirteen-year-old daughter is driving, and it's normal, as if I should have expected it.

At the house, Ren has laid out a banquet of tuna salad, peanut butter and jelly sandwiches, chunks of cheese, crusty bread, and sliced apples. I've never tasted anything so delicious. The abundance overwhelms me. The warmth of the house with comfortable chairs to sit in makes me melt with gratitude. I close my eyes and take in the sound of children eating, laughing, and chattering—the best sound on the planet.

When we're full, Owen helps Amina clear the table. Another surprise. My baby does chores. In one night, the children have reorganized themselves. They are functioning without me. I bask in their self-sufficiency, marveling how my brief absence changed the way they related to each other.

I start to nod off when we're stunned by a furious pounding on the front door—authoritative banging accustomed to being answered, a sound that expects surrender. We freeze for a moment, then Amina goes to the door.

I hear it open, hear my daughter say calmly, "Yes?"

"Out of my way, girl," a rough female voice says. Hard footfalls on the wood floor. In the next instant, a woman wearing a black and white checked flannel shirt over jeans and a crazy plastic mask contraption over her head that allows only her eyebrows and eyes to show barges into the kitchen.

"Jean Bennett," she bellows.

I automatically raise my hand, then, embarrassed by the thoroughness of my socialization, yank it down into my lap.

"Bennett, stand up." Her head swivels back and forth like she's trying to figure out if someone here is armed.

Dee struggles to her feet. "I own this house. You have no right to order anyone around."

The woman lurches over to Dee and puts her masked head close to her face. "You're not Bennett. Too old."

She turns her face toward me. "You," she barks. "You're under arrest by the authority of the United States Government." She grabs my arm and hauls me to my feet.

I jerk my arm away from her. Her grip is surprisingly weak, and I wonder if she's sick. The children immediately surround me.

"What are you talking about?" I yell back at her. I should know by now that talking doesn't get me out of any scrapes, but I've also learned some traits are indelible.

"You're wanted for fleeing the jurisdiction, murder, assault, breaking and entering, burglary, car theft. That's quite a crime spree you've had. It's over now. I'm taking you in."

"The US government? You have no authority here." I hope that's true. "This is Canada. Where are the warrant and extradition papers authorizing this arrest?" Stalling seems as good a strategy as any. Out of the corner of my eye, I notice Dee leave the room.

The children turn on the government agent. Mira tugs on her shirt, and a few snaps on it open to reveal a Kevlar vest. She came looking for trouble like she's Wyatt Earp going after the Clanton gang. Now, surrounded by little children, she seems bewildered.

"What's your name?" Mira asks.

She grabs Mira by the back of her neck. "Sergeant Diana Cooper, US Virus Protection Directorate." Her voice rasps as if she's been screaming for hours. "The sheriff in Sweetpine told me about you. Bunch of criminals, she said. Where's the one who assaulted her? I'm taking you in too."

"Let go of her," Ren says, stepping toward Cooper. He reaches for Mira's arm and pulls the child away.

Cooper looks surprised that he would confront her but is distracted by Pam saying, "That would be me. Do you mean she lived? Wow, that's great news."

She stares at the dressing on Pam's shoulder and the sling. "What happened to you?"

"I got shot."

"*Hmph*. Probably deserved it. You people have lost your grip. Assaulting a police officer is unlawful. You'll find that out right away where you're going."

Amina's face turns red. "That sheriff was going to shoot Mira!" She wraps her arm around Pam's waist. "You're not taking my cousin anywhere." The vein in her forehead pulses. Her eyes flash. "You don't know anything."

"Where's the rest of your outfit?" Pam asks. "Don't you normally have a head-to-toe costume? We saw it when you took our neighbors."

Cooper grunts. "I was attacked by a gang of hoodlums when I was staking out this house to make sure you were here. I was forced to shoot at 'em to get them to back off. My protective gear was ripped in the struggle, and I discarded it."

"Where's your gun?" Owen asks. He points to her empty holster.

Cooper stares at him. "I was relieved of my weapons by the local police when the shooting incident was reported by one of your nosy neighbors, and I was briefly detained. Professional courtesy doesn't apply over here, apparently."

"What does courtesy mean?" Owen asks.

Ren yanks off Cooper's mask while she's glaring at Owen. "You're not arresting anyone."

She runs her hand over her short blond hair and blinks like a possum confronted by light. Without her head covering, she looks diminished, like a normal human being. "Back off, kid," she grunts. "You've gone feral. You should be in custody."

Dee clears her throat. "You're not taking anyone anywhere." Standing with her back to the wall, she hoists a rifle to her shoulder. "My gun is aimed right at your head," she says calmly. "It's loaded, I'm a good shot, and I don't care if I'm arrested. I'm already sick. So take your hands off my family and get out of my house. Clock's ticking." She cocks the gun.

Cooper startles and whips around. Her hand goes to her empty holster, and her face pales.

"Time's up," Dee says. "Get going."

"Jesus!" Cooper backs up a few feet. She stumbles over a chair, rotates her arms, trying to get her balance, and falls into it. "If you infected me, you might as well shoot me." She coughs like she's trying to expel microscopic disease-laden particles she might have breathed in. The harder she coughs, the deeper she inhales.

Fury at being hounded from my home and chased across the country builds into a volcano of hate spewing enough fire to burn through her, to scald her skin, and tear through her body so she feels every bit of my fear and loss. I blame her for everything that's happened to us. The rage I felt about the groundskeeper was nothing compared to this; I could rip her apart with my bare hands.

My whole body trembles from the effort to contain my loathing. "Why are you still chasing us? What did we ever do to you?"

Cooper covers her face with her hands and breaks into tears, her shoulders bucking. It's like watching someone strip off her clothes in public. Shocked, I step back and look away to preserve her modesty.

"I can't stand this," she says between sobs. "I do everything right, I follow the law, and I end up with nothing. I'm the good guy; you're the bad guys. Don't you know that? I'm the one who's supposed to win."

My hate leaks out of me like air out of a spiked balloon, but I can't think of anything kind to say. The notion of good guys and bad guys died on the way here. All that's left is survival. Whatever helps us survive is good; everything else is irrelevant.

"All I wanted," Cooper says, "was one moment of glory where people acknowledged me and applauded, one little validation that I had as much right to be as important as anyone else. And you, you break a million laws, you crash through boundaries, and you get to have everything."

She glares at us as she dries her face with her hands.

"It's not fair. There should be a reward for sticking to my promises, for pulling myself out of that outhouse I grew up in and making something of myself. Instead, I'll get fired and have no place to live. I'll have to start all over again."

In a way, she's right. Even with everything I've lost, I have what matters—the children, my family. For a moment, I see she's like the rest of us, struggling to understand what to do next, desperate to stay alive. I take a deep breath and realize I'm tired of fighting; I just want her to disappear.

I put my hand on her shoulder, but she jerks away and dashes to the front door. "You people are crazy. You're not going to make me weak," she yells. "This was just a courtesy call to confirm your whereabouts and tell you I'll be back with local reinforcements to take you in. The Canadian government is going to deport you. Any day now. You won't get away from me."

From the front door, we watch her race to her bus as she swipes at her face.

"She won't come back," Ren says.

"She's wrong about us," Owen says. "We're the good guys. Right?"

Mira puts her hand in Pam's and leans against her sister. "She's scared of being sick like Momma was. I saw it in her face." Pam squats and kisses the child's cheek.

I hug Ren, just for the comfort of it. "I agree. That's the last we'll see of her."

)(

The next morning after breakfast, while the kids are clearing up, Ren leans forward, clasps his hands together on the table, and says, "Mom?"

I know what he's going to say, what he needs to do. I almost can't bear it, but I've borne everything else. During the night, I worked out what needs to happen, what I was trying to understand. This is what's next.

"Yes, Sweetie."

His face is so dear to me, his voice so urgent. "Mom, we have to go."

I nod to give him time to find the words.

"It's not going to be safe here. And . . ." He glances at Aunt Dee. "That kid was right about one thing. The virus is here. Adults are going to die. We have to find another place."

He's been thinking about what the scientists in Elyria said, that he's susceptible to the virus when he turns fifteen. Amina will be in danger right after he is, and then Pam. She watches us closely. They've talked about this. I put my palm on his face; his whiskers have started to come in. He can't be where people carry the virus, he can't be with me, and he knows it.

I woke up in the middle of the night knowing I couldn't stay with the children. It was as if Caro told me, that voice of God thing she does. They have to go where there are no adults, somewhere the virus has never been, so they won't be infected. That's the only way to save them. The whole reason I fled was to get them to safety, and they won't be safe until they're away from me.

I have to give them up for them to survive. The irony crushes me. That thought was chasing me in the hospital; that loss will kill me. My stomach turns over, and bile stings my throat. The apparition Caro saw hovering above the kids, did it mean danger or that something would watch over them?

Fatigue permeates every cell in my body. I didn't recover from the sickness; it mutated inside my body and continued its destruction. While we've been running, it's taken up permanent residence and owns me now. My head spins like the wheel on a TV quiz show, and the arrow stops on the answer I already know. I have to let them go into a future I can't see. If ever there were angels, if any of Caro's prayers meant anything, this is the time for their help. A chasm opens in my chest.

"Mom? Did you hear what I said?"

"Yes, Baby. *You* have to leave," I say, "but this is as far as *I* go. I'm going to stay here with Dee." Every word shreds me.

He looks at his knees and then up at me. "I know."

I tumble through memories of the children in no order—Ren's exaltation his first time on a bike, Amina's elegant repose, the tiny chirp of Owen suckling my breast, three-year-old Pam kissing Caro's foot, Mira's open-faced delight when her father lifted her into his arms.

Looking at anything but Ren, I see the thankful look in Dee's eyes. We're family; I can't leave her to die here alone or at the mercy of thieves. Those kids will be back, and they'll have weapons next time. But we do too. This time I'll remember to shoot first.

"I'm staying, too," Pam says, surprising me. "I'll stay with Jean and Dee till . . . I'm healed." She studies her apple slice. "And then I'll find you."

Ren nods as if he always knew this. "We'll work out a plan."

"It could be years before I come," she says.

Ren's eyes skitter away from me and Dee. "I don't think so. Make sure your shoulder is healed before you set out."

Pam's eyes fly open. "You think . . ."

He nods.

Pride and love swamp me. I don't have a name for this feeling yet, but it will come to me. Whatever it's called, it will sustain me even though giving the children up is far more lethal than the virus. This is the last thing I had to learn, my final act of courage, the only task left to me. My heart labors to beat regularly.

Caro wanted to know what I believe in. I know what it is now. It's the children and their future. They are my religion, the perfection of being that was so important to her. They are what makes me whole.

Ren leans over and embraces me. All my fears surge through me, chased by my love for him. My heart thunders in my chest so hard, I can barely breathe.

35

Ren

WE'VE chosen a large island in Lake Superior, about two hundred miles northwest of here, that is mostly forest. It doesn't even have a name on the map, and there's no sign of buildings or roads. There's a reason for that, maybe a dangerous force like the military has an underground installation there, or it floods every spring, or the winters aren't suitable for human habitation, but taking the satellite view to the highest magnification, expanding the image until we could see ants moving on the ground, we don't see any sign of people. I cross my fingers that we won't trespass on anyone's land, and a second later, I realize that wherever we go on this continent, someone was here before us thousands of years ago, and, for no reason I understand, the thought gives me hope that we'll make it.

We'll take Aunt Dee's car and drive west away from town and then north on Rt. 17 toward Batchawana Bay. At some point, we'll have to walk through the forest and then along the coast until we hit a beach to launch the boat Pam stole. That seems forever ago, like it happened in another life, or a game I outgrew. We plan a route on a paper map, one for us and make a duplicate to leave with Pam so she can follow us. My phone will be out of juice within a day or two after we leave the vehicle and probably won't work out there anyway, ending our access to the GPS lady. She's like another family member I have to leave behind.

I'll have to make maps in my head, footfall by footfall, memorize landmarks, and leave blazes on trees for Pam to follow. Sometimes, I zoom through a wormhole to eons ago, to the time of the earliest humans. People migrated; they walked across continents and found their way through jungles and ancient forests. For them, the world opened like pages in a book, their footprints marking their place. I hope that happens for us too.

For the next few days, we assemble what we need. Amina and I will carry backpacks with supplies, tents, and sleeping bags. I saw Amina packing a few books from Aunt Dee's shelves—*Bambi, Little Women, The Black Stallion*—but I didn't stop her. We'll need stories to tell the little ones, and Mom told us those were her favorites when she was young. When Pam comes, she'll bring the rest of the stuff on the list I made her. Every half-hour or so, I think how much easier this would be if Ruby were here—we could use her courage. Then I let it go.

Mom remembers all the things the hero didn't have in *Cast Away*, which we've watched like fifty times, and makes sure we take flashlights, batteries, lighters, a tent, prepared foods in lightweight pouches, a knife, inflatable life vests, and a small hatchet. I don't have the heart to remind her we'll be away for the rest of our lives. We watch videos about how to skin and butcher animals, how to build a lean-to shelter. The equipment she insists we take will break eventually, but I get what she's doing. We'll learn how to make replacements or get by without them; it's smart to have a head start.

She gets Georgia's Jeep fixed for her to run around in after we're gone. This is a lie she's telling me so I won't be scared for her. I can see with my own eyes that every day she's weaker, but she doesn't say anything about it. Pam will have to learn to drive the Jeep as soon as her shoulder heals.

"Don't let the fire go out," Mom says, her face sad but determined, the light in her eyes flickering. I don't think she's talking about an actual blaze. All these years, she's been looking out for us, planning, preparing, thinking we would grow up to do great things. That's what she always said. It's not just us she's losing, but her dreams about who we would be.

"Tell me again why we're doing this," I say, the pain in my chest as hard as a rock.

"Because adults carry the virus," she says, her voice steady like she's showing me the proof to a geometry problem. "If you go to a place without adults, there won't be any virus. You'll be able to grow up, to live a normal life. You won't get sick when you turn fifteen. You won't die."

"Are you sure about that, that we won't get sick?"

"No, but the farther you are from infected people, the safer you'll be. Dee and I are sick. Most of the adults here are infected. If you stay here with me, you'll die."

It seems so cold when she says it like that, but underneath it, I know her heart is as messed up as mine. I catch her staring at me when I'm packing our gear, and I see the pain, and then I see how brave she is.

On the afternoon we're ready, Aunt Dee gives me a hunting knife, a rifle, two handguns and ammo, her solar-powered watch that has a calendar on it, a box of matches to use when the lighter fluid runs out, and pats on the back. "You'll need to hunt," she says, but I know she's thinking about two-legged predators who'll come after us.

I split the weapons with Amina. She takes a revolver and the knife, "For close work," she says. She slips the knife sheath through Georgia's red leather belt and buckles it on.

I hug Dee and think for a minute I should stay here and defend her. She shakes her head like she's reading my mind. Steely-eyed, she says, "Stay alive. That's your job; it's what's important to us. We're counting on you."

"It'll be cold beginning in September," Mom says. "Remember to build a shelter right away."

She shows me printed instructions she found online, folds up the paper, and puts it in my shirt pocket. Her face looks like the blood has been sucked out of it. It's just hit her that this is forever. We're not just going away to summer camp. We'll never see each other again.

Her face wobbles as she tries to smile. I've given up trying. The truth is, I'm leaving my mother to die. I'm not a hero. This isn't the heroic thing; it's the only thing. I'm doing what we have to do.

We stand in a line on the front porch. Mom lifts Mira into her arms and rocks with her. "It'll be okay, Aunt Jean," Mira says. She strokes Mom's hair. "I'll take care of Owen."

Mom nods, reaches for Amina, and pulls her into the hug. "My beautiful girl," she says, and then neither of them says anymore.

When it's my turn, she wraps her arms around me and hangs on. She puts her face down on my shoulder. I feel her shaking. "You are my best thing," she whispers. "The best thing I ever did. I'm so proud of you."

"I love you forever, Mom."

She picks Owen up, and he puts his arms around her neck and nuzzles her face. Tears run down Mom's cheeks. He brushes them away with his fingertips.

"You're going on a great adventure, Owen," she says, "the greatest one any boy has ever had." He pulls his head back to check Mom's face. She nods. "Truly, the best adventure. You do everything Ren says, and you help Amina with whatever she needs because they can't do it without you. You're a big boy now. You have a job to do."

Amina tucks her head. Pam puts her good arm around her.

"We've got him, Mom," Amina says. "We'll take good care of him."

Mom closes her eyes and puts Owen down. "Go on then; go on."

Pam walks us to the car.

"Follow your map," I tell her, hoping my eyes are burning the instructions into her brain. "Watch for blue blazes on trees to keep you on target. I'll send you the GPS coordinates and put a flag in the ground where you should wait for me to get you. I'll come every three days until you're there. We *will* see you again."

"Got it," Pam says. "I'll be there."

In the rearview mirror, I watch Mom waving from the front porch until I can't see her anymore.

Two days later, I tie a blue flag onto a stick, pound it into the ground, check that everyone's life vest is secure, and push the boat out from shore. The lake is larger than any body of water we've seen except for the ocean. Our boat seems too small. There are waves, and Owen clings to Amina. The motor, of course, doesn't work for long enough because I forgot to juice it up. Dad always said, "There's no such thing as all you gotta do." I'm getting used to it.

I row in the direction that Mom told me to. "Head straight out, Sweetheart. You'll see the island when you're a mile away."

Five miles seems like a million parsecs. We're alone in a watery galaxy, far from home and on our own. It dawns on me this is what grownups do. They pretend they know what they're doing so their kids can feel safe. All this time, Mom pretended to be brave, just like I'm doing now. My heart feels huge.

The boat rocks. Amina has her arms around Owen and Mira. I look back toward the shore we came from, but we've gone far enough that I can't see it. My stomach lurches. What if I miss the island? What if I go in circles? What if a storm comes up, and the boat is swamped? My throat is dry.

"I'll take a turn rowing," Amina says.

We switch places, and I gratefully hand over the oars.

When I wipe away the sweat, blink a few times, and my eyes clear, I see another boat in the distance and then another and another. And floats and rafts, and on each one are children who look like us—exhausted and terrified.

I wave, and then everyone is waving, and Mira says, "There are people!" Ahead, I see the land covered in pine trees rising up from the lake. Amina dips the oars in the water and rows for the shore.

36

Pam

I wrapped the aunts in sheets and buried them in the backyard. Jean told me to leave her and Dee lying wherever they stopped breathing, but I couldn't do that. They meant too much to me. I owed them a ceremony, and the idea of burning them made me shudder. Memories of flames leaping up from my mom's body still jolt me awake, and I have to cover my mouth with my hand to hold in the screams.

Digging the hole wide enough for them to be together took days. Blisters popped on my hands, and I cried the whole time I did it, but I was ready on the day they died. They were heavy, but I managed. I'm more determined than I thought. I put a marker with their names on the grave and read Aunt Jean's favorite passage from *The Road* out loud.

I guess I'm the one carrying the fire now. Picasso is helping me.

I boarded up the windows and doors to make it harder for anyone to break into the house and spray-painted the infinity symbol on the front wall. I don't know why that mattered since I haven't seen anyone outside in weeks, but somehow, it did. It's important that everyone keep out because the house is sacred to me.

It felt like home there, maybe because Mom stayed at Aunt Dee's when she was young and left something of herself there. Aunt Dee told me about it, how Mom put on Georgia's clothes and jewelry and danced around the house singing at the top of her lungs. Georgia thought my mom was the bee's knees; that's how Aunt Dee said it, which I think means the absolute best.

If we return after a while, we'll need the place in decent shape. That infinity symbol should scare most squatters away, at least for a while. Anyway, there's no one to tell me what to do next, so I'm making it up as I go. Like Aunt Jean always said, I closed my eyes, asked myself what to do, and did that.

Dee's neighbor watched me from behind the lace curtain at her window, but she didn't say anything, and no cops came. Nobody called to ask about Dee the whole time I was there. I tried to imagine living totally alone with no one to talk to except Picasso, no one who cared about me, no hope of ever being with anyone, and I couldn't. Before, I never got how lucky I was. I was surrounded by people who loved me. The thought of living without them now makes me feel hollow inside. Even when Amina and Ren are annoying, they're my family; I belong with them.

I filled Dee's backpack with the gear Ren said I'd need, including warm clothes, food, and water. I took toilet paper, too, because Aunt Jean would have, and her phone for the GPS. The longest I should be in the woods on my own while I'm waiting for them is three days, but who knows for sure. Dee's sleeping bag, tent, and rifle, plus ammunition are as much extra weight as I can carry. Jean said there could be bears or bobcats in the forest. I'm not going to think about that. There could also be humans; they're scarier than animals, but I'm ready for them.

The Jeep was a little tricky to drive, but I got the hang of it by the time I got on the highway. No other vehicle was on the road with me the entire two-hundred miles. I followed Ren's map north to the place where he left Dee's red car on the side of the highway, so I could spot it. It stood out in all that green like a giant zit. I'm amazed it was still there after two months. From there, I drove the Jeep off-road west across the peninsula. Only the last four miles were the woods too thick with trees to get the vehicle through. I left the car but took the keys. It's like the house; we might want to return sometime when the infection is over, and it would be a long walk.

When I think about going back, about what we left behind, about my mom and dad, I get a twinge in my chest, like the stitch you get in your side when you run too long, and I have to stop and breathe gently for a few minutes to be able to stand. I touch my locket and focus on Mira's face to help me keep my place. To stay on course, I concentrate on where I'm going—to my family, to the people who are home to me, no matter what. Being with them is what's important. I don't care where we live or for how long, as long as we're together.

Following the blue marks Ren left on tree trunks, I think about him being careful to put the blazes where I would see them. I check the GPS map on Jean's phone every twenty minutes to make sure I'm on course. Picasso loves following his nose through the woods, running off, and veering back to me to make sure I'm still there. I couldn't imagine leaving him alone in the house or letting him go in the city. He's a people dog. How would he have survived without people to take care of?

Ahead of me is a clearing and a small beach lit by the rising moon. A piece of blue cloth tied to a stick in the ground flaps in the breeze. This must be the place Ren wants me to wait for him. Unless it's someone else's mark, but I can't think about that, or I'll be too scared to breathe.

Instead, I think about what I should say when Ren asks me how Aunt Jean died. I picture him with his eyes half-closed and the ends of his lips turned down. He'll watch the ground when I tell him.

"A little rough. Sad, mostly," I'll say. "She was brave. I held her hand, and she died in her sleep." Telling him about Aunt Dee will be easy. She died first with a smile, saying, "Georgia," clear as day.

I'm glad I was with them, that they weren't alone. Pictures of the last person on earth dying alone try to sneak into my mind, but I push them away. I focus on where I am right now. The lake is huge, and moonlight makes a path across it. Some bird sings and answers itself. I settle down by the flag, eat a granola bar, and try to stay awake, consoling myself with the thought that the longest I have to wait here for Ren is three days. I remember cuddling with Mom in my bed, listening to her read me a story, feeling her hand stroking my head and cheek, and fall asleep with Picasso curled up next to me.

When I wake, it's morning. There's a low-lying fog, and the lake is a pearly gray. I hear a steady, rhythmic splash and then giggling. Picasso jumps up and runs in circles, barking. I squiggle out of my sleeping bag and see Owen and Mira running toward me. Ren stands in the water, holding the boat. My family is here for me. In seconds, I'll be smothered in kisses.

Acknowledgments

I wouldn't find my way through the hinterlands of writing a novel without the feedback and insight of the writers, each with his or her own distinctive genius, who have been with me on this adventure of stringing sentences together: K.P. Robbins, Catherine Baldau, Tara Bell, the recently late Thomas Trumble, Lee Doty, Sean Murtagh, Lisa Taka Younis, Frank Joseph, Solveig Eggerz, Katherine Lorr, Linda Morefield, Catherine Flanagan, Leslie Rollins, Bob Gibson, Stanley Whatley, the late Phil Harvey, J.L. Dozier, Jeff Soloway, Kathleen Barber, Michael Rothrock, and John Thibault.

Not a page went by in this novel that I didn't think of my grandparents and parents, my children and grandchildren, my sisters and their families, and the fierce determination that living every day requires. They are the inspiration for this work.

Diana Cooper, a brilliant photographer based in Shepherdstown, West Virginia asked to be the named villain in one of my novels, and I've done my best to oblige her. I hope she forgives the liberties I've taken with her character and enjoys her namesake's story.

And, of course, I must thank Benee Knauer, Kimberly Coghlan, and Gabrielle Kirk, the skillful editors whose magic wands transformed my sentences. They have my undying gratitude for understanding what I was trying to do and helping me to realize it on the page. Gratitude also to all at the Sunbury Press who made this manuscript into a novel I'm proud to call mine.

About the Author

Award-winning writer GINNY FITE is the author of eight published novels, including the mildly addictive Detective LaGarde mystery series and the award-winning *The Physics of Things*, as well as a humorous book on aging, *I Should Be Dead by Now*, three collections of poetry, and a collection of short stories. With three other writers, she co-authored *Thoughts & Prayers*, which won the 2022 FAPA Gold Medal for fiction.

A graduate of Rutgers University with a master's from Johns Hopkins University, her 40-year career in communications included posts as founding editor of the Frederick *Gazette* where she won numerous newspaper industry awards; public relations director for Goucher College; press secretary and then district director for a member of Congress; the first female deputy press secretary for a Maryland governor, and media director for a robotics R&D company.

She also studied at the School for Women Healers and the Maryland Poetry Therapy Institute, completed the Novel Year program at the Writer's Center, and participated in workshops with renowned poets David St. John, Judson Jerome, Stanley Plumly, and Michael Cummings, and fiction masterclasses with Barbara Kingsolver and Marie Manilla.

Nominated for a Pushcart Prize, her writing has appeared in *McSweeney's*, The *Gazette Newspapers*, the *Herald-Mail*, the *Anthology of Appalachian Writers*, *Fluent Magazine*, the *Delmarva Review*, *Santa Fe Writers Project Quarterly*, *Heartwood Literary Magazine*, *Coffin Bell*, *Women Arts Quarterly*, *Masque and Spectacle*, *Frederick Magazine*, the *Arundel Observer*, *Spy Newspapers*, and *Temenos*.